DRAMA QUEEN

THE COURT BOOK ONE

SPECIAL EDITION

CHARLIE NOVAK

Copyright © Charlie Novak 2023

Cover by Natasha Snow

Cover photography by Wander Aguiar

Editing by Jennifer Smith

Formatting by Pumpkin Author Services

All rights reserved. Charlie Novak asserts the moral right to be identified as the author of this work.

This novel is entirely a work of fiction. Names, characters, places, and incidents are the products of the author's imagination or are used fictitiously. Any resemblance to actual events, locales, organizations or persons, living or dead, is entirely coincidental.

A NOTE FROM THE AUTHOR

Many drag performers use different pronouns in and out of drag, depending on their style of drag and their personal gender identity, and the performers in this book do the same.

To help you get to know them, here's a list of *Drama Queen*'s drag stars and their pronouns in and out of drag.

Bubblegum Galaxy, drag queen: she/her in drag, he/him out of it.
Bitch Fit, drag queen: she/her in drag, he/him out of it.
Eva Nessence, drag queen: she/her in drag, he/him out of it.
Peachy Keen, drag queen: she/her in drag, he/him out of it.
Legs Luthor, drag queen: she/her in drag, he/they out of it.
Violet Bucket, drag queen: she/her in drag, he/him out of it.
Moxxie Toxxic, drag king: they/them in and out of drag.
Incubussy, drag king: he/him in drag, she/her out of it.

Like many artists, musicians, writers, and performers, you'll also find many of the drag artists in this novel are referred to by their drag name, or a variation, while out of drag as well as in it.

For all the drag performers who continue to inspire me.

CHAPTER ONE

Bubblegum Galaxy

IF ANYONE ever tells you nobody will remember your most embarrassing moment, just know they're probably lying.

Especially if that moment happens in front of an audience.

The final verse of Sam Smith's "Man I Am" filled the airy rafters of Fox & Taylor as I watched Lincoln's newest and most amazing drag king, Moxxie Toxxic, strutting up and down between the restaurant's packed tables. The audience were absolutely entranced, but I wasn't sure whether it was because of Moxxie's voice, their strut, or the fact their cowboy hat, boots, and shirt glittered with so many rhinestones it was impossible to look at them without seeing stars.

I was kinda jealous because glitter and sparkles were my favourite things, but I couldn't deny how fabulous

Moxxie looked. It was the ultimate fuck you to the patriarchy.

Moxxie, Bitch Fit, Lincoln's resident trash goblin and one of my best drag friends, and I were all hosting Fox & Taylor's monthly bottomless drag brunch, where we each got twenty-five minutes to strut our stuff while the guests ate beautiful food and drank as many cocktails as they could stomach.

The restaurant was a newer addition to the high street, with huge windows, high ceilings, and a glitzy, art deco-inspired décor with gold highlights sparkling on the midnight blue walls and polished faux marble floor.

They'd only started running the drag brunches over the summer, but they'd already become a hit and had sold out within a couple of days of the tickets going on sale. Simon, one of the owners, had said they'd even started getting groups rebooking their table for the next month as soon as they arrived for the current one, which was wild to me, but in the best way. I loved seeing how much support Lincoln's small but passionate drag community was getting from the locals.

I'd done two of the four brunches since they tried to get a variety of performers in to stop the audience getting bored, but I was hoping they'd keep inviting me back. The money was pretty good for a few hours' work and they always fed us afterwards. There weren't many places that threw in a decent free meal as part of the arrangement, so I wanted to stay in Simon's good books.

And that meant serving absolute perfection.

Moxxie's set finished to thunderous applause and cheering, and they strolled into the little offstage area we'd been given, which was a couple of cordoned-off tables at the back of the restaurant nearest the kitchen, with an ornate art deco screen in front of it to give us some semblance of privacy.

They picked up one of the glasses of juice we'd been given and downed the whole thing in one before putting their hat on the table and sliding onto a chair.

"Fuck me, that was fun," they said, giving Bitch and me an exhausted smile. "It's roasting out there, though, and it's packed. I know they told everyone to tuck their bags away, but there's definitely a few stray bag handles. There's a bit of a sticky patch over by the window too. I think someone spilt something." They pointed in the direction they meant, and I nodded, making a mental note to avoid it if possible.

Wearing eight-inch glittering Pleasers might've made my legs look fucking amazing, but they weren't exactly the most stable things in the world.

"You were fucking amazing, though," Bitch said, plonking herself in the seat next to Moxxie and grabbing her own glass of juice. Bitch would go on last, so she had a little bit to wait, but she was also the perfect person to wait and watch with because, although she was as snarky as her name suggested, she was also very supportive and encouraging.

If I wanted anyone to be my cheerleader, it was Bitch Fit.

I'd just never suggest pompoms.

"How're you doing the splits in those?" Bitch asked, gesturing to Moxxie's fringed trousers. "Also, how the fuck can you do the splits?"

Moxxie chuckled. "I did gymnastics as a kid because my sister wanted to do it and my mum decided I could go too because it would keep me out of trouble. And I made the trousers so they'd stretch—the material has plenty of give in it. They're basically dance trousers."

"God, you can sing, sew, and do the splits. If you weren't my friend, I'd fucking hate you." Bitch winked at them and then looked at me. "You okay, hun? Ready to shine?"

"Definitely. I'm always ready to sparkle!" I grinned and did a little shimmy, making the star sequins sewn onto my skirt twinkle. This outfit was one of my favourites and had taken forever for my mum and me to finish it.

It had a corset-style bodice with baby blue satin covered in hundreds of white sequins and rhinestones, with a short tulle skirt made up of multiple layers and a handkerchief hem. The skirt was soft blue and white, and while it still glittered with sequins, they were fewer and further between.

It was like Elsa from *Frozen* crossed with pageant drag exuberance.

I always wore it with sheer glitter tights and an eye-wateringly expensive white-blonde wig, which if it hadn't been so irresistibly gorgeous, I'd never have considered spending so much on. I'd still never admitted the cost out loud and tried to be vague when people asked about it because there were *so* many people out there who'd think spending over three grand on a wig was fucking obscene.

But drag was my life and being Bubblegum allowed me

to indulge in all the pretty, sparkly things I'd loved since I was a child. Only now, I had adult money to spend.

Besides, if I didn't look good, I wasn't going to get booked and I was definitely not going to get onto the next series of *Drag Stars UK*. I'd been rejected last year, but this year I'd already made it through to the second stage, a phone interview, and I was crossing all my fingers and toes they liked me enough to progress me even further!

"By the way," Moxxie said, craning their neck to look out into the restaurant where the waiting staff were topping up drinks and starting to serve the main course. "There's a table off to the left full of the hottest men I've ever fucking seen. And they're all huge. One of them stood up as I was finishing and I swear he could've crushed me with his thighs." Moxxie sighed, a dreamy smile on their face.

"Oh my God, you're totally thinking about them dicking you down," I said, fighting to keep my voice quiet as I peered out at the tables, trying to see who Moxxie was talking about.

They were hard to miss. It was a table of six men, all of whom had the most amazing broad shoulders and bulging chest muscles, which were highlighted by their tailored shirts and well-fitting T-shirts. They were sitting off to one side, close enough to see everything well but just far enough away that it seemed like they were trying to avoid attracting our attention while we performed.

They all looked like they were probably in their twenties and thirties, but I was always hopeless with age, so I was taking my assessment with a pinch of salt. Each and every one of them was gorgeous as fuck, though, and I had no idea where they'd come from or why they were here. They didn't seem like our normal crowd.

One of them had a bruise on his jaw and another had some Steri-Strips over his eyebrow, suggesting it had been cut recently. I did a mental rundown of professions that tended to involve large muscular young men and violence.

My two options were sport and the mafia, and I didn't think Lincoln was the sort of city to have a thriving underground crime network. It was too boring for that.

Sport then.

I didn't think they were members of the football club since I occasionally went to games with my dad and brother, Christopher, and I couldn't remember seeing any of them on the squad. Lincoln didn't have anything like ice hockey, and the only American football stuff I'd seen was the university team, and they looked too old to be students. There were a few boxing gyms, though. And a rugby club...

A professional rugby club...

Sold. That was where my money was going.

"I'm not gonna deny it," Moxxie said, still grinning. "You can see them, and I know you wouldn't say no."

"You're right, I wouldn't. I'd let any of them do me. Or all. I'm not picky."

"Alright, Miss Sparkle Slut," Bitch teased affectionately. "You can go and flirt with them later. Just don't drop your panties in the middle of the restaurant."

"Damn, there goes my opening number," I said, flexing my feet and wiggling my toes. My feet were starting to ache and I knew if I sat down, I'd be in more pain when I got up.

"At least I only have to fight Moxxie for them. We can have three each."

"Sounds fair," Moxxie said. "And we can leave Miss Fit to go back to the arms of her beloved. Where is Tristan today?"

"At home," Bitch said, a soft smile sliding onto her face as she thought about her boyfriend, who was the most adorably wholesome man I'd ever met. How or why he and Bitch were compatible was a mystery not even science could solve, but they were so sweet together it was sickening. And not in a good way, more an actually about to chunder way. "He's spent all week building some new miniatures and I think he wants to prime them while the weather's not totally shit. Apparently, it's meant to piss it down all next week."

I groaned. Even though it was the middle of October and we were closer to Christmas than July, I desperately wanted more sunshine. I hated cold weather with a passion and all the layers I was forced to wear not to freeze to death. If I ever won the lottery, I'd spend every winter somewhere gloriously warm and sunny, lying out on the beach where a tall, handsome man in teeny, tiny swimwear could bring me endless cocktails with little umbrellas and big bowls of ice cream or plates of nachos.

"Bubblegum?" I turned as someone said my name and realised Simon was stood behind me looking at his watch. "Are you ready?"

"Absolutely!" I beamed at him, doing another excited little shimmy. I glanced at Bitch, who'd stood up. "Are you going to introduce me like you did Moxxie?"

"Sure," she said, winking at me as she took a portable mic from Simon. "Just so you know, I'm not using any official bio shit."

I snorted, checking my lipstick in the portable make-up mirror we'd propped up on the table. "It wouldn't be a true Bitch introduction if it wasn't wildly inaccurate and over the top." I blew Bitch a kiss over my shoulder and she laughed.

"We'll make a baby Bitch of you yet, Sparkles."

Bitch Fit stepped out into the restaurant and began chatting to the crowd, who laughed and applauded. It was easy to hear what she was saying, but I wasn't listening. My brain was running through my set list, mentally scrolling through lyrics for my lip syncs and slotting the dance moves, twists, turns, and drops into place. The restaurant had given us a runway to walk down between the tables as well as plenty of space to move around them, and I knew exactly what I wanted to do where.

All I needed was my cue.

"She's sweet, she's sparkly, and she's our very own shining star. It's Bubblegum Galaxy!" Bitch announced my name and my music cue, and the opening lyrics of Ava Max's "Million Dollar Baby" flooded the restaurant's sound system. I took a split second to compose myself and then, as the beat dropped, I strutted out onto the floor.

As soon as I stepped out, the perfect rush I got from performing hit me. I'd never gotten nervous about going out in front of people and I'd always been a natural show-off according to my brother. Being a drag queen let me live out every fantasy I'd had as a small boy bouncing around my living room to Girls Aloud and The Pussycat Dolls in my cousin's Princess Aurora dress and an old pink lipstick Mum had given me to play dress-up with.

I loved the feeling of people's eyes on me, the way they watched me as I strutted and twirled, keeping in perfect time with the music and lip-syncing meticulously to every word. I'd watched every single *Drag Stars* lip sync more times than I knew, and I'd learned something from all of them. Whether it was the absolutely legendary season seven finale of *Drag Stars US* where Venus L'Amour's dress had melted into flower petals and glitter, leaving her in a sheer bodysuit with perfectly positioned crystals, or the most recent season of *Drag Stars UK* where Barbie Summers had won a double lip-sync elimination and snatched the crown with her incredible performance of "Survivor" by Destiny's Child.

And I'd learnt even more from the bad performances: the lacklustre energy, the missteps, the wardrobe malfunctions, the poorly executed tricks, the not knowing the fucking lyrics. I'd studied them all and dedicated myself to becoming the best lip syncer I could be.

The only thing I'd never accounted for, in any performance, was a member of staff trying to duck behind me while carrying a large pitcher of Sex on the Beach…

And with one misplaced arm, a perfectly timed spin, and the worst luck in the entire fucking universe, I caught them and sent the entire jug flying straight into the lap of the most gorgeous man at the rugby table…

CHAPTER TWO

West

OF ALL THE things I'd been expecting to happen at my first drag brunch, getting a lapful of ice-cold cocktail hadn't been one of them.

I'd seen the whole thing happening in slow motion, but by the time I'd realised where the jug of flying liquid was headed, it had been too late to do more than hold my hands out in a pitiful attempt to catch it. The pitcher had emptied itself all over my crotch before clattering on the ground while the whole restaurant stared at me in disbelief.

"Oh my God! I'm so sorry," squeaked the poor member of staff as she clapped her hands to her face in horror. "I should… I didn't…" She stood frozen, like she had no idea what to do. I almost wanted to apologise for inconveniencing her as Mason, my best friend and the one who'd organised this outing and was now desperately trying not to laugh, handed me a napkin.

I didn't think it would do any good.

My dick was going to smell of cranberry juice, orange, and peach schnapps for weeks.

"Fucking hell, hun, are you okay?" asked another voice and I looked up from dabbing at my crotch to see a pair of beautiful grey eyes surrounded by rhinestones and glitter and a perfectly made-up face wearing an expression of shock. It was the queen who'd been performing… the one I hadn't been able to stop staring at since she'd appeared. "I'm so sorry!"

"Oh… it's fine," I said, taking another napkin off Mason and handing him a sodden one. I didn't think I was making any difference. "It was an accident. Don't worry about it."

"Generally when I want to get a man wet, I don't chuck Sex on the Beach into his lap," she said, grinning ruefully. I laughed. There was still music playing and I realised she was supposed to be performing. Behind her, I could see the poor girl who'd thrown the pitcher still frozen in place, looking between the two of us like she expected someone to start shouting.

"You, er, you don't need to worry about me," I said. "You can keep going." I gestured at the restaurant where people were watching us with interest. I hated being stared at and it was making me distinctly uncomfortable. Bubblegum Galaxy looked over her shoulder and then back at me, tilting her head slightly.

"I'll be back," she said, and before I could tell her that wasn't necessary, she walked back into the middle of the restaurant, heels clacking on the floor. Her whole body sparkled as she moved, and it was virtually impossible not to notice her long legs, nipped-in waist, and pert behind.

She lifted her hand and the music stopped suddenly. "Shall we try that again?" she asked the crowd, and I realised her voice was slightly lighter when she spoke to them. "And I promise this time I won't drench any of you in peach schnapps. Not unless you ask nicely." There was some laughter and applause, and then the track started again and she began to dance as if nothing had happened.

My eyes were transfixed by her, and I wasn't sure if I was more in awe of her looks, her dancing, or her ability to carry on as if nothing had happened. That took some serious professionalism.

"That's one way to get someone's attention," Mason said, handing me yet another napkin. I raised my eyebrow at him as I took it. He shrugged. "It's Jonny's. I've nicked everyone's."

I glanced around at the rest of the table, which was filled with other guys from the rugby team. All of them were smirking at me and I knew I'd never live this down. Rugby lads could always be trusted to be wankers about this shit. Not that I could blame them. I'd be doing the same if it'd happened to any of them. Besides, were people really friends if they didn't lovingly rip the ever-loving shit out of each other sometimes?

"It's not going to do anything," I said quietly, trying to dab at more of the liquid, which had soaked through both my jeans and boxers and was dripping off the chair onto the floor. There were ice cubes melting onto the tiled floor between my feet, making the sunset-coloured cocktail swirl and glitter. I didn't think it had even been meant for our table, and I hoped whoever had ordered it had been given a replacement. "I'll just have to wait until we get home."

"There's a break coming up," Mason said. "Once Bubblegum finishes, there'll be another break before the last act. You can sneak out then. I can ask them to box your pudding up and bring it back with me."

I glanced back at the table, noticing the last few chips on my plate had managed to avoid getting drenched. Luckily, I'd eaten my burger before the cocktail incident.

A couple of members of staff came hurrying up to me, one of them clutching a roll of blue paper towels and what looked like some tea towels. One of them wasn't wearing the same serving uniform as the rest of the waiting and bar staff, so I assumed he was part of the management. "I'm so sorry, sir," he said quietly. "That shouldn't have happened. Please accept our apologies."

"It's fine," I said, taking the tea towels from the other member of staff who was ripping off bits of paper towel to start mopping up the floor. "It was an accident. These things happen."

The man didn't look convinced, but if there were going to be any consequences, he wasn't exactly going to tell me. "Even so, it shouldn't have happened. We'll refund your ticket for today and compliment your bill."

"You don't have to do that," I said and behind me I heard Mason sigh. No doubt he thought I should shut up and take the free meal. But I felt bad. It wasn't anyone's fault.

"Thank you, sir, you're very kind but it's already been

arranged."

"If you're sure."

"I am." He looked around at the rest of the table. "If there's anything we can do for you gentlemen, please let us know."

I saw Jonny and Charlie both open their mouths, probably to ask for more drinks and maybe even some more food, but luckily they were interrupted by the end of Bubblegum's performance. The room burst into rapturous applause and even a few whistles as the queen did a little curtsy in the middle of the room. How on earth did she walk in those shoes without falling over? I'd have broken my ankle just trying to stand up.

I put the tea towels and the last of the wet napkins on the table, preparing to make a quick exit. It wasn't far to get home, but I didn't fancy walking through Lincoln with a visibly sodden crotch. I'd have to order a taxi and stand with my jacket carefully positioned so the driver didn't think I'd wet myself. The last thing I wanted was to be left stranded on the side of the road and blacklisted from every taxi service in the city.

But as I stood up and grabbed my jacket off the back of my chair, I realised Bubblegum Galaxy was striding towards me in her enormous platform heels. They were sparkly too, covered in a shimmering, opalescent glitter. And when she stopped in front of me, I noticed they made her nearly as tall as me, which was impressive considering I was six foot three.

"Did I scare you off then?" she asked, grinning. But there was a hesitancy in her eyes that was endearing, like she was trying to pretend everything was fine. "You wouldn't be the first man I've sent running, but at least you're not screaming this time."

I laughed. "Do you make a habit of throwing Sex on the Beach into men's laps or am I your first?"

"Well, it's not my preferred way to get a man's attention, but sometimes you have to take desperate measures." She grinned wickedly and then her expression softened. "I really am sorry about this. I feel like such a fucking twat."

"Seriously, it's fine. I'm pretty sure you didn't do it deliberately. And I don't think the poor girl holding it planned for it to happen either." I hadn't seen her since she'd been shepherded away by another member of staff. Hopefully she was okay and didn't lose her job—it wasn't like she'd been able to stop it happening.

"Oh shit, I hope she's okay," Bubblegum said, looking around trying to spot her. "I'll have to ask Simon."

"Simon?"

"Yeah, he's the owner. He's probably been over to see you."

"I think so, yeah." I heard a cough from beside me and realised we'd both been stood chatting in our own little world while everything went on around us. As I glanced around, I realised Mason was watching us with a smile while the others were pretending to look very interested in their phones, drinks, and whatever sudden bits of conversation they could come up with in a split second. Nosy bastards.

"Sorry," I continued, stepping slightly forward and ducking around a member of staff who was clearing the table next to us. "I didn't mean to keep you. I should let you go."

"You're fine. All that's waiting for me is a drink and a burger, although I'm not gonna lie—that burger is calling me. Wearing three pairs of Spanx and a waist-trainer while dancing is fucking exhausting."

"I'd have thought your feet would be killing you."

"A bit, but they've been worse. It's the price I have to pay for looking this pretty." She winked at me and I felt heat burst across my cheeks. I'd only ever seen drag queens on social media before and now I was face-to-face with one in real life and somehow I couldn't seem to stop staring. Or flirting. God, I was such a fucking mess.

"You're, er, you're very pretty," I said, trying really hard not to look at the floor like I was five. "I like your dress. And your, er, your gems." I touched my face just under my eye where Bubblegum had a mirrored line of silver gems.

"Thanks, you're pretty cute yourself." Her smile was bright, like the galaxy she was named after, and it stole all the breath from my lungs without me even noticing. "And the face gems look cute, but oh my fucking God, they're such a pain in the ass to take off. And sometimes they just fall off, so I keep finding them all around the house. I once found one in a mug of tea."

I chuckled. "Hopefully before you drank it."

"Just, but it was a close call."

"Oi! Sparkles!" The voice calling Bubblegum's name was hissed but demanding, not something to be ignored.

We both turned and I saw the other queen, the one who acted as MC and who'd be headlining the show, beckoning to Bubblegum and tapping an imaginary watch on her wrist. She had a bold punk-rock aesthetic that reminded me of the emo stuff I'd seen everywhere when I was about eight or nine. It was cool and obviously suited her, but I had to admit I preferred Bubblegum's sparkle and glamour.

It was beautiful and eye-catching, and I never wanted to tear my eyes away from her. I hoped she was local because if she performed regularly, I'd drag Mason along to see her. I hadn't been to a drag night before, but there was a first time for everything.

I'd have to find her on Instagram later and see where she'd be next. Fox & Taylor would've tagged her in their posts promoting today, so she shouldn't be hard to find. Maybe there'd also be pictures of her out of drag too. I bet Bubblegum was equally beautiful in boy mode.

"Ugh, I should go before Bitch Fit throws an actual temper tantrum," Bubblegum said. "You've got about two minutes to escape if that's still your plan."

"Yeah, I probably should head out. Everything's starting to dry and it's both weirdly sticky and crusty at the same time."

Bubblegum laughed again, then put her hand out to brush against mine. "It was nice to meet you. Sorry again about drenching you."

"No worries. It was nice to meet you too."

"Sparkles!" Bitch Fit hissed again and Bubblegum gave her a little wave.

"See you around." She blew me a kiss before she trotted off. I watched her go, a smile plastered on my lips.

"You know," Mason said in a low voice, leaning in close. "Next time you start flirting with someone in the middle of a restaurant, you should probably remember to give them your name."

CHAPTER THREE

Bubblegum Galaxy

"Roo? Is that you?" Dad's voice called as I slammed the front door and kicked off my trainers, silently wishing I could vanish into thin air. I was still half-dressed in drag because I'd wanted to get out as soon as possible, so I'd thrown my hoodie and joggers on over my tights, shoved my dress and wig in my bag, and hotfooted it to the car as soon as I was able to leave.

The cocktail incident kept playing over and over in my mind, and every time I thought about it, it got worse. If Simon ever let me anywhere near Fox & Taylor again, it would be a fucking miracle.

"Yeah," I said, dropping my bag on the floor. I wasn't even going to attempt to smile. Dad would see through it in a second. I could hear the sound of commentary and a crowd, so I assumed he and Christopher were watching the football. The smell of roast dinner wafted into the hall from the kitchen, making my stomach rumble. Even though I'd been offered a post-show burger, I'd turned it down out of sheer embarrassment. I kept running through every detail of my performance and my conversation with the guy I'd sort of splatted.

He'd been so gorgeous, I'd nearly swallowed my tongue. He was all broad shoulders, wide chest, and thick thighs, with sparkling blue eyes and a slightly crooked nose dusted with freckles. I hadn't been able to resist teasingly flirting with him, even though I'd known it could easily end horribly. There were a lot of guys out there who reacted badly when Bubblegum flirted with them because they hated the fact they found her attractive and underneath all the make-up, rhinestones, pretty dresses, and padding was a man.

Internalised homophobia was always *so* fun to deal with.

I'd wanted to kick myself for taking the risk, especially because I was the reason he'd been drenched in juice and peach schnapps. But then he'd flirted back in a soft, deep voice that made my knees weak. I was such a sucker for big men with soft hearts. It was probably why I'd been just a little bit obsessed with Kronk from *The Emperor's New Groove* as a kid before moving on to Thor from the MCU as soon as I'd seen Chris Hemsworth topless.

It was only afterwards, when Bitch Fit had dragged me away, I'd realised I hadn't even asked for his name.

I was the literal walking definition of a hot fucking mess.

"Roo? Everything okay?" Dad asked, snapping me back

from staring randomly into space. He sounded concerned and I knew I'd have to tell him everything. Dad might not have looked like it, with his bald head, grizzled features, and faded tattoos, including an England flag on the back of his neck, but he worried about Mum, Christopher, and me something chronic. I wasn't sure if it was because he was afraid we'd end up like him in his youth—starting fights, getting banned from pubs, and stabbed with broken bottles—or because he was worried we'd end up being subjected to something like that.

"Yeah. Fine." I wandered through into the living room where, as I'd expected, Dad and Christopher were watching the football. Both of them turned to look at me as I flopped onto the end of the floral sofa nearest the door next to my brother, and I felt their eyes boring into me, waiting for more details.

It was Christopher who broke first, nudging me with his elbow to get my attention before he started to sign.

"*That bad?*" he asked, a teasing smile on his face. "*Did you fall over?*"

"Worse," I said, speaking aloud and signing. Christopher had developed severe hearing loss as a child after a complication from an infection, and while he had hearing aids, he often preferred not to wear them at home because he complained they were uncomfortable. We'd all learnt British Sign Language alongside him, and these days signing was second nature. "It wasn't my fault but it feels like it was."

"What happened?" Dad asked, gently tickling Beans, our ginger cat, under the chin. Beans was cradled in Dad's arm like a baby, snuggled up against his round stomach and looking epically smug. It was her favourite place to sleep and we all joked that it was obvious who the favourite child was. "It didn't get nasty, did it?"

"No, nothing like that," I said, sighing deeply. I knew I had to rip the plaster off and tell them. Maybe it wasn't as big a deal as I was building it up to be in my head. "During my performance, a member of staff tried to walk behind me carrying a cocktail pitcher. I caught her with my arm and a spin. The pitcher went flying… and ended up landing in the lap of this guy at a nearby table. So yeah… not my best day. Don't think I've ever thrown an entire jug of cocktails all over someone before."

Christopher stared at me, eyes wide, desperately trying not to laugh. *"You didn't?"*

"Oh yeah, I did. Right all over his junk…" I flicked my fingers like I was mimicking the motion of the liquid as the poor guy's horrified face appeared in my mind. "The worst part was he was nice about it. Kept telling me it wasn't my fault."

"It wasn't, though, was it?" Dad said and Beans grumbled loudly as he moved his fingers away from her to sign. She tried to bat one of his fingers with an outstretched paw. "Not now, Beans, I'm talking. Gimme a minute."

"Love how you sign what you say to the cat like she understands," Christopher said. *"Demanding brat."*

"Watch it. That's my baby you're talking about. We can't leave her out."

"What about poor Sausage?"

"Sausage is a grumpy old bastard and doesn't want to be disturbed," Dad said. "And I know how he feels."

Sausage was our very elderly cat who spent most of his life asleep on either Mum and Dad's bed or in his bed on the kitchen windowsill where he could lie in the sun and watch the birds in the garden. Mum always put up several feeders and fat balls for them, and Sausage got endless hours of amusement watching the local bird population flit around our garden. Not that he'd know what to do with a bird if he ever came face-to-face with one since he'd lived inside his whole life and had once refused to come out of the living room because Christopher had left his toy penguin on the stairs. Apparently, penguins, in any form, were the most terrifying thing known to cat-kind.

"You're an old bastard too then?" Christopher asked.

"Yeah, and dealing with you two has taken twenty years off my life."

I laughed because we all knew being a dad was everything to him. There were photos of Christopher and me everywhere, chronicling both our lives from the day we'd been born. Considering my dad had grown up as a skinhead and football hooligan, some people probably considered it strange that he was so supportive of my sexuality and drag career and I hated that assumption. Dad was one of the most supportive people in my life and a fierce ally.

It was why he'd started so many fights in London pubs in the late eighties and early nineties during the AIDS crisis when he'd overheard men saying less than pleasant things about the queer community.

Dad wasn't one to give people more than one chance.

And he packed a wicked right hook, at least according to my Uncle Ian, who cheerfully regaled us with various stories from Dad's youth every Christmas.

"Are you worried they're not gonna have you back there?" Dad asked, turning his head to me and frowning. "Because if they are, then that's not bloody on. It wasn't your fault and I'm not having you being punished for it."

"Punished for what?" Mum asked, appearing in the doorway holding two cups of tea. "Hello, Rory, love. You all right?"

"Roo's worried Fox & Taylor won't have him back because a member of staff got in the way during his act and they ended up flinging a jug of cocktails onto one of the guests," Dad said as he adjusted his seat so he could take the cup of tea off Mum, wedging Beans in next to him so she wouldn't slide off. "You're an angel, Lou."

"*Where's my tea?*" Christopher asked.

"You didn't want one," Mum said as she signed, putting her tea on the end table next to her armchair, which was covered in sewing supplies and knitting needles. "And don't say you didn't see me ask, because you told me no. Alan, he told me no, correct?"

"He did."

"If you want a cup of tea, you can make one yourself," Mum said before settling herself into her chair. "Make one for your brother too. And give the roast potatoes a stir while you're out there."

"*Yes, Your Majesty.*" Christopher got off the sofa and did an elaborate bow towards Mum before wandering out of the room.

"I'm sure it'll be okay," Mum said as she picked up her tea. "Sounds like it was just an accident."

"I know," I said. "But... I feel like shit. Everyone saw it happen, and now I'll be forever known as the drag queen who threw Sex on the Beach all over some rando."

"Ah well," Mum said. "There's worse things to be known for."

I STEWED in my sulking for the rest of the afternoon, barely tasting my dinner even though Mum's Sunday roasts were the highlight of my week. Eventually, I took myself upstairs and threw myself on my bed, silently screaming into my pillow.

Bitch Fit and Moxxie had both messaged me several times to check in, and I'd promised them I was okay. Hopefully, both of them believed me. It was easier to lie over text than in person because all I had to do was add some exclamation points and emojis and it'd be the same as every other message I sent.

Rolling onto my side, I pulled my phone out of the pocket of my joggers, hoping that mindlessly scrolling through TikTok would help me zone out and forget. If anything could make me feel better, it would be endless videos of baby animals and pets doing silly things.

That or an entire packet of Maryland cookies.

There were a few notifications I went to dismiss offhandedly, including a couple of new followers on Instagram, when one of them caught my eye. It was the man from today.

I hurriedly tapped the notification to open his profile, willing my phone to work faster. My heart raced like I'd tried to run up three flights of stairs in heels. Why had he followed me? Surely it had to be a joke. Or maybe it was someone completely different who only looked vaguely similar. Profile pictures were pretty small, so it would be easy for me to be mistaken.

Except... I wasn't wrong.

It was him.

West Russell.

Hooker for the Lincoln Knights rugby team. And just as gorgeous in pictures as he was in person, especially in his kit when his shorts had ridden all the way up his thighs.

I hit Follow Back and then tapped the message arrow. I doubted he'd ever see it, but it was worth a shot.

> **Bubblegum Galaxy**
> Thanks for the follow! Sorry again about today. I hope you got home okay.

I scrolled back onto his profile and perused his photos for a few minutes. There were quite a lot of him at training or playing games, a couple from earlier in the month when he'd been at the beach in somewhere called Heather Bay, and when I ventured as far back as last year, I realised there were a couple of him from Lincoln Pride, decked out in rainbows with the bisexual flag painted on his face.

A giddy smile burst onto my lips as I stared at the pictures, absorbing every detail, and when my eyes flicked up to his profile and read the words "Rugby Player for

@LincolnKnights. Proudly Bisexual," I thought my heart might fall out of my mouth.

How had I missed that?

It explained the flirting at least.

A message notification appeared with a reply from West, and I hit it so hard I thought I was about to either break my finger or crack my screen.

> **West Russell**
> Hey! Yeah I got back fine. I put my jacket over my crotch so the taxi driver didn't ask questions. I think I got away with it!

> **West Russell**
> And don't apologise, it wasn't your fault. But next time I'm getting a table at the back.

Bubblegum Galaxy
Either that or I can get you a rain mac, like one of those cheap festival ponchos or the ones you get at Alton Towers! Maybe I should get branded ones.

> **West Russell**
> Lol I think that's asking for trouble. Unless you plan to squirt people with drinks regularly?

Bubblegum Galaxy
Not really my thing. If I'm going to throw anything at anyone regularly, it'll be glitter.

> **West Russell**
> Doesn't glitter get everywhere? I think that might be worse than soggy boxers.

I snorted, my stomach full of butterflies as I wiggled my toes. One short messenger conversation shouldn't have been enough to do this to me, but it had, and I wasn't going to question it. It had been forever since I'd felt like this while chatting to someone and I wasn't about to throw it away. After all, I'd had less conversation with some of the guys I'd hooked up with in the past.

> **Bubblegum Galaxy**
> Nobody ever wants wet underwear. At least not from being soaked in schnapps.

> **West Russell**
> Yeah definitely a waste of schnapps. Feel bad that whoever ordered it didn't get their drinks.

> **West Russell**
> Would you ever fancy getting a drink with me sometime? Boy you, not Bubblegum you. Would you be up for that?

A ridiculous scream burst from my throat and I bit my lip to stop myself, hoping nobody had heard me. That was the only problem with living at home; privacy was ridiculously hard to come by, even if my door was closed.

> **Bubblegum Galaxy**
> I'd love that! Sounds like fun <3

CHAPTER FOUR

West

For a Wednesday night, the bar Mason had suggested I take Rory to was much busier than I'd expected. But maybe that was a good thing. Then there'd be enough noise that nobody would hear me make a total fucking ass of myself in front of him.

Rory.

Bubblegum Galaxy's real name.

Or boy name.

Legal name.

Whatever the term was.

Rory.

It rolled off my tongue and sat comfortably beside his drag name in my mind. It suited him, which was weird because I'd never thought about how anyone's name suited them before. Maybe it was because I'd met Bubblegum first, and meeting Rory felt like getting to see something secret.

Which was again weird because they were both the same person and I was sure there were plenty of people who knew Rory as Rory, and Rory as Bubblegum.

I was definitely getting in my head and it wasn't helping my nerves. I didn't know what had caused the lightning strike of confidence that'd made me ask him out, but it was too late to back out now. Besides, it would be really rude of me to cancel after inviting him out.

At least this would shut Mason and Jonny up when they said I needed to get out more and not spend all my free time playing video games and watching whatever trashy reality shows Netflix and Channel 4 had to offer. I was currently working my way through *Married At First Sight: Australia* and trying to work out what on earth possessed people to sign up for these things if they were going to act like total fucking wankers.

Mason thought it was because the wankers were narcissists who thought they'd come off better than they did, coupled with a bullshit "alpha male" mindset that made men act like fucked-up dickheads. I had to agree. Why these men thought anyone would want to shag them was beyond me.

Mind you, I hadn't been out with any guys in a while and when I did hook up with men, we didn't usually get much beyond the names and sexual health part of the conversation. Maybe that was why I'd managed to avoid them. Or maybe I'd been lucky and they'd taken one look at my profile picture on Grindr and thought they wouldn't get far.

I didn't know why I was thinking about any of this. I

should've been keeping an eye out for Rory, not wondering why I'd managed to avoid the attention of some juiced-up, misogynistic cockwomble.

My eyes trailed over the other occupied tables, trying to guess what some of their occupants might be out for—dates, casual drinks with friends, work socials, midweek catchups with people who could only be pinned down every six months because life inevitably got in the way.

That amused me for a minute or two before I moved on to looking at the bottles behind the polished wooden bar and the eclectic selection of posters and photos adorning the walls, showing off everything from classic horror movies to sporting headlines to touring posters for indie bands.

A nervous itch pulled at my skin and I picked up my phone from where it lay flat on the table in front of me, double-checking to see if there was anything from Rory. I'd told him I was here and that I'd snagged a small table in the corner, but all he'd done was like my messages. I guessed that meant he was on his way. Maybe the traffic was bad.

To pass the time and distract myself, I opened Bubblegum's Instagram and scrolled through the reels and photos, finding the occasional one showing Rory out of drag. My eyes roamed over the curve of his jaw, the dimple in his chin, the fullness of his mouth—which I'd initially just assumed to be make-up but wasn't—and the way his grey eyes stared out of every image, dancing straight into my soul. I'd never seen such a pair of captivating eyes.

He had beautiful eyelashes too, long, thick, and dark.

If he fluttered them, it would probably cause a hurricane.

"Hey! There you are!" A bright voice caught my attention and I jumped, dropping my phone onto the table. It clattered loudly like it wanted to add dramatic emphasis to the moment.

"Shit, sorry!" I looked up to see Rory standing by my table, an amused smile curling the corner of his mouth. Despite the fact it was late October, he was wearing a white tank top under an oversized denim jacket with patches up and down the arms and across the chest and a stylish-looking pair of jeans. "I was totally zoned out there," I continued. "And now I look like a complete bellend."

"You're fine," Rory said, still smiling at me. His grey eyes seemed to be drinking in every inch of me and I hoped the glint in them meant he liked what he saw. I wasn't exactly the most fashionable person, but I could pull off a well-fitted pair of jeans and a T-shirt as well as the next man. "Can I get you a drink?"

I grinned. "Yes, but only if you let me get you one first. I invited you out—it seems only fair I buy you a drink."

"Such a gentleman," Rory said, sliding onto the chair opposite me and wiggling it around the edge of the table so we weren't sat so far apart. "I accept."

"Good, but I wasn't going to take no for an answer."

Rory's smile turned mischievous. "I do like a man who knows what he wants. To a certain extent."

"Don't worry," I said, picking up the drinks menu from the middle of the table and handing it to him. "I'm not going to choose for you or any of that bollocks. Besides, knowing my luck I'd order something you're allergic to or really fucking hate and that'd be shit. I'd become that guy you tell all your mates about, you know, like the worst date example."

Rory laughed as he took the menu. "Don't worry, you're already beating at least twenty percent of the men I've been out with."

"Only twenty percent? Damn, I better up my game. But also… I really want to know how someone can fail so epically."

"I mean barring all hook-ups where I'm not looking for their life story, the worst ones are like a two-way tie between the guy who took one look at me and said I was cuter online and needed to lose some weight, then offered me some coke because it'd really help suppress my appetite. Then there was the guy who brought two of his exes with him for no discernible reason, but it somehow simultaneously felt like I was being judged on *Britain's Got Talent* and lined up for sacrificial slaughter."

I stared at him, both astonished by the audacity of some people and captivated by how expressive he was when he spoke. "Yeah… I can't beat that."

"Most people can't," he said. "What about you? Got any bad date horror stories? You have to spill now."

I thought for a second, but my mind was suddenly blank. I'd had bad dates. Lots of them. But somehow, I couldn't think of anything that'd happened to me beyond the last five minutes. "I've had two marriage proposals before on first dates," I said finally, my tongue working on autopilot as my brain rebooted itself.

"Seriously?" Rory put his elbows on the table and interlinked his fingers together, resting his chin on them and giving me a delighted smile.

"Yeah… a girl whose best friend had just gotten engaged, so I think she was feeling pretty vulnerable, bless her. We actually ended up just getting some pizza and talking."

"Okay, that's kind of adorable but in a weird, slightly creepy way."

"Yeah, she was sweet. She apologised for it later, so I feel bad about making fun of her."

"Hmm, yes, we'll discard that one. That's more sad than anything. What about the other?"

"Er… that was a guy I went out for dinner with and we went back to his after…" I felt my face heat and my fingers tingle like they always did when I was embarrassed. At least this wasn't my most embarrassing moment, though. That was something only a select few people knew about and involved me rediscovering my older brother, who I hadn't spoken to or seen in fourteen years, via clips from his MyFans on Twitter… and not recognising him until I was halfway through his profile feed.

I didn't know if Theo knew, but his partner, Laurie, certainly did because he'd asked me several questions about how I'd found Theo again and it had been impossible to hide the truth. He'd been very nice about it, but that somehow made it worse.

"Oh my God," Rory said gleefully. "Did you seriously dick him down so good that he proposed? Are you that good? Or do you have a really big dick and he was a total needy size queen? Which I can totally understand, but still, that's impressive."

"Something like that," I said, knowing my face was the neon pink colour of cheap strawberry bubble gum. "Fuck, okay, that makes it sound like I'm bragging or something. Shit, pretend I never said any of that and add me to your list of really weird guys who tried to buy you a drink."

"Oh no, I'm definitely not letting you off the hook that easily." Rory slid a little closer, his eyes dropping down my body as he lowered his voice. "I feel like I need proof. If you're up for it?"

My heart raced and my cock swelled uncomfortably in my jeans. I wasn't sure if Rory could see it beneath the table but it would be really fucking obvious as soon as I stood up.

Having a larger dick was all well and good in porn, but in reality it could be a pain. Especially for playing sport. I'd become an expert in finding properly supportive underwear that didn't make every vein visible through my shorts, didn't cut off the blood supply to my balls, and didn't slip when I tackled someone and flash my dick to the crowd. And didn't repulse any man that looked at me.

"Yeah," I said with a nod, flashing him a smirk of my own. "As long as you promise not to propose to me afterwards."

Rory laughed and the sound sent butterflies fluttering through my chest and heat running down my spine like I was stood under a steaming waterfall. "I promise. Proposals are at least second dates for me. Third if I *really* want your dick again first."

I snorted and shook my head. "Good to know. I'll make sure I get a ring."

"Make sure it's a big one. I like my diamonds like my dicks and dildos: impossibly large." Rory winked at me and if I'd had a drink, I'd be choking on it.

That reminded me. We were in the middle of a bar... I looked around, not really caring if anyone was listening. I was more interested in seeing how busy the bar itself was, but although the staff seemed to be in a constant flow of making drinks and serving people, they didn't seem overwhelmed.

I glanced back at Rory and nodded at the bar, where neon lights glinted off the rows of bottles on display. "Did you want to get a drink first or..."

"Hmm, decisions, decisions," he said playfully, putting his hand on my leg under the table and sliding his fingers over my inner thigh. "Have a cocktail and then cock, or just cock?"

"Your choice. If you want a drink, I'll buy you whatever you want. And if you want to leave now, we can."

"You really are a gentleman."

"For now," I said teasingly. His hand was still pressed to my inner thigh, heat radiating out of his palm and into my leg. It was almost like he was branding me and I wouldn't have been surprised to take my jeans off later and see a mark burnt into my skin.

"Mmm, I like that implication."

"Have you made a decision then?"

"I have." Rory leant closer, his breath caressing my skin

as his words slipped into my ear. "Fuck the drinks. I'd rather you fucked me instead."

"I can do that," I said, twisting my head and bringing us nose to nose. This close, I could see every detail of his face in high definition. His eyelashes were even more perfect in person, and his irises had a ring of deep grey-blue around the edge of them while the rest of them were soft and bright. It reminded me of the sea in Heather Bay where my brother lived, cold and bright and glittering in the last of the autumn sunshine. It would be so easy to get lost in them. Maybe even to drown.

"Good," Rory said. He sat back slightly and bit his lip. "Ugh, this is the awkward part but are we okay to go back to yours? I'm still living with my family and if you don't want to be interrupted by my dad offering you a cup of tea and a box of condoms, then I'd suggest we go elsewhere."

I chuckled softly. "Sure. I've got three housemates, but they're just guys from the team. I don't really give a shit what they think. And my bedroom door has a lock." I knew if they heard us, they'd rib me for it in the morning, but I didn't care. I needed Rory in my bed more than I needed to breathe.

Besides, Jonny and Guy brought girls home all the fucking time. To the point I'd started keeping a pair of earplugs beside my bed so I didn't have to listen to Jonny's headboard slamming into my bedroom wall. If I had to put up with that shit two or three times a week, Jonny could damn well listen to me getting laid for once.

"That's fine with me. Definitely better than my house,"

Rory said, his smile returning. "Need to get anything on the way?"

"No, I'm good." I reached my hand under the table and slipped my fingers into his, jerking slightly as static electricity sparked between us.

"Perfect." Rory's gaze was so full of heat and need I almost melted onto the floor. "Let's see if you can make me propose."

CHAPTER FIVE

Bubblegum Galaxy

West's bedroom door banged shut as he pushed me up against it, his fingers fumbling for the lock as his mouth met mine in a desperate, hungry kiss. Need buzzed under my skin, making my body thrum like a live wire as my hands caressed his broad, firm chest. West was a big man and if the rest of his body, and his adorable, embarrassing story, was anything to go by, I was in for a hell of a night.

Fuck, it had been a long time since I'd taken a properly big dick. Not unless you counted the life-model dildo of Jake Summers I had in my bedside table, in which case the answer was last week when I'd had the house to myself for a few blissful hours.

But I wasn't counting that. Because as amazing and fun as getting myself off with Jake's dildo was, a dildo couldn't kiss me like they were a starving man and I was the sweetest peach, couldn't trail its lips down my neck and suck a mark into that spot on my collarbone that made my knees buckle and a needy moan burst from my throat, couldn't brush my jacket off my shoulders with a caress that sent electricity racing through me, couldn't slide its hands under my tank top and rest a thumb in the groove of my hip, stroking the skin and slowly undoing me one atom at a time.

West was the perfect amount of desperate and demanding. He was eager and sweet, like he needed to please me but there was power and hunger there too, bubbling underneath. It felt like he was holding it in check, as if letting it go was too risky. It made me want to push every single button this beautiful man had just to see what happened.

I was ninety-nine percent sure the result would be fucking fabulous.

My fingers grabbed the hem of his T-shirt, trying to tug it up and out of the way as West sucked another mark onto my chest. He realised what I was trying to do and straightened up, helping me shrug the annoying piece of fabric over his head to expose his muscular barrel chest covered in thick dark blond hair, broad shoulders, and giant upper arms that I was pretty sure would allow him to pick me up without a second thought.

The idea of him holding me up and fucking me against the door made my cock pulse in my jeans, my balls aching with the need to come.

I wasn't the smallest, twinkiest guy ever, but I didn't think my size would be an issue for West. He could probably throw me onto the bed without needing to take a breath.

"What're you thinking?" West asked, stepping closer to pin me against the door. His bright blue eyes seared into my soul, but there was a softness behind them too, like his question was less of a veiled demand and more of a gentle check-in to see what I wanted. He was so fucking sweet and I knew I was in trouble. West was like that first toffee apple of autumn—I always told myself that one or two would be enough, but they never were.

"I'm just thinking about how you could probably lift me up," I said as I reached out to trail my fingers across his chest, feeling the heat of his skin, the softness of the hair, and the thundering of his heart. "And fuck me against this door."

West smirked and bent slightly, his hands wrapping around my thighs and gripping my ass, casually squeezing it before standing up and lifting me into the air. "Like this?" he asked as he pushed my back against the door. My legs wrapped around his waist as my hands instinctively went to his neck, but I didn't feel the urge to cling on like a desperate koala. I felt totally safe in his arms.

"Yes," I said with a groan. I wiggled slightly, pressing my crotch against his abdomen so he could feel how much I wanted him. West kissed me again, holding me against the door and nipping my lip, his tongue teasing mine. He shifted and I felt the head of his cock pushing against my ass, and I groaned in delight. "More. Fuck, I want more."

"More?" West asked, his voice deep and teasing. "You're wearing too many clothes for more."

"I can fix that. You'll just have to put me down."

"I have a better idea." I wanted to ask what, but West wasn't one to hang around. He turned away from the door and carried me over to his bed, gently setting me down on the mattress before putting one knee between my legs, leaning over me, and casting me in shadow. He was still smirking, and fire danced in his eyes as he lowered his head, brushing his lips against mine as he spoke. "Now I can reach all of you."

His fingers casually reached for the hem of my tank top, sliding up and gently pulling it over my head, then throwing it off the edge of the bed. "You're so gorgeous," he said as he leant down to trail his mouth down my chest, each kiss burning into my skin like a brand. I gasped as he ran his tongue down the groove in my hip, pushing my body up and begging for more. West kissed across the waistband of my jeans, quickly popping them open and tugging them down, taking the tiny skintight pair of briefs I'd worn with them. I was almost sad he hadn't gotten to see me in them because they made my ass look deliciously fabulous and insanely fuckable.

Not that West needed any more convincing to fuck me considering I was already naked on his bed.

"Fuck," West said, throwing my clothes onto the floor and running his hand up my thigh. "You're…"

I grinned, sitting up and scooting forward so I was perfectly positioned to undo his jeans. "If I've stunned you into silence, then I'm totally taking that as a good thing."

"It is." West's voice melted into a low groan as I pressed a kiss to his bulge through the straining denim. I popped the button open, scarcely able to contain my delight as I slowly drew the zip down and released his cock.

West hadn't been exaggerating and honestly, I'd have proposed marriage too if I got to be fucked on a regular basis with what he was packing.

I pressed another kiss to his thick shaft through his boxers, which clung so tightly to him he might as well have been naked. I could see every ridge and vein and the way his foreskin had already pulled back to show off the wide mushroom head. I grinned up at West, who was watching me with awe and trepidation as if he half expected me to run screaming at the sight of his dick. I assumed some of his hook-ups had in the past. But they weren't me. I was a horny, determined size queen who was desperately in need of cock.

Winking at West, I reached for the waistband of his boxers and tugged them down, taking his jeans along for the ride. His beautiful dick sprang free and slapped against his abdomen, and I let out a ridiculous gasp. He probably thought I was a psychopath for being so excited. Or maybe it was a normal response to him.

West opened his mouth to say something, but whatever it was dissolved into a broken moan as I wrapped my fingers around his shaft and gave it a teasing, experimental pump. Not only was his cock thick, but it was long and gently curved too. I wasn't exactly about to whip out a tape measure, but it had to be at least nine or ten inches. It looked longer than my highest pair of heels and they were eight inches. Heat and excitement whipped themselves into a frenzy in my stomach, and my own cock twitched between my legs.

Leaning forward, I ran my tongue across his soft, silky cockhead, collecting his precum and savouring the taste of it. West gasped, his hand instinctively reaching for my hair as I wrapped my lips around him, sucking gently. I didn't know how much of him I'd be able to swallow, but luckily for West I'd trained myself out of gagging on cock as soon as I'd turned eighteen and gotten my hands on my first dildo.

West's fingers sank into my hair, brushing against my scalp and tightening on the golden-brown strands. I loved having my hair pulled and played with during sex, and his touch made me take him deeper, slowly sliding his beautiful big cock into my mouth. I swallowed around him and West moaned at the constricting sensation. Smiling to myself, I hummed around his shaft as I began to move my hand and mouth in perfect rhythm.

"Fuck," West said, the word a drawn-out whisper that sent shivers across my skin. "Shit, sweetheart... you have a fucking talented mouth. You're taking so much of me."

I moaned around him as his fingers rubbed the back of my head and I pushed into his touch. It was such a soft gesture, a praise through touch that made me tighten my stretched, aching lips and redouble my efforts. I didn't want him to come, but I wanted to show him exactly what I could do.

I wanted West to remember me long after tonight.

I wanted to be the one he compared everyone else to. For the rest of his life.

"S-shit. Oh fuck… Rory…" West groaned and I loved the way my name sounded dripping from his tongue. Sweeter than honey and as addictive as sugar. He gently pulled my head backwards, stepping away to ease his cock from my mouth. I moaned in desperation because I didn't want it to end. I looked up at him with pleading eyes and slick lips, strings of saliva hanging from my mouth and connecting me to his shaft.

He smiled as he looked down at me, running a thumb across my bottom lip and collecting the saliva on his skin. "Fuck, sweetheart, you look so beautiful like this. Even prettier than when you had my cock in your mouth." He leant down and captured my mouth in a deep kiss, pushing me back onto the bed and covering me with his body. "Now it's my turn," he whispered, trailing his lips down the shell of my ear. "Do you still want me to fuck you?"

"Honey, if I can get that much of your dick in my mouth, I'm definitely getting it in my ass. I want all of it."

West snorted and laughed into the bed beside me. "Good to know."

"Trust me," I said. "I can take it all. And I'll be moaning your name when I do."

"Mmm, I want to hear that." He slid a hand down my side, reaching for my ass and squeezing it playfully. "My name will sound so good on your lips, sweetheart."

I groaned, melting into the bed as he began to kiss down my body. He sucked more marks into my hips like he wanted me to remember him tomorrow. But I'd be thinking about him for a lot longer than that.

He pushed my thighs apart, spreading them wide as he

teased my aching cock with his tongue. I wanted him to suck me, swallowing me down until I came, but that was only because I was desperate. Waiting until he was deep inside me would be sweeter, but fuck I hated waiting. I probably could've done both, because while my refractory period wasn't as instantaneous as it was at eighteen, it never took me that long to get hard again.

But that thought was brushed aside as soon as West lowered his head between my thighs and began to eat my hole like it was his last meal. His tongue teased and flicked over the furled skin, sending pulses of pleasure racing through me. He pressed his tongue inside me, working me open with soft licks and sucking kisses, saliva dripping down my skin. My body felt like an exposed live wire, crackling and dangerous. My chest was tight, as if I couldn't breathe, and my legs had melted into jelly. If West expected me to move any time soon, he was going to need to hold me up.

I looked down my body to see him watching me, and when our eyes met, he winked at me.

If I could've died from a look, it would've been that one.

Fuck West remembering me for the rest of his life—I was going to be the one remembering him.

I moaned loudly as he flicked his tongue again, my cock jerking and leaking precum onto my skin. I needed more… anything… everything… And then his mouth was gone and it was like the fucking world had ended.

"Don't worry, sweetheart," West said, running his hand over my thigh. "I just need to get some lube and a condom."

I almost wanted to tell him I'd be fine, that I'd taken guys with just spit before. But then I remembered the size of West's dick and the fact I had to go to work tomorrow and decided not to argue.

West slipped off the bed with grace and speed, rummaging in a drawer before throwing a bottle of lube and a Durex XL condom on the bed. The lube was an expensive brand I loved and I almost complimented him on his taste. But my mouth seemed to have forgotten how to form words and my brain was firmly offline.

The only thing I could do was roll onto my stomach and push my ass into the air, resting my head on my hands as I lowered my shoulders as much as possible.

West groaned appreciatively, running his hand up my thigh as he knelt behind me. "You have a gorgeous ass. It's fucking perfect."

I grinned and wiggled it teasingly, gasping as West gently spanked it and squeezed my cheek. "You should fuck it then."

"I will," he said and I heard the bottle of lube click open. "I'm sorry if this is cold."

I wanted to tell him I didn't care, but all that came out was another gasp as he trickled the thick liquid across the sensitive skin, a large finger rubbing it on my hole. I groaned as he slowly pressed his finger inside me, starting to work me open with a gentle care and attention I'd not always experienced. West didn't seem to be in a rush, which was adorably sweet, but holy shit I wanted him to fuck me.

I moaned as he added a second finger, stretching me wide and scissoring me open. My fingers gripped his sheets and I pushed back onto him, desperate for more. West added a third, which I'd normally have told him was unnecessary, but I couldn't formulate anything more than his name and a small selection of phrases to beg for more.

It was almost a relief when West pulled his fingers out of me and rolled on a condom, because it gave me a few seconds of respite. I was so on edge one touch was all it would take and I wanted to last more than ten seconds once his cock was inside me.

West moved closer to me, and I felt the blunt, thick head of his cock brushing against my hole. I tried to push back against him, but his hand gripped my hip and stopped me. "Slowly, sweetheart," he murmured. "I don't want to hurt you."

"Y-you won't," I said, lifting myself up enough to look over my shoulder at him. "I can take it. Please, give it to me."

"I will," he said with a warm smile that set a swarm of butterflies loose in my stomach. "Slowly."

My eyes lingered on him as he pressed the head of his cock inside me, and holy sucking fit he was big. I'd seen his cock, of course, and had it deep in my throat, but there was no way to compare those feelings to the way his dick was splitting me open.

I moaned and whimpered as West pushed into me, his pace achingly slow as he gave my body time to adjust. I pushed my hips back and lowered my head, pressing my shoulders into the bed. I reached back with one hand to grasp my cock and stroke myself. The pleasure mixed with the burn and stretch, making my skin tingle and hum.

"Fuck," West said, groaning as he tightened his grip on my hip. "I'm getting so deep in you... you look so good taking my cock. Mmm, fuck, you're so fucking tight, sweetheart. God, it's like you were made for it."

"Y-yes…" My fingers tangled in the sheets, holding on tightly. It was like I was afraid of what would happen if I let go, but it wasn't like I could fall. West was making me fly. "I want… fuck, I want all of it."

West let out a slow breath, squeezing my hip, and I felt the heat of his body against me. "That's it," he said, voice low and soft. I groaned, relishing the feeling of every millimetre of his perfect, heavy cock filling me up. West ran his other hand down my spine, his fingers trailing over every vertebra. "Is that what you wanted?"

"Fuck yes," I said, nodding my head. "It's… fuck… so fucking good. I can see why people want to marry you."

West laughed and the sound vibrated through my body. "Want me to show you what I can do with it?"

"Please. Fuck me, West."

West began to rock his hips. The movements were small at first, like gentle waves brushing against the beach, but then he started to pull further out, holding me tightly as he slammed back into me over and over. His hand on my spine pressed me further into the bed as the one on my hip pulled me onto his cock, and I was powerless to resist. My moans were getting louder and I buried my face into the bed, trying to at least be vaguely considerate of his roommates.

"You don't have to try and be quiet," West said, leaning down over me and brushing his lips over the top of my shoulders. "Let me hear you. I want to know how much you love my cock." He ground deep into me, his cock rubbing against my prostate and making stars burst behind my eyes. I gasped, the sound filling the room. "That's it," he said in a voice that sounded dark and hungry. It threatened to consume me and I would willingly have thrown myself to it. "Let it all out, sweetheart. Tell me how much you want it."

He adjusted his position, holding me tightly as he started to fuck me again, thrusting deep and hard inside me. I howled with pleasure as his cock rubbed over my sweet spot with every move he made. Any words I tried to speak became nothing but begged pleas for more and needy sounds of delight as West took me apart. My blood boiled under my skin, my body super-heating, burning up from the inside out.

My orgasm barrelled towards me like a heat-seeking missile. I still had one hand on my cock, but it wasn't doing anything except holding it tightly.

"I know you're close," West said. "I know you want to come for me."

I whimpered, gasping out a response that made no sense to anyone. Not even me. I started pumping my cock, jerking it wildly and knowing that it wouldn't take much to push me over the edge.

"Come for me, Rory," West said. "Come on my cock like the good boy you are."

His words sank into me and that was all it took. My body stiffened as pure bliss hit me like a motherfucking fireball, a muffled scream tearing out of my mouth as I buried my face in the bed and ribbons of cum splattered on my hand. It was like someone had set off a box of fireworks inside me, but not the crappy, cheap kind, the kind used by professionals on New Year's Eve.

West fucked me through my release before chasing his own with wild desperation. It was almost too much, but at the same time, I never wanted him to stop. His fingers tightened on my hip, gripping me so hard I'd probably bruise, and with a final deep thrust, he came with a growl as he pushed me deeper into the mattress, emptying into the condom inside me.

For a long moment, all I could hear was my heartbeat and our breathing.

Then West slowly eased out of me and gently released his grip on my body. I sagged onto the mattress, stretching out and blinking before rolling over to watch him. West pulled the condom off and reached for a box of tissues, offering me one, which I took.

"Are you still tempted to propose to me?" he asked, tying the condom off and wrapping it in a tissue before dropping it in the small bin in the corner.

I chuckled hoarsely, wiping the cum off my hand. "Maybe… but I think I might need a few more test runs first. You know, just to see what I'm getting into."

West grinned as he walked back over to me, leaning down to press a gentle kiss to my mouth. "I'd be down for that. This was a lot of fun."

"It was," I said, kissing him again and savouring the taste. "I'd offer to stay for round two. Or even three. But I have work tomorrow and I'm apparently a cranky bitch if I get anything less than six or seven hours."

West chuckled. "Next time we'll make it a weekend then. One where I don't have a match."

"I like that plan." I gave him a final kiss before sliding past him to start collecting my clothes. West watched me for a moment, then pulled on a pair of loose shorts and a T-shirt.

"I'll walk you out," he said when I was dressed. "Got everything?"

"I think so."

We walked through the house to the front door. There was nobody else around but I could hear movement from somewhere. I didn't care if anyone had heard us, though, because it wasn't like I knew any of these people. At the door, West stopped and frowned. "Do you need help getting home? Want me to call you a taxi?"

"It's fine," I said, my heart melting at his sweetness. It wasn't every day I met a man who would fuck my brains out one minute and offer to make sure I got home safe the next. "I can walk. It's only half an hour and Lincoln's very safe. And if I have trouble, I'll just call an Uber." Or Dad, but I didn't say that out loud. It weirded some guys out to know that my dad would happily have picked me up from a hook-up and not said a word about it. Then again, Dad had always said he'd rather collect us from wherever we were than us get lost or get into trouble.

Both Christopher and I had reminded him more than once we weren't the type to start bar fights or get stabbed. Just because Dad had a list of pubs he was banned from in

East London didn't mean we were going to follow in his footsteps.

"Okay." West drew me into another kiss in the open doorway. "Goodnight, Rory," he said softly. "Sweet dreams."

CHAPTER SIX

West

"Hey, hey, Jonny said you had company last night," Danny said, leaning against the weight rack with a delighted smile on his face. Smug bastard. If there was one man on this team who could gossip for England, it was Danny Wheeler. All he needed was the tiniest hint of something, and he'd go into full sleuth mode. Nothing was safe from him.

He'd give Coleen Rooney a run for her money any day.

"Did he now?" I asked, trying to ignore Danny and continue with my squat set.

"He did. Said they were quite loud."

"Yeah, well, Jonny should try living on the other side of his bedroom wall." I racked the bar and stepped out from under it, shaking out my legs and grabbing my water bottle. I had two more sets of squats, four sets of RDLs, then four of traditional deadlifts, and lunges to do before I could escape, and if Danny was going to interrogate me throughout all of them, I was going to lose my patience really fucking quickly.

Leg day was hell enough already without having to answer questions about my sex life.

I loved Jonny, but I was going to have to ask him why the fuck he'd told Danny when it was nobody's bloody business who I took home.

"Don't make this about Jonny," Danny said, waggling his finger at me like an old man. "You got laid last night, not him."

"And if I did?" I raised my eyebrow and folded my arms. "Why do you fucking care?"

"You know me."

"Yeah, you're a nosy fucker."

Danny laughed as I took a long swig from my bottle before putting it down and stepping back under the bar. My thighs were warm, my muscles already anticipating the burn. "Not gonna deny it. But seriously, who was it? Was she hot? He hot? They hot?"

I snorted and shook my head.

"What? I'm an equal opportunities kinda guy," Danny said. "I don't care who you shag."

"Then why are you so interested?" I asked, grunting out the words as I pushed through my set. The weight on the bar was the same as normal, but today it felt like someone had doubled it. Was it just because I was tired after spending half of last night lying awake thinking about Rory? Or was it because I was also carrying the weight of this conversation?

"Because he can't get fucking laid to save his fucking

life," Charlie said, clapping Danny on the shoulder and grinning at him. "So he gets off on hearing about everyone else."

"Fuck off, you wanker," Danny said as he shoved Charlie sideways. "I get laid."

"Yeah, since when?"

"Just ask your mum."

"Seriously? That's all you've got?"

"If you fuckers haven't got anything else to do, can you go and harass someone else about their sex life?" I asked as I pushed through the last squat of the set, slotting the bar back into the rack. My breathing was coming heavier now and I felt the familiar burn setting in down the sides and backs of my thighs.

"But annoying you is fun," Danny said, still wearing that smug smirk. "Plus you're being really coy about it. And that makes me wanna know more."

"So just because I'm not like half you bellends who come in and talk about the size of your hook-up's tits and whether she sucked your dick, I'm being coy? It's called having manners, dipshit."

"He's got you there," Charlie said.

"You used to do the same," Danny said.

Charlie shrugged. "Maybe I did, maybe I didn't."

Danny rolled his eyes. "Yeah, you fucking did. Then you met Amanda and turned into a proper lovesick bastard."

"See, Danny, if Charlie can learn to be a gentleman, there's hope for you yet," I said, winking at him before downing half my water and setting the bottle down before stretching against the bar. If I'd been training on my own,

I'd have been straight on my phone the moment I'd put the bar down, seeing if there was anything from Rory before debating whether I should message him.

Would it be weird to send him something today and see how he was doing? Usually I didn't message my hook-ups unless we planned on meeting up again, but even thinking about Rory made my fingers itch. While we hadn't exactly done a lot of talking last night, it felt like there was more between us than just incredible chemistry.

Maybe it was because I hadn't gotten laid in a while, but part of me wanted to believe there was something there. Rory was funny and sharp and drop-dead fucking gorgeous. I wanted to know more about him, not just what he liked in bed or his worst dates.

I didn't know how to ask, though. I didn't want to come off as needy or clingy. A couple of people had accused me of being that in the past, and I was trying my hardest not to let history repeat itself.

"Hey, can I ask you a question?" Danny asked as I hefted the bar onto my shoulders for my final squat set.

"I don't know, can you?" I asked, steadying my breathing and making sure my feet were correctly placed before pushing my hips back and down, lowering my body.

"Ha-fucking-ha. Do you prefer hooking up with men or women? And when you fuck around with guys, do you—"

"Danny!" Mason's voice was a sharp, clear snap. "Put a fucking sock in it."

"What? I was just asking!"

"Shall I start asking you about your sexual preferences?" Mason asked. Out of the corner of my eye I saw him standing on Danny's other side, effectively sandwiching the winger between him and Charlie. "Favourite positions, if you like getting pegged or using a dildo, or maybe a vibrator. What about nipple clamps? Maybe we could start on your kinks too."

"Hey, that's totally different."

"Is it? How?" Mason folded his arms and I froze halfway through my set, my muscles burning as I watched with abject fascination. Mason was usually pretty chilled, but every now and then, if you pushed him enough, he could tear you apart with a look.

"That's, like, I don't know, personal?" Danny didn't sound sure and I internally prayed for his soul. I wanted to feel bad for him, and then I wondered if I should just feel pissed he'd asked me that shit, like I hadn't been asked a thousand times before if I preferred men or women, bottoming or topping, and the inevitable question of when I was going to pick a side and stop pretending to be gay. Or straight.

Usually, the people asking were straight guys, most of whom were dealing with more than a smidge of internalised homophobia and couldn't understand why someone who looked like me—masculine, muscled, and built like a brick shithouse—wanted to take other men to bed.

It was why I'd been so hesitant about coming out as bi, because there was always at least one prick who seemed to think I wanted to shag him. Funnily enough, they always took it as a personal insult when I said I'd never be interested.

They didn't want me to objectify them, but they also didn't want to be told they weren't attractive.

Men could be really fucking weird sometimes.

"And the questions you're asking West aren't personal?" Mason asked, his voice deathly calm and quiet. "Come on, explain it to me."

The whole gym had gone quiet and I finally found the strength to finish my squat and rack the bar before my legs gave out.

"Mason, it's fine," I said. Everyone was watching us and I wanted the ground to open up and swallow me whole. "Danny didn't mean any harm."

Mason glared at me. "Doesn't mean he wasn't being an asshole. We've been through this, Daniel, and we're not going through it again."

"Please, Mason. Just leave it." I put my hand on his arm and tried to smile at him. "It's fine."

"All right." Mason's nostrils flared as he breathed out. "Fuck off, Danny. I don't want to see your face for the rest of the morning."

Danny looked between the two of us. He opened his mouth but Charlie grabbed his arm. "Drop it, Danny."

"Listen to Charlie," Mason said coldly. "Haven't you got work to do?"

The two of them turned tail and suddenly the whole gym burst into life again like nobody wanted to be caught listening in even though I knew they'd all been doing it.

I sighed and picked up my bottle, which was now virtually empty, and walked across to the water fountain to fill it up, avoiding everyone's gaze as I did.

Mason followed me. "Why did you let him do that?"

"Do what?"

"Ask you that shit."

"I wasn't going to answer him," I said as I unscrewed the bottle lid, slid it onto the grill under the tap, and pushed the button. "And you know what Danny's like. He's just a nosy shit. He doesn't mean anything by it."

"Doesn't mean he should ask it," Mason said, leaning against the wall next to the fountain. He watched me closely, a frown etching itself into his broad features. "Come on, man, you can't let him get away with that shit."

"Look, I know you mean well, but doing stuff like that just makes it worse."

"How?" Mason asked. He folded his arms and fixed me with the same look he'd given Danny. "How does calling out their biphobic bullshit make it worse?"

"Because now I just look like a dickhead who can't take a joke," I said quietly. I hated saying those words out loud, hated the way they made me feel. Mason was right—I shouldn't have let Danny, or anyone else, ask me shit like that—but compared to some of the other comments and questions I'd had hurled at me over the years in the guise of banter, Danny's had been nothing.

"Look," I continued, picking my full bottle up and screwing the lid back on. "I get it. I probably should be calling them out, but it's just... where do I start? What's considered just a joke and what's them actually being biphobic? I don't think they actually know themselves. But if I start, then it's constant. And then I get labelled a problem, that guy who you can't have a laugh with, the one nobody wants to work with because they might offend him. And if nobody wants to work with me, I'm fucked. Rugby's a team sport, Mason. I can't play if nobody wants me on the team."

"Fucking Christ, West. So you're just going to let them treat you like that?" Mason's voice was hissed but I could feel the seething anger coming through.

I chuckled dryly. "Trust me, this is nothing. I'll let you know if it ever gets to be a real problem."

Mason muttered something under his breath that sounded like "It's never fucking getting to that" but I wasn't going to ask. I loved that Mason was willing to stand up for me, it made him such a great friend, but sometimes I wished he'd think about the consequences before he opened his mouth.

Or maybe I was just being a coward.

I was out for a reason, and it was through my own choice, not anyone else's. Coming out had cost me a lot, including my relationship with my parents, but it had given me a lot of things too. Like reconnecting with my brother, Theo, who until recently I hadn't seen since he'd left our parents' house the day he turned eighteen.

And the only reason I'd found Theo was because I'd been watching gay porn on Twitter.

I liked being bisexual, loved it even. The only thing I struggled with was advocating for myself in situations like this. Deep down, I was still the people-pleasing little boy I'd always been. The one who desperately wanted people to like him and let him play with them, even if it meant letting them treat him like shit. Because being the subject of people's jokes and teasing was better than being left out.

Mason was still looking at me. His expression softened and now he just looked worried. That was almost worse than him looking pissed off, because when Mason was worried about you, he tended to smother you until you gave in and told him what was wrong.

"Are you sure you're okay?" he asked.

"Yeah, I'm fine." I wasn't, but I would be. Maybe not right this second, but there was always later. And tomorrow. "My thighs are fucking burning, though. I did the same weight as last week, but it's killing me today."

"Come on, we can switch in and out," Mason said, patting me on the shoulder. "Give ourselves better breaks between sets."

We walked back across the gym to the rack I'd been at, which was still empty, and Mason began moving the bar and weights around for RDLs. I stood and watched him for a moment before glancing down at the floor where my phone was sat.

I bent down and picked it up, pretending I was just moving it out of the way. As I did I tapped the screen.

There was an Instagram notification from Bubblegum Galaxy.

I pulled it down far enough to see it, trying to keep the smile off my face as I read.

> **Bubblegum Galaxy**
> Still thinking about you this morning.
> Feeling you too ;D Let's do it again
> soon <3

CHAPTER SEVEN

Bubblegum Galaxy

"Try that one," I signed, pointing to the socket on Christopher's right-hand side. "*See if it works now.*"

Christopher plugged the socket tester in and flicked it on, the pair of us watching to see if the three lights on the front illuminated. I let out a sigh of relief as they lit up. "*Thank fuck. Try the next one.*"

"*Whoever did this wiring was a dick,*" Christopher signed before he swapped the socket tester over. "*Why the fuck do people think they can do it themselves? Fucking cowboys.*"

I didn't know but it was a question we asked each other regularly. If I had a quid for every job we got called out to where people had tried to do complex electrical work themselves with nothing more than some determination and a YouTube tutorial and had horrible results, I'd probably have enough for a new high-end lace front wig.

I got that people wanted to save money, especially these days, and for people living in a shitty rented property with an asshole landlord, they didn't always have a choice, but electricity wasn't something to play around with lightly. Dad had more than one story about someone frying themselves.

Working as an electrician might not have been the first thing people thought of as a day job for a drag queen, but I really enjoyed it. Dad had been teaching me to take things apart since I was a kid, and as I'd gotten older, there hadn't been a doubt in my mind that I'd go to college and follow him into the trade. The money wasn't bad, Dad was a pretty flexible boss, and it gave me a handy set of skills to put to use, like wiring in the most amazing LED make-up mirror above my dressing table.

I was also Phil's go-to electrician for The Court, Lincoln's best, and only, drag bar and queer club. It'd happened by accident. I'd been getting ready when one of the trip switches in the fuse box had gone, shorting out the whole front of house. Phil had been *this* close to cancelling the whole night but I'd just grabbed my tools out of the car and done a bit of detective work to find the problem—some loose wiring in a plug socket that someone had plugged a hoover into.

Fixing some wiring while half dragged up had been a new one for me, but I hadn't been about to get changed or take my make-up off first.

After that I'd politely asked Phil when the last time he'd had the wiring checked in The Court was, since the building was a couple of hundred years old and had been refitted numerous times in the last twenty years alone. I hadn't even wanted to imagine what might be in the walls.

One conversation later and Dad, Christopher, and I had spent two weeks rewiring the whole place.

Today, Christopher and I were dealing with some cowboy's attempt to wire in a fancy garden office with double doors, polished wooden floors, and solid, dark wood furniture. The whole thing had probably cost more than my yearly salary.

The cowboy had done just enough to hide all the shit for about six months, and what we'd thought was a case of one dodgy socket had led to Christopher and me uncovering a litany of electrical horrors. I'd thought the property owner was going to cry when we'd told him the damage and what it would take to fix it.

But the alternative was leaving it as a fire hazard, so here we were on day two of rewiring the entire thing.

If I ever came face-to-face with the asshole who'd done the first round, I'd be taking a leaf out of my dad's book.

"This one's good too," Christopher signed and I felt myself relax. That was all the sockets dealt with, and now we just needed to finish the lighting and tidy up. But first, I needed a break.

"Tea?" I asked.

Christopher looked at his watch. *"Lunch?"*

I hadn't realised how late it was. No wonder my stomach was starting to grumble.

We packed a few things away and walked out to the

van, which was parked on the street outside the house, to grab the boxes of sandwiches Mum still insisted on packing us every day. I'd told her I was perfectly capable of making my own lunch, but she always brushed me off. Christopher hopped up into the passenger seat and started scrolling through his phone, ham and pickle sandwich in hand. I climbed into the driver's side, leaving the door open so I could hang my legs out the side. For the end of October, the weather wasn't bad.

Retrieving a sandwich out of the tub, I pulled my phone from one of the pockets of my work trousers. I wasn't expecting anything exciting. West and I had messaged a few times since our hook-up last week, mostly little things about our day or sending reels we'd seen, but there was nothing today.

There was an email, though.

From the producers of *Drag Stars UK*.

A nervous feeling churned in my stomach, and I felt like I was about to be sick. I'd hardly told anyone about applying to the next season because that had felt like jinxing it. This was the second time I'd answered the casting call and really hoped this was my shot. Last time, Bubblegum hadn't been nearly as polished, and I'd made some rookie mistakes with the audition tape. But this time, I'd spent hours making sure it was as close to fucking perfect as possible.

If I didn't make it this time, I didn't know what else I could do.

Christopher must have noticed me fidgeting and

fiddling with my phone, turning it over in my hands while I plucked up the courage to open it. He nudged me with his elbow and nodded at my phone.

"*Drag Stars emailed me,*" I signed, resting my sandwich on my knee.

"*Did you get in?*"

"*Don't know. I haven't opened it.*"

Christopher raised his eyebrow and gestured at me to get on with it. He was one of the few people who knew because I'd made him watch my audition tape since I knew he'd be honest with me about whether it was any good. And we'd watched all five previous seasons together, along with all the US seasons, so he knew what they were looking for.

My stomach churned as I closed my eyes and tapped the notification. If I couldn't see it, I couldn't read their answer.

Christopher nudged me again and when I opened my eyes, he was grinning at me, mouth full of sandwich. He looked like a hamster. "*Only I'm allowed to do that,*" he signed, referencing his infuriating way of ending arguments where he just closed his eyes and walked away so he couldn't see anyone signing at him. "*What did they say?*"

I glanced down at my phone, the words coming into focus.

Dear Rory,
Thank you so much for submitting your audition tape for season six of **Drag Stars UK**. *After careful consideration, we regret to inform you that…*

My heart sank through my stomach and into the floor. There was no nausea anymore, only a vast empty feeling threatening to swallow me up like a black hole.

I'd given it everything. Spent hours on my audition. Worn all my best drag. Tried so hard to tell a story about who I was and what being Bubblegum meant to me. And it had meant nothing.

I felt Christopher's arm wrap around my shoulder as his fingers plucked my phone out of my hand. He must have read it, because I hadn't locked the screen, but he didn't say anything. All he did was squeeze me tightly and rest his head against me.

Numbness crept into my muscles, draining the life out of me.

Getting on *Drag Stars* wasn't the be all and end all of drag, but it was a dream I'd held on to for as long as I could remember. The US version had started airing fifteen years ago when I was seven, and when I'd discovered it in my teenage years, I'd binged every episode on repeat. It was part of the reason Bubblegum existed, and when they'd announced they were doing a UK version, I'd danced around my living room, praying I'd get to be there one day.

And maybe I still would.

But it wouldn't be this year.

My eyes stung as tears started to well up in the corners. I tried to push them away, fluttering my lashes and taking a couple of deep breaths, hoping somehow to suck them back into my body. But all it did was make it worse.

"Shit," I muttered, wiping my face as the first few tears

started to run down my cheeks. Christopher lifted his head, leaning forward to look at me.

"*It's okay,*" he signed. "*You can cry. It's fucking shit.*"

I snorted because my brother was never one to mince words, and another stream of tears bubbled down my cheeks. Part of me felt stupid for crying because it was only a TV show, not the end of the world, and there was always next year.

But that voice was drowned out by the rest of my brain, which screamed and howled because I'd wanted this so fucking much it hurt. It felt like my dreams were being smashed into a million pieces on the pavement in front of me, and no matter how hard I tried, I'd never be able to stick them back together.

Christopher let go of me for a second and rummaged around in the glove compartment, pulling out a handful of old McDonald's napkins from the last time we'd gone through the drive-through. He handed them to me with a soft smile and I started to dab my face dry. The napkins weren't exactly the softest on my skin, but they'd do. It was better than walking round all afternoon with dried tears on my cheeks and a snotty nose.

Once I'd cleaned up, Christopher handed me back my phone and dropped a bar of chocolate into my lap. I didn't know where it'd come from, but I wasn't going to turn down free chocolate.

"*Eat that and look at hot boys,*" he signed. "*And message that guy again. The one with the massive dick you hooked up with last week. A good dicking will make you feel better.*" I laughed and Christopher smirked. "*You know I'm right.*"

"Yeah, sure." I hadn't meant to tell him about West, but he'd still been awake when I'd come home and he'd noticed the blooming hickeys on my neck and the way I was walking. I tried to ignore him but he'd just followed me into my room until I'd given in and told the nosy bugger some very brief details.

He did have a point, though. Sex would be a good distraction and it'd make me feel better, especially if it was as good as last time.

And West and I had already talked about doing it again.

Ignoring the half-eaten sandwich on my lap, I opened the bar of chocolate and Instagram messenger.

> **Bubblegum Galaxy**
> Hey, what're you doing tonight? Fancy blowing off some steam? I've had a shit day and I could do with getting pounded!

I didn't expect a response straight away because I assumed West was probably in the gym or throwing himself around a rugby pitch. It wasn't a sport I was totally familiar with and part of me wondered if I should at least try and get a vague overview of the game. All I knew was they all wore really short shorts, had beautiful thick thighs, and grappled with other men while trying to get a ball up and down a pitch.

Snapping off a few squares of chocolate, I opened TikTok and started scrolling through the rugby tag, hoping it'd come up with something useful. I was halfway down a rabbit hole of watching men wrestle each other at speed and realising just how violent the sport was when a message from West dropped into my inbox.

> **West**
> Fuck, I'm sorry your day sucked! Yeah I'm free tonight, want to come over about eight?

> **West**
> Anything you want to vent about?

I smiled to myself, my heart fluttering to life. It was sweet of him to ask because most guys wouldn't, especially when being offered my ass on a plate. But that didn't mean I was going to pour my heart out to him—I didn't want to be one of those ridiculously needy, clingy bottoms and scare him off.

Although I hadn't proposed marriage yet, so I could've been worse.

> **Bubblegum Galaxy**
> Just got rejected from Drag Stars and feeling like shit.

> **West**
> That's bollocks. You're so fucking talented! And gorgeous! That's definitely their loss.

My heart skittered and skipped, my stomach twisting itself in knots. Fuck, what was happening to me? I'd never felt this for a hook-up before. I wasn't supposed to get butterflies about something casual, but clearly my body hadn't gotten the message.

Another message popped onto the screen and I grinned, biting my lip.

> **West**
> Don't worry, I promise to make you feel better later ;D

CHAPTER EIGHT

West

"Why are you lurking in the kitchen?" Mason asked, pouring himself a cup of tea and watching me shrewdly. "Did you order a takeaway or something?"

"No," I said with a shake of my head as I checked my phone again in case Rory had messaged me. It was just before eight and I hadn't heard from him since lunchtime, but there was a strange sensation sitting on my chest and I couldn't work out what it meant. "Anyway, you saw me make dinner."

"So, you could've ordered a sneaky snack."

I chuckled to myself. Technically Rory was a snack, and one I'd definitely enjoy eating, but he probably wasn't what Mason was thinking.

Or my best friend knew exactly what I was waiting for and was trying to get me to admit it.

I didn't feel the need to hide Rory, though, or the fact he was coming over to hook up.

"Rory's coming over," I said. "He's had a shit day and wanted to blow off some steam."

Mason snorted and muttered, "I'm sure he wants to blow something."

"I'm not going to say no."

"I didn't think you would," he said with a grin, chucking the teabag from his mug into the bin and grabbing the milk out of the fridge. There were a few shouts from the living room where Guy and Jonny were playing *Call of Duty* together. Knowing Jonny, he was probably kicking Guy's butt from here to the moon and back. "When's he coming over?"

"Any minute," I said, glancing at my phone again. An odd bubble of nerves rose in my stomach. It wasn't about what my housemates might say or about Rory coming over, but it had *something* to do with him. He'd had a terrible day, probably worse than he'd let on, and I wanted to do whatever I could to make him feel better—whether that was fucking his brains out or wrapping him in my arms and holding him tightly until he let everything go. And that was an odd feeling.

I wasn't a stranger to hook-ups or booty calls, but this was the first time I'd felt anything more than desire for one of them.

Maybe it was just because Rory was a sweet guy and I didn't want him to be miserable.

My phone flashed with a message saying he was outside

and I smiled. I reached for the front door, glancing back at Mason, who was rapidly adding sugar to his tea.

"Let him in. I'll distract the Chuckle Brothers," Mason said, nodding his head in the direction of the living room where loud bursts of swearing accompanied the crackle of explosions. "At least then they won't corner you until tomorrow."

"Cheers," I said, watching him walk out of the kitchen, tea in hand, to ask Guy loudly if he was bored of getting his ass kicked yet. Pulling the door open, my heart leapt to see Rory standing on the pavement. He turned as soon as he heard me, and while he was smiling, I could see the slump in his shoulders. He didn't seem as bouncing and vibrant as the last time I'd seen him, like someone had snuffed out his sparkle.

"Hey," he said.

"Hey." I stepped back and held the door open. "Wanna come in?"

"Definitely." His grin brightened as he strolled into the house, sliding past me and running his hand across my stomach, sending a shiver of anticipation coursing through me.

Another explosion sounded from the living room along with a chorus of groans and creative swearing. Rory looked at me quizzically. "I'm guessing your housemates are around?"

"Yeah, they're playing *Call of Duty*," I said as I shut the door and grabbed Rory's hand. Luckily, we didn't have to go through the living room to get to the stairs. "Let's go upstairs."

"God yes," Rory said, following me towards the stairs and up them. "Today has been utterly shit. I just need you to fuck me until I forget everything."

I chuckled softly as I pushed him into my room and closed the door behind us, throwing the lock across in case any of the wankers downstairs got any ideas. "I can do that." I stepped into Rory's space, putting my hand on his waist and drawing him against me. "Need me to make you feel good, sweetheart?"

"Fuck yes." Rory grabbed the front of my T-shirt and dragged me into a heated kiss, nipping my lip and groaning as my tongue slid into his mouth.

I reached for the bottom of his hoodie, tearing it over his head along with his T-shirt and throwing them both to the floor. I dipped my hand into the back of his joggers, squeezing his ass and smirking. "I see you skipped underwear," I said, teasing Rory's bottom lip with my teeth as I slid my finger into his crack.

"I figured I wouldn't be wearing it for long," he said. "There wasn't any point putting some on."

"You were right." I kissed him again, sinking to my knees and dragging his joggers down around his thighs, releasing his cock. Rory wanted me to make him feel good, and I wasn't going to waste time. Wrapping my hand around his half-hard shaft, I pumped him slowly as I flicked my tongue over the shining head of his cock, licking up the precum collecting there.

Rory gasped, one hand tangling in my hair, the other gripping my shoulder. "Fuck!"

My mouth curled into a teasing smile as I ran my tongue

down his shaft to tease his balls, sucking them into my mouth one at a time, loving the way he moaned. Rory's fingers dug into my shoulder as I kissed back up his shaft and enveloped his cock with my lips.

Rory's moan was loud and low as I took him deeper into my mouth, tightening my lips and fingers around him in a slick, tight tunnel. I slid my other hand up the back of his thigh, caressing his ass cheek as I sucked his cock and dipping two fingers into his crack, brushing them over his hole.

"F-fuck, West," Rory said. "I… fuck, that feels good."

Pride fluttered in my chest because all I wanted was for him to feel good. Not that it was a hardship for me. I loved bringing my partners pleasure and sending them soaring into ecstasy.

I sucked his cock as deep as I could, saliva slicking my fingers at the base of his cock. He gasped again, his breath hitching and shaking.

"I'm… West, I'm getting close."

I wasn't ready for that. Not yet.

With a final suck, I released his cock, looking up at him from my knees. Rory already looked wrecked, with flushed cheeks and swollen lips where he'd been biting them. His chest was heaving as he tried to catch his breath.

I grinned at him, winking as I put my other hand on his thigh, gently pulling him around. "Turn around, sweetheart," I growled. "I'm not finished with you yet."

Rory pivoted slowly, presenting me with his perfect ass. It was round, firm, and covered in soft light brown hair, reminding me of a peach. I wanted to sink my teeth into him, or at least my tongue, until he was riding my face and begging for more.

"Fuck, your ass is perfect," I said, lightly spanking his cheeks and making them jiggle. "I've been dreaming about this ass."

"Y-yes," Rory said as he pushed his hips back. The nearby chest of drawers rattled as Rory's hands shot out, balancing himself against it. "Take it."

I grinned as I gently pulled his cheeks apart and buried my face between them. My tongue laved over his hole, teasing the sensitive skin and slowly pressing inside him. Rory groaned, pushing his ass back onto my face, desperate for more as he moaned and whined.

My cock throbbed inside my joggers, aching to be inside him, and I wished I'd had the sense to get naked before we'd started.

I'd still be on my knees, though, the taste of Rory on my lips as his moans reverberated through me like a deep bass line. Every one was exquisite and made me want to do more. I wanted him to forget all the shit of today and focus on nothing but the feel of my tongue opening up that tight ring of muscle and teasing every nerve until he was ready to explode.

Rory gasped as I slid a finger down his crack, using it alongside my tongue and teasing his slick hole. Slowly, I pressed the tip of my finger inside him, just enough to make him want more.

"Fuck," Rory said, pushing his hips back even further as he rode my tongue, trying to get more of my finger inside him. "I want... fuck, where's your lube? I fucking need you inside me."

I wasn't going to tease him by pointing out I already was, because I knew it wasn't what he meant. He wanted my fingers stretching him wide and my cock filling him up. "Bedside table," I said hoarsely as I lifted my head for a second. "There's condoms too."

I felt him stretch as he reached for them, and then a bottle and the foil wrapper of a condom was shoved in my face. "Here," Rory said.

"Still want me to fuck you?"

"God yes," Rory said. "I want all of it. You know I can take it."

"I do." I kissed his left butt cheek. "You take me so well, and your ass feels so fucking good around my cock."

I sat back on my heels, squirting some lube onto my fingers and drizzling a little down his crack. I kissed his ass again as I slid a finger down the slick skin, teasing his softened hole before slowly pushing inside him.

Rory groaned, letting out a sigh of pleasure as I began to stretch him open. Unlike before, I wasn't going to spend longer than I needed working him open. I loved the noises he was making and the feel of his tight channel squeezing my fingers as I pumped them in and out, but I needed more.

Desperation bubbled under my skin, making my muscles tense and cock ache. I wanted to bury my dick deep inside the beautiful man in front of me and feel the heat of his body envelop me. I needed to fuck him deep and hard until both of us were dripping in sweat and utterly spent, until we had nothing left to give and could only lie on the bed panting for air.

By the time I had three fingers inside him, I knew neither of us had much patience left. I just needed to get fucking naked.

Slowly, I pulled out of him and pressed a final kiss to the base of his spine. Then I rose, ignoring the pins and needles in my feet as I began to yank my clothes off, not caring if I ripped anything.

Rory watched me over his shoulder, eyes wide with need and lips curling in delight as my cock sprang out of my joggers. "God, that cock," he said with a little sigh. "Can I ride it?"

"You can have it however you want," I said. "As long as I'm inside, I don't fucking care how we do it."

Rory laughed and turned, pulling me into a deep kiss. "Get on the bed, baby. I can't wait any longer."

I didn't think anyone had ever called me baby before. I kind of liked it.

I clambered onto the bed, stacking the pillows behind my shoulders before rolling a condom down my shaft and slicking myself with lube. Rory stroked his cock lazily as he watched and as soon as I finished sliding the condom on, he climbed into my lap, his slim thighs spread across my broad ones.

He reached down behind him to grasp my cock, slowly lowering himself down, and I groaned as I felt the head of my dick pressing against his hole. Rory's expression was nothing but raw pleasure as he began to sink onto my cock, slowly taking my thick shaft inside him.

Heat and pressure enveloped me as his ass squeezed me, and my hands grasped his hips so tightly I worried I'd leave bruises. The urge to pull him down and fill him up in one deep thrust was almost overwhelming, but I didn't want to hurt him.

And I was enjoying watching Rory take what he wanted from me, seeing the way his mouth went slack, eyes closing and head tilting back as he took more and more.

His ass cheeks brushed against my thighs and he shifted his position like he wanted to make sure I was as deep in him as I could be. He looked down at me and smirked playfully, leaning down to kiss me and sliding his tongue into my mouth as his hands rested on my chest.

"Mmm," he murmured against my lips. "I needed this."

"Yeah? You missed me filling you up?"

"You have no idea." He rolled his hips in a way that was so filthy it nearly made me come. "You're so fucking big. God, I can't even think properly."

"Good," I said, kissing him. "Don't think, just feel." I caressed his hips, gently starting to rock them. "Ride me, sweetheart. I want to watch you use my dick. Make yourself come for me."

Rory groaned, rolling his hips under my hands. His hands were still on my chest, using my pecs for balance as he tucked his toes under his feet and began to bounce on my cock. I moaned, gripping his hips tighter, not quite moving him but supporting his movement.

Rory threw his head back, a decadent moan sliding from his lips as he rode me, fucking himself deep and hard on my cock. He angled his hips and cried out as the head of my dick nudged his prostate as he sank back down onto me.

"Fuck yes, right there," Rory said. "Right fucking there."

"You look so good like this," I said, growling as he rolled his hips again in the filthy way that sent pleasure running through me, setting my body alight. "You're so fucking sexy."

"Yeah? Like watching me?"

"Yeah. Like hearing you too."

He grinned. "I'm not good at being quiet."

"I don't want you to be."

Rory's grin widened and he winked at me as he started moving faster, using my body to chase his release. He wasn't shy about making noise as he did so, gasps and curses filling the air around us. We both knew they'd be able to hear us downstairs and maybe that was inconsiderate of us, but I didn't fucking care. I was too lost in Rory's body to think about anything beyond the feel of his ass on my cock and the way he was milking me so exquisitely that I knew I wouldn't be able to last.

Rory slid his hand down his chest, making a show of reaching for his cock. My eyes followed and I licked my lips as I watched. Rory saw me and held out his hand. "Lick it."

I brought his hand to my mouth, our gazes locked as I ran my tongue across his palm, sucking each of his fingers before spitting into his hand. Rory smirked and lowered his hand, leaning back to grasp his cock. He started to pump it fast, moving his hips at the same rate, slamming down on my lap as he fucked me hard.

"Oh fuck… fuck!" He bit his lip, eyes fluttering closed.

"I'm gonna... fuck, West!" His body tensed as he sank down onto me again, his ass squeezing around me as his cock shot thick ropes of cum across my stomach, decorating our skin.

"Holy shit," Rory gasped, eyes flying open and chest heaving. "Shit..."

"Yeah? Was that good?" I asked, like I couldn't feel the way his channel was pulsing.

He snorted and buried his head in my shoulder. "That's a fucking understatement." He shifted his body, kissing my neck. "Fuck me, West. It's your turn to use me."

I growled, gripping his hips and lifting him slightly so I could put my feet flat on the bed. I rocked my hips up experimentally and when Rory moaned, I held him tightly and began to pound him.

My orgasm had already been on the horizon, and now it rushed towards me at the speed of light. Heat barrelled down my spine, my balls pulling up tight as I thrust deep into Rory. He gasped and moaned, sucking kisses into my neck and whispering, "Yes, more," over and over until everything collided in the perfect storm.

I pulled Rory down onto my shaft, burying every inch inside him as I came, his name a deep, broken growl on my tongue.

CHAPTER NINE

Bubblegum Galaxy

"You don't have to shoot off."

I turned to look at West, holding my crumpled-up T-shirt in my hands. He was watching me from the bed, stretched out in all his naked glory and propped up on one elbow. "I mean, if you wanted to, you could stay for a bit," he continued, glancing down at the bed like he'd suddenly gone all shy. There was a pink flush to his cheeks, but I didn't know if that was from embarrassment or leftover from the exertion. "You don't have to, obviously, but yeah… I'm not kicking you out."

I rolled my lips together, trying to hide the smile threatening to burst onto them. West was so fucking sweet he was going to rot my teeth. How could I say no to a man who'd fuck me until I came apart at the seams, pouring absolute filth in my ears, and then blush when asking me to stay for a bit?

"Budge up then," I said, dropping my T-shirt back onto the floor. West wiggled over and I slid onto the bed beside him, wearing nothing but my hastily collected joggers. I hoped I wasn't going to leave a lube stain on them, but at least we'd used a condom, so there wouldn't be as much mess as if we'd gone bare. I wasn't going to mention it, though, because some guys got really weird when you brought up the side effects of sex to them.

There were definitely some tops out there who didn't even want to consider that their bottom might have to do any kind of prep work or that they might drip cum into their underwear afterwards if they went raw—which was one of my least favourite things ever, especially when it went wet and cold.

"Do you want anything to eat?" West asked. "Or drink? I've got plenty of stuff downstairs."

"Are you sure?"

"Yeah." He looked bemused by my question. "I wouldn't offer otherwise. It's not a trick question."

"Then sure, a drink would be great." My mouth was a little dry from being so loud, and it was making my tongue feel fuzzy.

West smiled brightly at me and it was cute to see how excited he was about me staying. "What do you fancy? I've got things like water, tea, coffee. There's some fizzy too, and I think I've got a couple of beers. And maybe a few fruit ciders. Yeah, I think there's a couple of bottles of pineapple and raspberry cider. I got them in the summer, but they're a bit sweet for me."

"And nobody else drank them?"

"Nah, Mason only drinks when we're out, Jonny's a beer snob, and Guy's a bit of a wanker, so I don't think I'd let him have them if he asked."

I laughed, a little snort escaping my nose, and I slapped my hand across my mouth. West leant across and pried my fingers off my face. "Sorry," I said. "That snort is—"

"It's cute," West said, kissing my nose and then my mouth. "Genuine. I like it."

"You'd be the first."

"Good." He smiled again and my stomach flipped. "It's mine then." He kissed me again, his fingers cupping my jaw. "Did you want a cider then?"

"I think I should," I said quietly. "If only to save them from your wanker housemate. Can I have a glass of water too, please?"

"Sure." Another kiss. Then he drew back slowly, leaving my lips feeling like they were burning. He shuffled over to the edge of the bed and grabbed his boxers off the floor. "I'll be right back."

"Don't worry, I'm not going anywhere."

He chuckled. "I mean, I'd be impressed if you can climb out that window. It only opens about six inches."

"Guess I'll be breathing in extra far then," I said. "It'll be like I'm wearing my best corset."

West laughed again, the sound so bold and bright it was like drinking the best Baileys hot chocolate. "'Get those corsets laced properly! I can hear you speak without gasping.'"

"Oh my God!" I shot forward, practically toppling over in excitement. "You're a fan of *Corpse Bride*?"

"Yeah. I had a friend at school who loved it. She used to make me watch it all the time. I think I can pretty much quote it line for line."

"Okay, first drinks, then we have to talk because I have questions."

He opened the door and disappeared through it, and I heard his footsteps on the landing as he headed towards the stairs. My phone was somewhere on the floor, having fallen out of my pocket, and I couldn't be bothered to fetch it, so instead I looked around West's room, trying to glean details about his life.

Since the house was obviously rented, the walls were a traditional, boring beige and probably hadn't been painted in a while. There weren't any pictures on the walls, but there were a few photos on top of the chest of drawers I'd been leaning against, including what looked like an official line-up photo from the rugby club. There were a few knick-knacks, books, and graphic novels stacked on some small shelves along with a row of game boxes for various consoles, and wedged in beside them was a slightly scraggly-looking stuffed monkey that had clearly been well loved throughout the years.

It made my heart do a little flip because honestly, it was adorable as fuck that West had kept his childhood toy. He clearly felt no embarrassment at having it on display either, which probably meant it was important to him, and that made it somehow sweeter.

West hadn't left many clothes lying around, so I had to assume he was pretty tidy, and his bedside table only had a lamp, some tissues, a charging cable, and a pulp novel that looked like it was about zombies lying on top, along with an open box of condoms. I presumed the lube was still somewhere on the bed.

I couldn't see anything fun, like a dildo or fleshlight, but West didn't seem like the kind of person to just leave them out in public. And even though my fingers were itching to go through his drawers, that would cross so many boundaries I could kiss goodbye to any future invitations.

Another set of footsteps on the landing interrupted my thoughts, and West reappeared in the door holding a glass of water with two bottles tucked into the crook of his arm… and a tub of ice cream with two spoons.

"I remembered I had this in the freezer," he said, gently dropping the unopened tub of Ben & Jerry's onto the bed before handing me the glass of water and a spoon. "I know you didn't say you were hungry, but you had a shit day and in my experience, ice cream usually makes it better."

"Thank you," I said, because I was genuinely stumped for anything else. It definitely wasn't what I'd expected to happen, but nothing West had done since we'd fucked had been. Every time he opened his mouth, it threw me for a loop, and I was curious to know where he'd go next. "That's really sweet of you."

West shrugged and handed me one of the bottles. It was already open, with condensation pooling on the pink and yellow label. "Don't worry about it." He sat down on the edge of the bed, making the mattress dip slightly. He took a swig of his drink, which I assumed was beer, and then reached for the ice cream, tearing off the plastic wrap around the lid. "Do you want to talk about it?"

"About today? Not really." I sighed and sipped my cider. It was sweet and cold, the taste of fruit bursting on my tongue. "Have you ever watched *Drag Stars*?"

"Little bits," West said as he popped the lid off the ice cream and inspected the contents to see if it was soft enough to dive into or whether it was likely to bend the spoon. "Mostly just clips on TikTok and Instagram. I don't think I've watched a whole episode, but I know the premise. It's like a reality show for drag queens, right?"

"Yeah. The US version has been running for fifteen years, and they started a UK version five years ago—they're just casting for season six at the moment."

"Which is what you applied for?"

I nodded. "Yeah, it was the second time I'd applied too. I really thought this time I'd nailed it. I spent fucking forever on the application, made sure my tape was fucking Oscar-worthy, or like, whatever the drag version is. But nope, still didn't get it." I sighed again, my chest aching as I remembered the email. *We regret to inform you...* yeah, like they meant that. *Let's just shoot your dreams out of the sky with a fucking cannon and offer you some vague platitudes so we sound polite.*

"Fuck, I'm sorry," West said and he sounded like he meant it. "That's really shit."

"Thanks."

"If it helps, I think you're fucking incredible. As both you and Bubblegum Galaxy." He shot me a gentle smile and held out the ice cream. "How long have you been doing drag?"

"About five years," I said as I took the tub. It was a little awkward with the glass of water, but as I was looking for somewhere to put it, West plucked it out of my hands and set it on his bedside table. "Thanks."

"No worries." He smiled at me again. "So is drag something you've always wanted to do?"

"Kind of, I mean I remember watching bits of Lily Savage as a kid and just loving her, and then I found *Drag Stars* when I was a teenager on YouTube. They all looked so fucking amazing, but I never thought I'd be able to do that, even though my mum'll tell you I've been dressing up in princess dresses and lipstick since I was about five." I snorted softly and dug into the ice cream, scooping out a heap of chocolate and marshmallow, the tail of a chocolate fish just visible. "I was about seventeen when I finally plucked up the courage to get some make-up to try. I remember sitting on my bed watching YouTube tutorials and trying to work out what the fuck to do. I'm pretty sure there's some really bad selfies of me somewhere, but they're never seeing the light of day."

West laughed and took the ice cream as I handed it to him. "I'm sure you looked great."

"No, I looked like a six-year-old who'd gotten into his mum's make-up for the first time," I said. "But it just kind of went from there. I got more make-up, wigs, shoes, some clothes. The more I did, the more I loved it. And then my parents found out and I thought they were going to be *seriously* weirded out or mad or something, but all my dad said was that he thought I looked very nice and Mum's reaction was to start teaching me how to sew."

I looked down at the bed as I remembered the fear

that'd pulsed through my body when they'd come home early and I'd been dressed up in my bedroom singing along to Little Mix. I'd been so sure they'd hate it, but Dad had just smiled and said I looked very pretty but maybe my skirt should be a bit longer so I didn't show off my ass to the whole of Lincoln.

West was quiet and I glanced up at him. The expression on his face was almost sad, like there was pain lingering behind his eyes.

"Are you okay?" I asked.

"Yeah." He nodded and pushed some ice cream onto his spoon. "I'm glad you have supportive parents. It's important."

The way he said it made something pull in my chest and I put my hand on his broad thigh. "I'm guessing yours aren't?"

"You could say that," he said dryly. "I haven't spoken to them in nearly four years, since I first came out as bi. And they pretty much threw my brother away as a kid because he was obviously gay. I mean, they didn't kick him out, but yeah…"

"Shit, I'm so, so sorry." I wiggled closer to him and threw my arms around him, not caring that it was awkward or that there was a cold tub of ice cream pressed against my stomach. "In the nicest way possible, fuck them. They don't deserve you. Or your brother."

"Thanks. It's definitely been weird and at times I kind of miss them, but I think the hardest part is the fact they always told me they loved me, pushed me to excel at rugby, told me they were proud and then…"

"Love shouldn't be conditional," I said, squeezing him tightly. "Ever. And I hope you don't think this is your fault, because it's not."

"I know... Logically, I know anyway. Reality is harder sometimes."

I nodded as I sat back. "Reality is a bitch!"

"Yeah, it is."

We sat in silence for a few minutes, passing the ice cream back and forth. It wasn't awkward, more like that kind of silence where you're just processing everything.

"Was the drag brunch your first drag show?" I asked, handing West back the tub and taking a swig of my cider.

He nodded. "Yeah, it was Mason's idea. He thought it might be like a fun team-bonding thing for a few of us."

"And did you enjoy it? What you saw anyway. Before I kinda ruined it."

"You didn't ruin it," he said. "If you hadn't done that, we wouldn't be here."

"True and I'd be deprived of your dick, and that would be a travesty."

West laughed and nudged me. "How would you have survived?"

"I'd be alive. I just wouldn't be living." I grinned. "But if you enjoyed it, you should come down to The Court one night. The show we do there is a bit more... not family friendly? It's bolder, a bit more over the top. More fun."

"The Court?" West frowned, like he knew the name and was trying to place it. "That's the gay bar, right?"

"Yes! Lincoln's one and only gay and drag club," I said. "We do drag shows like, two or three nights a week. There's club nights too, variety shows, special events, tours. I'm there pretty much every weekend, and we've started doing some fun things on Wednesday nights too, like karaoke or drag bingo, so I'm sometimes there hosting that with one of the others."

"Drag bingo?"

"Yeah, it's just bingo but hosted by drag performers. And there's usually prizes too, like free drinks."

West nodded, then smiled at me. "Okay then, I'll have to come down one night. Would I need tickets?"

"Depends. But if you want to come to something, message me and I can get a couple left at the door for you. Bring Mason too, then you'll have someone to sit with." If West hadn't been to a show before, it might be good for him to have a friend for support. Not that we got wild or anything, but I had a hunch he might find it a bit overwhelming.

West smiled and handed me the last of the ice cream. "Sounds fun."

"Good," I said, eating the last spoonful and leaning over to kiss him. His hand slid down onto my waist and he slowly pulled me onto his lap, his cock starting to grow hard underneath me.

"Do you need to go?"

I shook my head and let out a breathless whine, heat kindling in my gut. "No… I can stay."

West smirked and started kissing down my neck.

CHAPTER TEN

West

"Do I look okay?" I asked, pulling my shirt across my chest as Mason and I followed a crowd of people into The Court. It was just over a week since Rory had suggested we come, and this was the first Saturday night I'd had free in a while, so it felt like the best way to use it.

"You look hot," Mason said with an exasperated smile, probably because I'd asked the same question twenty times in the last hour. "Bubblegum will love it. And so will Rory."

"You think?"

"I fucking know. And if you keep asking me, I'm going to make you buy me a drink every time."

"I'll buy you a drink anyway," I said. "I really appreciate you coming."

Mason shrugged. "Don't worry about it. It sounds like fun."

We walked through into the main part of the downstairs

and I nearly stopped in my tracks. I wasn't sure what I'd been expecting, but it hadn't been this.

It looked like something out of an old movie.

There was a little stage at the front with huge red velvet curtains hung from each side, trimmed with gold tassels. The wooden floor in front of it was filled with round tables and gold chairs with red cushions. The chairs looked fairly solid, but I said a silent prayer that they'd be able to take Mason's and my weight.

That was the one problem with being rugby forwards. We were both six foot plus of solid muscle.

There was a bar in the corner that was already doing a solid amount of business, with staff in dark T-shirts serving up a storm to the crowd.

"I'll grab a table," Mason said, clapping me on the shoulder. "You get some drinks."

"What do you want?" I asked.

"I don't mind. You know what I like."

I watched him stroll across the floor, skirting around the tables. I'd meant to ask him not to get one too near the front, but luckily most of them were already taken. Besides, I had a sneaky feeling that if I'd asked, Mason would've ignored me and tried to sit as close to the front as possible.

Turning back to the bar, I took a few steps forward and joined the vague queue that had formed, letting my eyes roam across the crowd in a way I hoped wasn't noticeable. There was a real mix of people here, and the bright hum of chatter and relaxation in everyone's bodies made it obvious this was a place they felt safe.

I bit my lip as I stepped forward, wondering if I looked

out of place and if that would put people off. I'd always been aware of my size and the fact I looked incredibly masculine, but in the past few years, I'd come to realise just how accidentally threatening I looked to other people.

I wasn't visibly queer in the way I dressed or in my mannerisms, and I knew most people thought I was straight. But apart from draping myself in rainbows, I wasn't really sure what to do.

My thoughts were still occupied by the time I reached the bar, and it wasn't until a member of staff waved a hand in front of my face that I realised it was my turn.

"Shit, sorry," I said, shaking my head with an apologetic smile. "I was miles away."

"No worries," the man said. He had a name badge pinned to his T-shirt with his pronouns underneath it in bold pink lettering. He was sporting a buzz cut that'd been dyed neon green, and when he spoke I could see a metal ball glinting on his tongue. "What can I get for you?"

"Er, can I get..." I glanced behind the bar and at the taps in front of me. "A double rum and coke and a double gin and lemonade, please."

"Any preference on the rum or the gin?"

"No, just whatever you can reach."

Usually we stuck to things like beer when we went out, but I wanted something a bit stronger. Now I just had to remember to sip it slowly. Although it wasn't like drinks were expensive round here—having grown up in London, where the cost of a pint was eye-watering, the price of anything outside the city still threw me. The first time I'd only paid a fiver for a drink, I'd had to double-check they'd charged me for the right thing.

Drinks in hand, I wandered across the room looking for Mason. I finally spotted him sitting at a table off to the left, around about halfway back, chatting to a couple of people at the table next to him. I smiled because it was typical of Mason to make friends wherever he went. He didn't seem to have any of that British awkwardness about striking up a conversation with a random stranger.

"Here you go," I said, handing him the tall glass of rum and coke before gingerly lowering myself into the seat next to him.

"What did you get?"

"That's a double rum and coke, and this is gin and lemonade."

"Perfect." He sipped it and smiled.

"Making friends?" I asked, gesturing at the other table, who'd gone back to their conversation.

"Just saying hi," he said. "And asking about the show. Seems pretty popular."

"Yeah." I took a sip of my own drink and looked around, realising most people had taken their seats. I pulled at my shirt again and Mason raised an eyebrow at me. "What? I didn't ask."

"You were thinking about it."

"Maybe, but I didn't."

Mason rolled his eyes but any admonishment he'd been thinking of giving me was cut off as the lights dimmed. The audience cheered and clapped as sweeping classical music began to play, welcoming a curvaceous older queen onto the stage. She was wearing an enormous lavender wig decorated with flowers and a tiny fascinator hat perched on top at an angle with purple feathers sticking out of it. Her dress also had flowers on it and a fair amount of rhinestones too, and she was waving to the crowd like camp royalty.

"Hello, my darlings," she said, lifting the microphone she was holding. "How are we all this evening?" Everyone cheered. "Continuing to drink me out of house and home then. I must say you're making this whole cost of living crisis much easier on my wallet." I laughed softly, and it was echoed around the room. "For those of you who are new or who've forgotten since last time—in which case I suggest you get your head checked because I'm quite memorable—I am your hostess and MC for this evening, Violet *Bouquet*." I smiled at the perfect nod to *Keeping Up Appearances* as Violet lifted her hand to the tiny hat on her head. "Now, I must ask, do you like my hat? I thought it was rather fetching and very suitable for this evening."

Everyone laughed and there were a few shouted comments. Violet leaned in and listened.

"You think it should be bigger? I see. Well, I'm sure you'll appreciate size isn't everything," she said. "And you think what? More feathers? Oh well, that might look nice, but I don't want it to be too much. I don't want to look like a peacock. And you... what's that? I look like Marie Antoinette... definitely not, I'm not letting any of you lot eat cake. You can do that on your own time."

I choked on my gin, my laughing turning into broken coughs as Mason thumped me on my back. Violet was hilarious and I loved the way she chatted with the crowd, bringing us into her world of sequins and snark.

"Now, we do have a fabulous show for you this evening," Violet continued, "and kicking it off is our brand-new arrival all the way from Cornwall—and yes, they apparently do have drag down there. It's drag's very own maniacal super villain, Legs Luthor."

A cheer went up from people around me as Violet waltzed offstage. The lights flashed and whirled as a techno beat dropped a remixed version of the original *Superman* theme, and onto the stage strutted a tall queen with a shaved head and elaborate make-up that made my eyes pop. She was wearing thigh-high lace-up boots and a toxic-green latex bodysuit that ended in tiny shorts that clung to her dark skin, showing off every inch of her perfectly sculpted thighs.

"Fucking hell," Mason whispered, his eyes transfixed on the stage as Legs started to dance, dropping into the splits and bouncing on the floor.

"You okay?"

"I… shit, man… no, I don't think I am." Mason swallowed as Legs swivelled, pulling herself up as the music transitioned into a sexy dance version of "Sway With Me," throwing a wink to the crowd.

I'd foolishly always assumed Mason was straight, but I got the feeling I'd missed the mark. Although maybe Mason was just starting to figure that out for himself.

"She… she's fucking incredible," Mason said in awe, stars in his eyes. I smiled into my glass, draining the last of my drink. Legs was gorgeous and very talented, but in my eyes, she couldn't hold a candle to Bubblegum.

Maybe it was unfair of me to judge and compare since they were so different, but there was something about Bubblegum that made my chest warm and insides squirm. I'd only seen her perform live once, but I'd watched enough of her reels and TikToks to know there was something special about her, and I hated that *Drag Stars* hadn't been able to see it.

The whole world deserved to see how amazing she was.

And if I was lucky, maybe I'd get to be there when it happened.

After Legs Luthor came another queen, then a king, and by the time his set had ended, I was practically vibrating with anticipation. Mason hadn't said much since Legs had left the stage except to ask if I wanted another drink, and it seemed like his mind was more than a little melted.

Violet was back onstage again, but it was only when she mentioned Bubblegum's name that I started to listen.

"Our next performer is someone we all love very much here at The Court, and she just seems to get prettier as she goes—I'm sure it's all that bathing in almond milk and twink blood. It's not like we're going to find many innocents round here." She shot the crowd a deprecating look with raised eyebrows to a round of laughter. "Please put your hands together for the very sweet, and very sparkly, Bubblegum Galaxy!"

Bubblegum bounced onto the stage to rapturous applause and my jaw dropped. If I'd thought she looked beautiful the last time I'd seen her, then today she looked like a goddess.

Her hair was an apt shade of bubblegum pink, styled in soft waves like a Golden Age Hollywood movie star and glittering under the lights. Her outfit was also pink but more of a pastel, with a corset top that had tiny puff sleeves on her upper arms and a stiff tutu skirt, making her kind of look like a ballerina Barbie, especially since her sparkling pink shoes also had ribbon ties that wrapped around her ankles.

I was completely mesmerised, drinking in every detail over and over, from how long and perfect Bubblegum's legs looked, to her beautiful plush lips that looked like they'd been painted to accentuate them, to the vibrant energy that radiated out of her. Bubblegum had harnessed the power of the universe and brought it to her performance, enchanting everyone in her presence. It was like seeing a meteor shower for the first time, or maybe even the Milky Way. Something truly out of this world and so beautiful and perfect that no words would ever be able to describe it.

Bubblegum moved seamlessly with the music, lip-syncing every word as if she was the artist and dancing up a dizzying storm. I wished we were sat closer because then it would feel like there was nobody else here.

The song changed and Bubblegum sashayed down a small set of steps at the side of the stage and into the crowd as she sang about dripping in diamonds. The spotlight followed her, throwing patches of light onto the floor from her glitter and rhinestones. She danced through the tables, interacting with the people around her, and as she turned away from one, she looked across the room and her eyes locked onto mine.

She smiled.

And my heart exploded, a new galaxy forming in my chest.

CHAPTER ELEVEN

Bubblegum Galaxy

EVEN THOUGH I'D known West was coming this evening, seeing him in the crowd hit harder than I'd thought it would.

There was something about the expression of awe on his face as I danced through the tables. Part of me wanted to say it was just because he'd never seen anything like it before, since the brunch at Fox & Taylor had been his first drag show, but it looked like more than that. The way his eyes were fixed on me, as if I was special, shook me all the way down through the soles of my Pleasers and into the floor.

It was like being struck by an errant bolt of lightning, and I channelled every drop of that into my performance.

If I'd had time, I'd have waltzed over to him, but my routine was carefully choreographed down to the last beat and if I stepped out of place, I'd never have time to get back to the stage before the song changed. Then my brain would get stuck and I could kiss any sense of timing and showmanship goodbye. And if West had come to see my show, I wanted him to see *my show*. I wanted to completely blow him away so he'd never forget me.

And then I wanted to drag him back to his bedroom so I could blow him away all over again.

I began to head back to the stage, every line of the song word-perfect on my lips. But as I walked, I threw in a little twirl and blew West a cheeky kiss and a wink, giving him a shot of signature Bubblegum sweetness. And when I climbed the steps, I made sure to find him in the crowd.

It might have had something to do with the lights, but I could've sworn West was as red as the stage curtains.

Refocusing my mind, I slid straight into my next song and strutted across the stage. This was one time I *really* wished we had backup dancers for every show. Sometimes Phil could wrangle some for special occasion shows like Halloween, Christmas, Valentine's Day, and our Pride celebration, as well as the odd variety show, but he'd drawn the line at having them two or three days a week.

Which I could understand from a cost point of view, but it would be really fucking perfect to have some sexy guys in glittering booty shorts and harnesses dancing beside me and lifting me up like a proper showgirl. I just wanted my vintage Marilyn Monroe moment. Was that too much to ask?

The final song in my set kicked in and I dragged up every single drop of energy left inside me as I geared up to my big finish. I changed my set list fairly regularly, mixing together old and new stuff that I adored, and my current finale was Mariah Carey's absolute classic, "Fantasy." It was one of the first songs I'd learnt by heart when I was a kid dancing around the living room to whatever CDs my mum had. I'd had an awesome babysitter too, Melissa, who'd always brought round her NOW CDs, her iPod, and her tiny crackling portable speaker so we could listen to stuff together and pretend we were in music videos.

I really wished we'd kept in touch because I wanted to be able to thank her for encouraging me and never telling me boys weren't allowed to like things like Girls Aloud, Little Mix, Beyoncé, and Britney Spears.

As the song reached its final chorus, I danced across to the centre of the stage and struck my final pose as the music came to an end. My chest was heaving, sweat dripping down my back and making my tights cling to my thighs in all the wrong places, my feet starting to burn from the exertion of doing a whole routine in seven-inch platforms, and my wig itching where my head was overheating from the stage lights.

Whoever said women, and drag queens, didn't suffer to look pretty was a fucking moron who deserved to be thrown into an oubliette to be forgotten about.

Or maybe they should just be drenched in glitter and sent packing. They'd be finding that shit everywhere for the rest of their lives.

My ears echoed with the sound of applause mixed with the thumping of my heart. I gathered myself, taking a steadying breath before waving to the crowd, doing a little curtsy, and skipping offstage to where a couple of the others were waiting in the wings.

Violet gave me a beaming smile and said, "Well done, darling, that was spectacular," before strolling back onto the stage. Bitch Fit was watching her closely, waiting for her cue as she straightened her skirt and brushed a stray wisp of hair away. I had to say, ever since Bitch's best friend Orlando had started styling her wigs, there'd been a marked improvement in her appearance. Not that they'd been bad before, but Orlando had a way of making even cheap wigs look like they were worth considerably more.

He'd done a couple of mine recently and every one was a work of art.

"Good job, Sparkles," Bitch said with a wink. "The kiss is new. That wouldn't happen to be the guy you dumped drinks over, would it?"

I felt my cheeks heat and hoped it wouldn't show through my make-up. Of course Bitch would notice who I'd directed it at. She never missed anything, shady bitch. "Maybe," I said, trying to play it cool. Even though I kind of wanted to tell Bitch everything, because West was hot as fuck and sweeter than a whole bag of candyfloss, I didn't want the man being mobbed by drag performers at the end of the night. And Bitch Fit was definitely the sort of person to interrogate him, probably accompanied by at least two of the others.

Eva was definitely the sort to get involved. And Legs.

The only one who might stop them was Peachy Keen, but I doubted it. Peaches, as she was known, seemed sweet, but she was as nosy as the rest of us.

Thank fuck the murder twins weren't here, or I'd be in trouble.

"We're *so* not done with this," Bitch said as she took her mic from one of the techs. "We're picking it up as soon as I'm done."

"Not if I'm not waiting," I muttered as Violet announced Bitch Fit and she sauntered onto the stage like she fucking owned it. Which she kind of did at this point.

Violet saw me lurking and headed straight for me, flicking her mic off as she stepped into the wings. "Oh darling, while I remember, if you've got two minutes, drop in and see Peaches and Ink before you go. They're organising something fun in the run-up to Christmas and wanted to ask you about it. It's a bit last minute, but there you go."

I frowned. "What're they doing?"

"That would ruin the surprise if I told you," she said. "They're just in the second dressing room if you want them. I'd go now, or Peaches will corner you while you're half-naked. She has a habit of doing that."

I laughed and tottered away towards The Court's backstage area where there was a series of small dressing rooms. Violet had one of her own, which doubled as Phil's office, there were three for the club's regular drag performers, and then two for visitors or when we needed extra space. I usually shared with Bitch Fit and Eva Nessence when she was here, Moxxie, or sometimes the murder twins, aka Scary-Kate and Slashley.

My feet were killing me, so I leant against the wall to take my shoes off, breathing a pained sigh of relief at the feel of the cold floor through my tights. Holding them in one hand, I started walking down the corridor when a door opened and I saw a familiar face sticking his head out.

"Perfect timing," Ink said, his blue rhinestone stubble glinting in the light of the corridor. Ink, or Incubussy, was a drag king who'd joined us at the start of the year when he'd moved back from London, and I adored his dry humour and camp style. "We were just about to come looking for you."

"Violet said something about you and Peaches having plans?"

"Yeah, come in and we can talk about it." He gestured at the door to the dressing room and ushered me inside, where I found Legs Luthor chatting to Peachy Keen over a shared packet of sweet chilli crisps, a tube of paprika Pringles, chocolate buttons, and two cans of Pepsi Max. The pair of them were half-dressed, with Peaches still wearing her wig and make-up but then nothing else but a pair of grey jogging bottoms and some fluffy slippers. Legs was still wearing her bodysuit but had removed her make-up and incredible boots.

They turned and looked at me and grinned. "You all right, love?" Legs asked, stealing a handful of crisps as she sat back in her chair and gestured at me. "I love this, by the way. Very sexy."

"So cute," Peaches said. "Sorry, I didn't get to see all your set—I wanted to corner Legs before she headed out. Grab a seat, if you can find one."

"She'd have more luck if you didn't put your shit everywhere," Ink said with laugh, picking up Peaches's hip pads and waist shaper off a chair and throwing them at her head. "There's meant to be room for four of us in here."

"I'm not the only messy one," Peaches said, laughing as Ink hefted her gel breast inserts in his hands.

"Christ, how much do these weigh? I think they must be as big as mine." He prodded his own chest and winced before reaching for the bottom of his chest plate. "I'm going to get undressed. Ignore me getting my tits out."

"We always do," Legs said as she stole another handful of crisps. She picked up the bag and offered it to me, and I took a few before sliding onto the now empty chair that Ink and Peaches had cleared, putting my shoes on the floor next to me.

"Okay, so…" Peaches turned to face me. There was a notebook resting on her knee and I could see various bullet points scrawled across the pages. "Ink and I have been looking at ways that we can bring a little more queer joy to Lincoln and get performers involved in the local community. Now, I know it's a bit short notice, but we'd love to do something before the end of the year, so we're looking at organising some holiday-themed drag story hours throughout December. Right now, we're looking at doing anywhere between three and six, depending on how many people we can get involved. Venue-wise, we're hoping to use Lincoln Library and a couple of bookshops and cafés across the city to really make sure we're involving as many people as possible. And I wondered if you'd be interested in hosting one? All you'd need to do is pick a book or maybe two to read, something suitable for kids, and make sure you're happy to interact with them. You wouldn't be on your own either. At least one of us will be there at all times, and we'll be able to supervise, answer questions, make sure it all runs smoothly."

"You don't have to answer right now," Ink said. He'd removed his chest plate and binder and thrown on a sports bra and tank top instead, although he was still wearing his leather trousers and blue rhinestoned codpiece. "You can take a few days to think about it. But you're cute and fun, and in those photos I saw of you at Fox & Taylor, you kinda looked like drag Elsa, which I think people will love. Also, we could trust you to behave and not swear."

I snorted because there were definitely a few people who nobody would trust with a ten-foot barge pole to keep their tongue in their head. Not all drag was family friendly, nor did it have to be, but this was one occasion that would call for more sweetness than salt.

The pair of them were watching me and I could see Legs stealing chocolate buttons out of the corner of my eye.

"Who else is involved?" I asked. It wouldn't have a massive bearing on my decision, but I was curious. The whole thing sounded like a lot of fun, and while I didn't have a ton of experience working with children, the idea of getting to pretend to be a Christmas princess definitely appealed.

"I'm doing one," Peaches said. "Then Moxxie and Eva. Bitch is a potential backup, because she's apparently pretty good with kids, but she might be busy—apparently one of her brothers is getting married, so she might not have time, although she offered to blow him off for us. She even offered to go by Miss Fit because she did that when she was out in Tennessee earlier in the year. Then Legs is going to do all the graphics and design work."

"Strange as it sounds, I can see Bitch being good with kids," I said. "Mostly because she's still one at heart. I'm kinda surprised about Eva, though."

"Yeah, but she's a paramedic, isn't she?" Legs pointed out. "And the whole gothic queen thing would be really fun."

"We're getting a whole fairy-tale cast here," I said with a laugh. "Eva's the evil queen, Peaches can be the good fairy, Moxxie can be the knight in shining armour, and Bitch can be their comic relief."

"I guess that makes you our princess," Ink said, leaning on the top of Peaches's chair and grinning at me. "What do you say, Bubbles? Want to go storm a castle with us?"

"Absolutely," I said. "But there's no way I'm letting Moxxie kiss me."

CHAPTER TWELVE

West

"IF YOU THROW one more fucking grenade at me, I will personally shove one up your arse!" Alex cried as his character ducked the comically smoking grenade that Lane had thrown at his head.

"Not my fault if you keep standing in front of the bloody zombies," Lane said. "Move yourself!"

"How about both of you get out the way and let me handle it, m'kay?" Theo, my brother, asked as his cheerleader neatly somersaulted over them straight into the zombie hordes surrounding us and started cutting off heads with ruthless precision.

We were playing our weekly game of *Age of Blood* online, which involved Mason, Theo, his two friends, Alex and Lane, and me all attempting to fight our way through legions of the undead and survive as long as possible. Usually, this involved Theo, who ran a Twitch channel for fun, which definitely made him the most competent gamer among us by a mile, and Mason, who was silent but deadly, making sure that Alex, Lane, and I didn't get mowed down within the first two minutes.

It was a fun way to spend an evening, and I loved getting to spend time with my brother.

This had been his suggestion during our first video call, after we'd made the leap from emails and messaging, and I'd been glad I'd taken him up on it. There was something weirdly soothing about sitting on my bed, laptop on my thighs, headphones on, completely shutting out the world while I mashed the keyboard and launched rockets randomly across the screen. It was one of the best forms of stress relief I'd come across.

Apart from Rory.

I wondered if he was a gamer. I'd never asked him and I didn't want to judge based on his appearance. After all, Theo was adorably femme and wore dresses with ruffles and bows and owned pink cat-eared headphones, but he was also the biggest fan of gory zombie horror I'd ever met, owned a selection of stuffed animals, and worked as a mortician on a day-to-day basis. He was a walking paradox, and I loved him for it.

"West!" Theo screeched, jolting me from my thoughts, and I realised I was being chewed on by at least three zombies. My health bar flashed critically at the top of the screen, along with the bright chemical yellow dial that showed the character's infection rate. I was about two chomps away from joining our enemies, which would end the game and we'd have to start all over again.

"Shit, sorry! I'm on it!" I hit a few keys, my American football player avatar spinning around and charging through the zombies, trampling two of them underfoot. The third tried to follow me until Mason slid up behind it and neatly dispatched it.

"Are you okay?" Alex asked. "Did your connection drop out?"

"Nah, it's just me," I said, finding some space and quickly cycling through my character's inventory to grab a med pack and an antiviral one. They'd give me enough health and lower my infection rate enough to get me through the rest of the level.

"Is something wrong?" Theo asked, his cheerleader neatly slicing off more heads. "Do you want to talk about it?"

"There's nothing wrong, honest. I just got distracted, sorry."

"You don't need to apologise," Lane said.

"I nearly got us all killed," I said.

"It's just a game," Lane said. "And if we have to start again, then maybe Alex will be less shit."

"Ha-fucking-ha. My kill count is higher than yours," Alex said with a laugh. From what Theo had told me, Alex and Lane had known each other since they were at primary school and had been friends for about twenty years. Listening to them always made me smile because you could tell that even when they ripped the shit out of each other, it was always done with love, never malice, and whatever they said they always had each other's backs. Literally, in this case.

"What's distracting you?" Theo asked. I closed my eyes for a second and tried not to sigh, wondering how long I could get away with not bringing up Rory. After all, it wasn't like we were dating. We were just friends who fucked. But Theo wasn't the sort of person to leave things alone, not if he thought he was missing out on something.

"He's thinking about Rory," Mason said, so fucking casually it was like he was talking about the weather or what he'd had for dinner.

"Oh?" Theo sounded far too delighted. "Who's Rory?"

"He's just a friend," I said quickly. Too quickly.

Mason snorted. "Yeah, sure. *Friend*. The sort of friend you rail regularly. And loudly."

"Jesus Christ, Mason," I muttered. "Can you not?"

"I've had that kind of friend before," Theo said, slicing off the last zombie head as the level came to an end. "But I'm pretty sure West isn't running a secret MyFans account. And if he is, I'd definitely want to know. Then I can tell all my friends!"

"I'm not running a secret MyFans!" I exhaled, watching the screen as our characters walked into the next safe house so we could heal and stock up on supplies. "Rory is a drag queen I met a couple of weeks ago and we started chatting and stuff. He's really talented and gorgeous too. Mason and I actually went to see his show last weekend."

"You're missing a lot of details there," Mason said. Fucking shit stirrer. "But West's right—he's really talented. Everyone was. If you guys ever come down, we'll have to take you."

"Oh my God, I'd love that!" Theo said. "We don't really

get many drag queens here. We should totally mention it to Colin and Soren, see if they'll do a drag night at the pub."

I assumed his last comment was directed to Lane and Alex since I didn't know who Theo was talking about. Hopefully, the idea of setting up a drag night in Heather Bay would distract him enough that the next level would start and we could leave this conversation behind. Because while I liked the idea that Theo and I were getting close enough to talk about relationships, I didn't know how I felt about my brother interrogating me about my sex life. Especially because Theo didn't seem to do things like boundaries. At least, not according to his boyfriend, Laurie.

"We can ask them tomorrow," Alex said. "Or we can get Anders to ask since Soren's his brother."

"You could do something at Novel Tea," Lane said. "And I'm not saying that to be a dick, but Oliver mentioned he's seen places doing those drag queen story hours. Could be fun."

"Yeah, might be," Alex said as his character pulled out a med pack. "We'd actually need to find someone willing to drag their ass all the way out here, but it might be fun." He thought for a second. "I think Henry said something about one of Lewis's brothers being a drag queen… Bitch something."

"Bitch Fit?" I asked.

"Yeah, you know her?"

"Not really, but I think she's a friend of Rory's. She was at the show we went to the other day. Kinda like an emo-girl style?"

"Yeah, sounds about right." Alex chuckled. "Small world."

"Okay," Theo said, sounding like he was about to start issuing orders. "New plan: Alex asks Henry to get us a drag performer or two and then we have a fabulous drag day in Heather Bay. And then West can come with Rory."

"No." I shook my head vigorously, even though I knew they couldn't see me. "We're not dating. I can't ask him that."

Theo sighed and I heard the eye roll. "Yes, you can! It's not difficult. Anyway, if you like him, you should tell him."

"You do realise the irony of *you* saying that, right?" Alex asked. "You, who lived with Laurie for six fucking years and did fuck all about your feelings for him while being so deep in each other's pockets that we all thought you were married?"

"No, you can't use that against me," Theo whined. "And anyway, Laurie and I told each other we loved each other all the time. That counts."

"No, it fucking doesn't and you know it."

I chuckled. Alex had a point. When I'd first reached out to Theo, his very first response had mentioned Laurie, and I'd assumed he was Theo's partner right from the start. Then when we'd finally met in person, I'd just assumed they were married from the way they interacted with each other. I'd been astounded when Laurie had told me they'd only just started dating because it had seemed so contrary to everything I'd seen.

This situation with Rory was nothing like that and given everything, I didn't think Theo could really lecture me on relationships, so I decided I'd take his advice with a pinch of salt.

A large one.

"Theo's kind of right, though," Mason said. "You obviously like the guy, and you couldn't stop staring at Bubblegum on Saturday. You should do something about it, and I don't just mean bringing him back here and having a drink together after you've fucked."

"Rory was having a bad day," I said. "He wanted to blow off some steam."

"Best way to do it," Lane said with a dry chuckle. "But the guys have a point. If you like him, you should do something more than just hook up."

"Yeah but…" Nerves bubbled up in my chest and I didn't know whether to voice my thoughts. In my head, they sounded kind of ridiculous. It wasn't like I hadn't dated before, but asking Rory to do more than hang out and have orgasms felt like facing down one of those army climbing walls. Only this one was about thirty feet tall. "What if he says no?"

"He's not going to say no," Mason said. "He blew a fucking kiss to you in the middle of his routine on Saturday night. In front of the whole club. And you're always messaging each other. You can deny it, but you get that bloody stupid look on your face whenever you look at your phone. It's like you've seen the world's cutest puppy or eaten fifteen bags of gummy worms."

I couldn't believe we were having this conversation now, over voice chat in the middle of a game when we were literally three rooms apart.

"You should definitely do something together," Lane said as we all finished gearing up for the next level. A countdown time appeared in the corner of the screen, ticking down the seconds until we returned to the zombie apocalypse.

"Agreed," Alex said as his avatar reloaded his guns and adjusted his hat. "Just do something simple. Get a takeaway or go out for dinner. Like you're just hanging out, only with all your clothes on and not in your bedroom."

"Oh yes, you should definitely do that!" Theo's avatar bounced on the spot in a perfect recreation of its player's excitement. "Have dinner, a few drinks, lots of kisses—it'd be perfect. And you can ask him about coming to Heather Bay too!"

I laughed softly. "One thing at a time, Theo. Let's start with dinner."

"Ask him now," Theo said. "I can pause this. But if you don't do it now, I bet you won't do it at all."

"Basically, if you don't do it now, Theo will nag you about it all evening and be an adorable pain in the arse," Alex said with a snort.

"No, I won't!"

"Don't lie," Alex said. "I know you too well."

"Technically, I'm not lying," Theo said insistently. "I'd just remind West he needs to ask Rory out now before Rory gets busy. Or sad that West hasn't asked him yet."

I shook my head as they all began bickering, but since Theo had already hit pause, I grabbed my phone from where it was resting beside me on the bed. My fingers felt weirdly clammy as I pulled open our message thread and began to type.

> **West**
> Hey, so, not sure if this would be something you'd fancy but would you like to maybe have dinner at some point? No worries if you just want to stick to casual though.

> **Bubblegum**
> That sounds fun! I'm definitely down for that <3

> **West**
> Awesome, cool. Are you free maybe Friday? Or next week?

> **West**
> And how do you feel about Greek food?

CHAPTER THIRTEEN

Bubblegum Galaxy

"Please tell me you're having as much trouble choosing as I am," I said, tearing my eyes away from the menu of The Olive Grove to grin at West across the table.

The smells wafting out of the small Greek restaurant's kitchen were making me drool, my stomach rumbling as it reminded me I hadn't eaten anything since I'd hastily shovelled a sandwich into my mouth about twelve-ish while Christopher and I were driving between jobs.

"Yeah, I don't think it's possible to just pick one thing," West said, returning my smile and setting off fireworks in my chest. That smile was the reason I'd spent forty minutes choosing something to wear tonight. "Do you want to get a meze? Then we'll get a load of different things to share."

"Wait, where's that? I can't see that," I said, scanning the menu again and trying to spot what West was talking about.

West reached across the table, plucking the menu out of my hands and flipping it over to where I'd naively assumed they'd just have drinks listed. Instead there was a whole page of food I'd missed.

I laughed, glancing away and picking up my cocktail, hoping I could somehow hide my embarrassment. "Can you pretend that didn't happen and I do actually know how to read a menu?"

"You're fine," West said. "I did it too the first time I came here. Mason thought it was hilarious."

"Okay, well, I'm glad it's not just me who's a total numpty."

"Definitely not." West was still smiling at me. It was almost fond, like what I was doing was cute. "The meze is good, though. Jonny, Mason, and I came here in the summer for Mason's birthday because he didn't fancy doing the whole team-night-out thing, and it was enough to feed the three of us. You can't really swap anything out unless you've got an allergy, but there's nothing here that I hate."

"Me neither, unless something randomly turns up with melon in. I think we're safe from sneaky burger pickles here."

"Don't you like pickles?"

I pulled a face and stuck my tongue out. "Ugh, no, they're so gross! One minute you're eating a good burger, and the next minute you're dealing with a slimy slug thing sticking to your tongue." I shuddered. "I've put a lot of things in my mouth and *nothing* is as bad as burger pickles.

Not even the cat food my brother dared me to eat when I was twelve, and that was disgusting."

"Please tell me it was cat biscuits?" West asked with horrified amusement.

"Nope, it was from a pouch of Whiskers," I said. "I made him run around our garden starkers in revenge. Then our mum caught us before we could do any more stupid shit."

"I still can't believe you ate cat food."

"And it was still better than burger pickles!"

West chuckled and took a sip of his beer. "I'll remember that if we go out for burgers. Or make them."

"You make your own burgers?" I put the menu down and leant on the table, watching West with fascination and lazily sipping my drink. The cocktail was a simple strawberry daiquiri and they'd dusted the rim of the glass with sugar and added strawberry slices. I picked one off while West watched, sliding it slowly between my lips with one finger.

"Er… yeah… yes… well… I don't usually make the burgers themselves. I mean we've done it a couple of times but it's a bit of a faff, so we just get really good burgers, all the toppings we want, nice burger buns—not brioche ones because they're too sweet for me. Burgers shouldn't be sweet. We get some good chips too, and some onion rings. Then we make whatever we fancy. It's cheaper than going out, and I'm not risking still being hungry by the end."

I nodded, sliding another slice of strawberry onto my tongue and tasting the rum alongside the sweetness. "There's a burger place in Nottingham that Eva took me and Bitch to when we did a show there that's got this whole menu of weird and wonderful combos, including a burger that's got peanut butter and jam on!"

West pulled a face and I laughed. "I'm not gonna judge anyone who likes it," West said. "But at the same time, that's fucked up."

Our waiter arrived, and we ordered the meze and a couple more drinks. The small dining room around us was nearly full, which was unsurprising for a Friday night, and a hum of chatter surrounded us. I looked around as I sipped my drink, taking in our surroundings for the first time. West had already been here when I'd arrived, and I'd been so focused on him, I could've been on Mars for all I'd have noticed.

The dining room was green and white with bright prints in dark frames placed here and there and warm lighting that made me feel like I was sitting in someone's house rather than a restaurant. The tables were close enough together to allow them to fit plenty of people in but not so close it felt like we were sitting in our neighbours' laps or were part of their conversation, which was something I found awkward as fuck in restaurants. I hated it when I was trying to eat dinner or get to know someone while all I could focus on was the argument the table next to us was having or, even worse, their sickeningly twee conversation about how much they loved each other.

I told West all this and he chuckled, smiling wryly at me and holding his beer. "You mean you don't want to hear people coo over each other while you're trying to eat dolmades?"

"God no!" I pulled a face and then laughed as a memory sprang to the front of my mind. "The worst one, hands down, has to be the time I went on this really awkward date and the couple next to us were practically fucking on the table. Yeah, everyone still had their clothes on, but they kept feeding each other and stopping to make out and whisper, not at all fucking quietly, what they wanted to do to each other when they got home. Trying to eat spaghetti while the guy next to you is talking about how he's going to eat his girlfriend's pussy is enough to put anyone off. I'm sure her vagina was lovely, but I didn't want to hear it described in explicit detail in the middle of dinner."

West sniggered and I rolled my eyes, playfully nudging him with my foot under the table. "Come on, like you'd be able to do anything except sit there awkwardly and wish you were somewhere else?" I asked.

"I can think of a few things," West said. "If you were game."

"Ohh… I think I'd be down… I could definitely describe giving you a blow job in agonising detail."

"And I could talk about just how perfect your tight little hole is," West said in a low voice, leaning across the table. "How much I love playing with your ass, eating you out… making you take every inch of me and scream my name."

"Okay, you're not playing fair," I said, trying hard not to squirm in my seat. Thank fuck super-tight skinny jeans were out of fashion or I wouldn't be able to stand up without showing the entire restaurant I wasn't wearing underwear.

"Why not?"

"Because my dick is getting hard," I hissed as I glanced around, hoping nobody was listening. I didn't want to become someone else's horror story. "And—"

I cut myself off abruptly as a member of staff arrived with our second round of drinks, closely followed by another bringing a basket of toasted pita bread and colourful dishes filled with tzatziki, houmous, and tirokafteri—which was a spicy, creamy dip made with feta and chilli I'd never had before. There were also two different salads: tabbouleh, with bulgar wheat, herbs, tomatoes, onion, and various seasonings that definitely included lemon, and a Greek salad packed full of fresh leaves, tomatoes, cucumber, onion, juicy olives, and huge chunks of feta.

And this was only the first selection of dishes.

At this rate, my desire for West to fuck me senseless after dinner might be overridden by the fact I'd likely be full to bursting. And yeah, I could eat less and get dicked down to my heart's content, but I was fucking starving and everything looked and smelt too good to resist.

Maybe I'd see if I could stay overnight and West could fuck me before I went home to get changed for work. If I was going to go home and shower, West might as well get me sweaty and covered in cum first. It would be the gentlemanly thing to do.

West was still smirking at me as he dipped a chunk of pita into the tzatziki, the yoghurt dip clinging to his lip as he pushed it into his mouth. I tried to think of a way to change the subject, but that fucking smirk was making me hard again and all I could think about was West laying me out on the table and feasting on my hole.

"You're still thinking about me fucking you, aren't you, sweetheart?" he asked, leaning across the table and keeping his voice low.

"You're making it difficult to think about anything else." I picked up a piece of pita and toyed with it.

"I'll stop," he said. "It's a bit bloody rude of me to ask you out for dinner and not let you eat anything." He nudged the dish of tirokafteri towards me. "Try that. It's really good."

I did, and West was right. The dip was rich and creamy with a warming hint of chilli, and one taste made me want to eat a bucket of it.

"How's your week been?" West asked. "Is work busy?"

"Yeah, really busy. Loads of people suddenly want things done before December, and sometimes it's just small things like wanting outside lights fitting because it's so dark when they get home, but they all add up and I'm spending half my days in the van going from job to job," I said. "And I've agreed to take part in this new drag story hour thing that Peaches and Ink are throwing together for December, so I need to start thinking about what I'm going to wear. And read. Shit, I've not even thought about what I should read."

"What's a drag story hour?"

"It's basically what it says on the tin: a drag queen, or king, reads a story to a bunch of kids for an hour. We get to dress up, be silly and funny, and play pretend. I mean, most of us are a bunch of clowns and kids are a fun audience, and their parents often get really into it too. It's a really good way to introduce kids to things like diversity and drag, but in a fun, colourful way they'll connect with. I've not hosted one before, but I've been to one a friend hosted in Leeds a few years ago."

"That sounds really cool!" West said, and it was clear his interest was genuine. My heart did a little backflip. "I guess it'll depend what age the kids are and how confident you are reading aloud. Is there a theme? You said it's in December, right? So is it all Christmas stories?"

"I think we might be doing a fairy-tale theme? But I'm not sure if Ink was joking. I hadn't even thought about reading a Christmas story."

"Hey, don't worry. You've got plenty of time." West smiled at me encouragingly. "And I can help you practice. I can't sew, though, so my help with anything outfit related will be limited to telling you how beautiful you are."

I glanced away, hoping to hide my embarrassment.

"Don't do that," West said, hooking his foot around mine under the table. "Bubblegum is absolutely stunning, and Rory is gorgeous as fuck. In drag or out of it, I think you're the most beautiful person I've ever met."

"Thanks," I said. "It's nice when you talk about me and Bubblegum together, like we both matter to you."

West's forehead crinkled in confusion as he reached for the bowls of salad, dishing some out onto the colourful, patterned plate in front of him. "Why wouldn't I? It'd be really weird if I acted as if she didn't exist. Bubblegum is a big part of who you are, and I can't imagine pretending she isn't. You're the same person, and that means you both matter to me."

Those words shouldn't have been such a big deal, but

they were because I'd heard so few people say them in the past. Dating as a drag queen could be tricky, not only because it often meant long hours over evenings and weekends but because so much of my time, money, and energy went into my craft. Drag wasn't just a hobby for me; it was part of who I was. And I needed someone who understood that.

"Thank you," I said. "That means a lot. Not everyone gets it, and the fact you do…"

West reached out and took my hand across the table, his touch sending sparks dancing across my skin. "I might not always understand all the details, but I want to try. Because I like you Rory, I really do."

"I like you too. A lot."

"Good," West said, a playfully relieved smile on his lips. "Because otherwise the rest of dinner would be really bloody awkward."

I snorted out a laugh and reached for the Greek salad as another member of staff returned with more dishes for us to try.

CHAPTER FOURTEEN

West

"If I eat anything else, I think I might actually explode," Rory said, putting his napkin on the table next to his plate, which had half a piece of baklava resting on it, syrup pooling on the painted-on flowers underneath.

"I think I might too," I said with a deep exhale, like it would magically stop my jeans from digging into my stomach. "It was so good, though."

"Amazing. We'll definitely have to come here again."

I smiled at the way Rory had so casually said "we", like it was a certainty. We still hadn't talked about what we were doing, but in my head this felt a bit like a first date. Except one where we'd already fucked multiple times, eaten ice cream in bed, and talked about everything from Rory's obsession with Dua Lipa to our favourite places to visit and the trashy reality shows we'd decided to binge-watch together on Netflix.

"What do you want to do now?" I asked. "Did you want to come back to mine? We don't have to fuck. We can just chill."

Rory reached over the table, his fingers caressing mine. "You have no idea how much it pains me to say this, but I think if you fuck me, I might throw up. Not because I hate your dick, but any kind of strenuous movement is going to make me feel like I'm on a rollercoaster, and I'm not a rollercoaster person."

I chuckled and squeezed his hand. "Noted, no trips to Alton Towers then."

"God no," he said. "Although I have been on rollercoasters before because Christopher loves them and I'm a sucker, so I always volunteer to go on them with him because Mum and Dad won't. The worst one was this one in France that turned you upside down nine times in thirty seconds! Dad was stood underneath and said he'd never heard such creative swearing before."

My chest shook as a rumbling laugh rolled through it. "That sounds horrifying."

"But you're still laughing."

"Sorry," I said, trying to school my face into a serious expression but that made Rory laugh instead. "What? I'm trying to be serious here."

"You look like you're constipated," Rory said, laughing so hard he snorted. He put his hand up to cover his face, then stopped himself. "God, I hate that sound."

"I think it's cute," I said, leaning across the table to kiss him quickly. "Like you."

"I want to say you're lying, but I don't think you are."

I shook my head. "I'm not. I wouldn't lie about something like that. When I tell you you're cute, or hot, or the most gorgeous person I've ever met, it's the truth. And I mean every word of it."

Rory's cheeks flushed and he glanced away for a second. "Thanks. And for the record, I think you're hot as fuck. Like whenever I see you, I want to jump you."

"Except when you're full of Greek food," I said, flagging down a passing member of the wait staff to ask for the bill.

"Except then." He smiled, a little spark dancing in his eyes. "Although… I think I can work around that. I'm pretty creative."

"I'm listening."

He smirked, leaning in closer. "I know I said no strenuous movement, but hand jobs don't have to be strenuous. Neither do blow jobs. And cum doesn't count as food."

"We'd better go back to mine then," I said. "So I can take you apart."

It didn't take us long to settle the bill and order an Uber to pick us up. I didn't know what any of my housemates had planned for their Friday night, but when we got back, only Mason was there playing *Starfield* in the living room.

He gave me a knowing look and a wink as I walked past before reaching for his headphones and I almost rolled my eyes.

Rory was already halfway up the stairs and I loved watching the way his butt wiggled in his jeans as he climbed. It felt like forever since I'd gotten my hands on him but, in reality, it was less than a week.

I couldn't get enough of him, and I didn't think I'd ever be able to.

I threw the lock across my bedroom door as soon as it closed and when I turned around, Rory was already sitting on the bed. He patted the mattress.

"Come and sit down," he said. "We're going for lazy tonight, and that means no standing, no leaning on furniture, and no kneeling on the floor."

"Want me to take my jeans off first?" I asked. "Save the awkward wiggling and shit."

"Good point." He grinned and reached for his waistband. "Get naked, then get over here."

"You're feeling bossy tonight, sweetheart."

He shrugged and pulled his slim-fit jumper over his head, exposing his lightly tanned chest. "I know what I want, and I don't want to wait for it."

I unbuttoned my shirt and slid it off my shoulders, tugging the cuffs over my wrists and dropping it to the floor. "I won't keep you waiting then." My jeans and boxers were next, and it only took seconds to shove them down my thighs and step out of them, quickly pulling my socks off to leave me completely nude.

Rory watched me hungrily, and a shiver ran down my spine. He was still wearing his jeans but as I looked at him, he stood on the bed and unbuttoned them slowly, making a show of sliding them down and revealing what was underneath.

"I see you decided against underwear again," I said, moving closer to the bed as Rory kicked off his jeans. With him stood on the bed, his abdomen was head hight and I leant forward to press a gentle kiss to his stomach.

"Yeah, I find it gets in the way. Besides, it's not like I spend much time in it, so what's the point of putting it on if it's just gonna come straight off?"

"Can't argue with that."

His fingers stroked through my hair as I kissed his stomach again, trailing my mouth as high up his chest as I could reach. "Lie down," Rory said. "I want to suck you."

"What if I want to suck you?"

"Afterwards. I know sixty-nine-ing is a thing, but I really hate it. It's so fucking awkward and I can't concentrate."

"One at a time then," I said, sitting down on the bed and stretching out with my legs apart so Rory could kneel between them, which he did very gracefully. He leant forward, hands resting on my chest, and kissed me softly, his tongue lazily sweeping my lips. I sighed into his mouth. "I love kissing you. You have such a beautiful mouth."

Rory moaned quietly. "You have a filthy one, and your tongue… mmm, the way you use it." He kissed me again, sweet and languid, taking his time to explore every tiny bit of my lips.

When he was satisfied, he moved his mouth along my jaw, down my neck, and across my chest, kissing and licking the muscles I'd spent so long building. I groaned as his tongue flicked over my nipples, sucking them lazily into his mouth one at a time. My nipples weren't the most sensitive in the world, but I still enjoyed it when people paid attention to them.

Rory wiggled backwards on the mattress as he began kissing down my broad stomach. I'd never be a chiselled gym rat, but there were still muscles there under a layer of softness. But since part of my job involved linking up with other men to shove against another group of equally large men, being big was a good thing.

I'd never been self-conscious in bed because if people wanted to fuck me, they already knew what I looked like, but the way Rory was worshipping my body made me feel things I'd never experienced, like I was somehow extraordinary.

I groaned as Rory's mouth moved lower. He licked the muscles of my hips, getting ever closer to my cock, which had grown hard between us. Rory looked up at me as he stretched out between my legs, his face lingering inches above the swollen head of my cock.

He winked, catching me off guard and making my heart jolt as he slowly, deliberately extended his tongue and licked over the head. I growled, my hands balling into fists in the sheets beside me.

Rory smirked and wrapped his lips around the head of my dick, sucking gently and sending a bolt of pleasure up my spine. He wrapped the fingers of one hand around the base of my dick, holding it in place as he slowly began to work my cock, taking more into his mouth.

Filthy wet sucking sounds filled the room as Rory played with my cock. Saliva dripped down my aching shaft to coat his fingers as he slid me in and out of his mouth. It was slick and messy and so fucking hot I couldn't take my eyes off him.

"Fuck, sweetheart," I said, gently pushing his hair back off his face. "You make me feel so good."

Rory hummed around my shaft, the vibrations making pleasure ripple though me, and I groaned. He tightened his lips and his fingers, not taking me deeper or working me faster but squeezing and sucking me so beautifully I knew I wasn't going to last.

"Rory..." I moaned, losing myself in the onslaught of sensation. "Sweetheart, I'm close."

Rory tightened his lips again, redoubling his efforts until my body was wound tight, my orgasm coiling in my balls like a spring. He sucked me deeper into his mouth, the head of my cock bumping against the back of his throat. Then he swallowed around me and it was game over.

I came down Rory's throat with a deep grunt, my body releasing all the tension at once and sending white-hot bliss rushing through me, a sweet ecstasy of pleasure flooding my muscles.

Rory kept sucking me, drinking down every drop of cum until I was empty and panting for air. He released my cock slowly and pressed a last long kiss just under the sensitive head.

I grinned at him and extended my hand, curling my fingers and beckoning him towards me. "Come here."

Rory climbed out from between my legs and moved to kneel beside me, his cock hard and waiting. I adjusted my position, making sure my head was still propped up but that I was low enough for what I wanted.

"No, sweetheart," I said, gently reaching for Rory's

thigh and pulling it towards me. "Here. I want you to straddle my chest."

"Are you sure?"

"Yeah, I am. You're not going to break me." I tapped his thigh again. "You can hold on to the headboard if you're worried. But I want you here, on my chest with your dick in my mouth."

Rory moaned and nodded, swinging his leg over my chest to straddle me. His cock bumped against my lips and I opened my mouth willingly, letting his aching shaft slide into my warm, waiting hole.

He gasped, his hands slamming into the headboard as I put my hands on his thighs, gently controlling how deep his cock went as I closed my lips around him and started to suck.

"Oh shit… shit, West…" Rory said, trying to rock his hips to go deeper. I stopped him with a firm hand on his thigh. He'd said no strenuous movement, so I wasn't going to let him move more than necessary.

I bobbed my head, sucking him deeper and flicking my tongue across his slit. I kept one hand on his thigh and worked the other between us, teasing his balls with my fingers and sliding them down his taint.

Rory groaned and pushed his hips forward, desperate for more. His thigh was starting to shake under my palm and I knew he was close. I took him as deep as I could, sucking him hard and swallowing around him.

Rory gasped out my name, his body trembling and his cock thickening between my lips. I swallowed again and that was all it took to send Rory tumbling over the edge. He came with a broken moan, cum spurting across my tongue and down my throat.

I coaxed him through his release, taking everything he gave me until he was wrung out and spent. I put my other hand on his thigh, supporting his weight as he sagged back into my touch, his softening cock slipping from my lips.

"H-holy shit," he said as I gently helped him slide down my body and into my lap. It was a little awkward to wiggle up into a position where I could hold him, but we managed it and I wrapped my arms around him, pulling him against my chest.

"Good?" I asked, kissing him softly. The taste of our cum mingled on our lips, salty but not unpleasant.

"Mm-hmm." He nodded, snuggling against me. I rolled the two of us onto our sides so we were lying on the bed, my arms still around him so I could hold him close. "Tonight was… it's been amazing."

"Good, I'm glad." I kissed him again. I didn't want him to leave because the thought of spending the rest of the night alone made a gaping hole open in my chest. Yes, I had training tomorrow before our away match on Sunday, but that was hours away with a yawning chasm of time between then and now. "You should stay."

Rory looked up at me, a sweet smile on his plush lips. "Okay."

CHAPTER FIFTEEN

Bubblegum Galaxy

"What about this one?" West asked, holding up a book with an orange and pink dragon on the cover wearing an apron and a tall chef's hat and carrying an elaborately decorated three-tiered cake in its claws. He turned it over to read the back cover blurb. "It's about a dragon that loves baking, only dragons aren't supposed to like baking, but he decides he's going to try and get into cake school so he can make his dreams come true. That sounds cute."

"It does," I said, putting down the book I was holding and walking over to him. He flicked through a couple of the pages so we could look at the beautiful artwork and I giggled at some of *The Great British Bake Off* puns the author and illustrator had hidden in the characters. One of the examiners for the baking school was clearly a parody of Paul Hollywood. "Okay, we're definitely getting this one."

"I'll add it to the pile."

"How many have we got now?"

"That makes four," West said, sliding the dragon book into the stack tucked under his arm. "Do you want to look for any more?"

I thought for a moment, looking over the shelves of colourful books. West had volunteered to come with me and spend Thursday afternoon trying to hunt down the perfect book to read for my drag story hour. Peaches had taken the fairy-tale theme we'd joked about in the dressing room and run with it, so we'd all been tasked with finding suitable fantasy or fairy-tale books, preferably with a fun twist or LGBTQ+ message.

As the group's official princess, I wanted to read something featuring royalty or dragons since princesses and dragons were often closely associated. Although I'd much rather have a dragon as a friend or pet than be held hostage by one. I thought a pet dragon would be adorable, and if it was small enough, I could carry it around in one of those baby papoose things on my chest.

Maybe I'd see if I could find a dragon plushie and bring it with me.

"Maybe one? Then I'll have a good selection to choose from. And I can always read more than one if I need to."

"Sounds good," West said, kissing the side of my head before walking down to the next bay and starting to peruse the books there. I stood there in shock, my fingers reaching up to brush my temple. West had never done that before, and the casual intimacy of the gesture stunned me. We hadn't exactly talked about what we were to each other or what we were doing, yet here he was, kissing my head in the middle of a bookshop like it was no big deal.

To me, we'd gone beyond the casual hook-up stage on the day West had brought me ice cream in bed, but I wasn't sure whether we were still in the friends-who-fuck stage or if we'd started dating without realising it.

I pulled my lip between my teeth, ignoring the churning in my stomach and the way my brain was fizzing like I'd drunk four double espressos back to back. If we weren't friends, I definitely wouldn't have invited West to The Court and we wouldn't be here now, browsing children's books in the basement of The Lost World, a small fantasy and LGBTQ+ bookshop near the top of Steep Hill where I'd be doing my story hour.

Would we have gone out for dinner together if we didn't want more?

Yes, friends could definitely go out for dinner, but when I went out for food with my friends, we didn't hold hands across the table or share bites with each other. And we didn't go back to their house afterwards for incredible blow jobs and conversations that lasted long into the night when most of the city was asleep.

Somewhere, the lines between hook-ups, friends, and boyfriends had blurred. And while part of me wanted to know where this was going, the rest of me didn't want to jinx it by asking.

After all, I didn't have a problem with what we were doing, so why change it?

I turned back to the bookshelves, deciding to lean into

whatever was going on with West, roll with it, and see where it went.

My eyes scanned the colourful selection of covers, searching for a hidden gem neither West nor I had noticed. I didn't have a ton of experience with kids except for my cousins' children, who were two, three, five, and seven, but I only saw them a few times a year. The oldest two lived in London, where most of Dad's family lived, and the youngest two were in Leeds, where my cousin Katie and her husband had moved a few years ago.

Maybe I should've sent them all a message asking what sort of things their kids liked. At least that would've given me a starting point.

The bright corner of a cover on the middle shelf caught my eye, and when I pulled the book out, I realised the cover had snow on it. The illustration showed a beautiful young woman in a red dress and an old-fashioned hooded cape trimmed with white fur holding hands with another young woman, who was wearing a deep green and blue tartan suit with a cape. There was a dog at their feet with a bow round its neck, because there was always a dog in Christmas stories.

The book was called *All I Want For Christmas*, and the title shone out in sweeping, embossed gold lettering with a little snowflake dotting the *i* in Christmas.

I turned it over to read the blurb before flicking through a few pages towards the end. It was for a slightly older audience than some of the picture books we'd picked out, but that was good because I still didn't know what age the kids turning up would be. Peaches had said they could be anywhere from two upwards but couldn't advise any further, which was really fucking helpful.

"What did you find?" West asked, materialising by my shoulder and making me jump. "Shit, sorry, I didn't mean to scare you."

"You're fine," I said as I rubbed my chest, my heart thumping painfully against my ribcage. I'd never been good with jump scares, and Christopher took great delight in using that against me because he was my little brother and therefore a right asshole at times. "I just… er, I scare pretty easily sometimes. Especially when I'm thinking about something else."

"I'm sorry, sweetheart." He put his arm around my waist, gently pulling me back against his massive chest. "I thought you'd heard me, but I'll make sure I call your name next time."

My cheeks burned and my skin tingled. "It's fine, I promise. I was just looking at this." I held up the book so he could see the cover. "It's about a princess and her best friend who keep trying to find each other the perfect Christmas present. And by the sound of it, they go through all the usual things, you know, jewellery, chocolates, swords, craft things, plants—normal lesbian presents—until right at the end they finally realise what they really want for Christmas is each other. Then they get married and move to a house in the forest…" I looked at the final page and last illustration. "And apparently adopt a small horde of pets. Doesn't look like they've got a pet dragon, though, so that's sad."

"A pet dragon?" West asked, his voice soft and warm against my ear.

"Think about it, a tiny dragon about the size of a house cat. It would make such a cute pet!"

"As long as it didn't set me or my house on fire, then yeah, I'd be down for that. I've never had a pet before, so starting with a dragon wouldn't be any different to starting with a kitten. I'd still be clueless."

I chuckled as I turned in West's arms and handed him the book. "I'm trying to think what Sausage and Beans would be like if I brought a tiny dragon home. I don't think Sausage would even notice and Beans would want to play with it. Nothing I owned would ever be safe again."

"Does Beans get into everything?" West asked as he stepped back and we started heading towards the stairs in the corner since the counter was upstairs in the main part of the shop. Part of the reason we'd come here, apart from book shopping, was to give me a chance to see the event space, and Jay, the owner, had talked me through how he was thinking of setting it up.

We only had just over three weeks to go, but I wanted to be prepared.

All I needed to do now was actually make my dress. Trust me to save the biggest thing until last.

"Yeah, she's an adorable nightmare sometimes," I said as we climbed. I made sure to walk behind West so I got to watch the way his butt moved in his jeans. I swore the man had butt dimples, and I wanted to bury my face in his behind and let him wrap his thighs around my head. "It's because my dad babies her something rotten. She was cross with me over the summer because I wouldn't let her sit on the kitchen table while I was sewing, so when I got up to make a cup of tea, she jumped up and pushed a whole pot of glitter onto the floor. So now she has a little bed on the chair next to me when I'm sewing so she doesn't feel left out."

I sighed. I'd been furious because Beans had trailed glitter across the whole fucking house, but Dad had just scooped her up, kissed her nose, and told her she was his precious baby and that I was a right bastard for ignoring her when she wanted to help.

Honestly, that cat got away with more than Christopher or I ever had. And she was a million times smarter than Dad gave her credit for.

"I've never had cats," he said. "But you make it sound interesting."

"Beans is like living with a very smart, fluffy criminal mastermind. Sausage is more like a teddy bear who happens to breathe, eat, and fart loudly when you're making breakfast," I said. "I wouldn't live without them."

"That sounds familiar," said Jay from behind the counter. He was a softly spoken man with fluffy black hair that stuck out at odd angles, thick-rimmed glasses, and a lip ring that glinted in the light. The sleeves of his dark blue jumper were rolled up and it had Read More Books emblazoned across the chest.

"Do you have cats too?" I asked as West put the books down near the till.

"Nope, but I do have Rupert," Jay said, gesturing down beside him. I leant over the counter to see a chunky

Staffie in a knitted jumper doing his best impression of a cockroach on a cosy-looking tartan bed, a stuffed giraffe tucked in beside his head and his tongue lolling out. From where I was standing, it didn't look like Rupert had any ears except tattered stumps. "He's supposed to be my assistant but all he does is beg for treats, lie on my feet when I try and restock, and snore very loudly." He smiled fondly down at the dog. "My fiancé, Leo, and I actually have two of them—one for each of our businesses. Rupert stays here with me, and his sister, Angie, goes down to Wild Things."

"Aww, that's so cute," I said. "Do you think Rupert would like to come to story hour too? We could find him a costume."

"Depending on the amount of people, I think he'd love that," Jay said. He looked sad for a second but then he smiled again. "People think he looks scary because of his ears and his scars, but really he's as soft as a marshmallow and an absolute cuddle monster. A couple of our friends have kids and Rupert adores them. He follows them around everywhere. Although that might be because he knows the kids will share any food they have with him, and if there's anything Rupert loves more than cuddles, it's food."

"That's perfect then. I can be a princess and Rupert can be my adorable animal best friend, because all princesses have them."

Jay chuckled as he began to ring up the books and slide them into a paper bag. "I'll make sure he wears his best bow tie. I've got some posters in to put up this afternoon to start advertising the event, and I know a few other shops around here have got them too. And I think Peachy Keen said they'd be announcing it on social media today."

I nodded, although truthfully I'd forgotten the announcement was today. I'd meant to put it in my calendar and completely forgotten. Hopefully Peaches or Legs would tag me, and then I'd be able to repost without it looking like I'd forgotten. As I pulled my phone out of my pocket to pay, it looked like my dreams had come true.

"Looks like they've already done it," I said, swiping to dismiss the notifications before pulling up my payment app and tapping it on the card reader. "Hopefully we get a good response. I know it's a bit last minute."

"Fingers crossed," Jay said. "I know one of the other queens doing it and Eli's very excited."

"Eli… Bitch Fit?" When people were in drag, I usually used their drag name or a variation, and it felt strange thinking of Bitch Fit as Eli, even though I'd known Bitch for several years. I didn't even know what some of the performers' real names were. Peachy Keen was Peaches to everyone I knew and Moxxie was always just Moxxie. And I didn't think Eva would ever tell anyone her real name.

Jay nodded. "Yeah, he's my friend Lewis's older brother. We've been down to The Court a few times to see his show, and there's a few of us who've all had dinner together before."

Beside me, West let out a surprised noise and when I looked at him, he was laughing quietly and shaking his head. "Lewis wouldn't happen to have a brother-in-law called Henry, would he? With a boyfriend named Alex?"

"Yes…" Jay frowned suspiciously. "How did you…"

"My brother, Theo, is friends with Alex. They live up in Yorkshire."

Jay's face relaxed instantly and he chuckled softly as he slid the bag across the counter to me. "It really is a small world."

"You're telling me," West said, picking up the bag before I had a chance. He slipped his spare hand into mine and squeezed it gently, making my whole arm tingle.

"Thanks again," I said to Jay. "I'll pop in and see you a couple of days before the event but let me know if you need anything before that. You can always drop me a message on Instagram."

"You're welcome. I'm looking forward to it."

I followed West out to the street, my hand still tightly clutched in his. The sun had already started to set and around us the streetlights flooded the cobbled street with a cosy yellow glow. "Do you have anything to do now?" West asked.

"Not really. You?"

"No." He looked down at me and smiled. "Fancy a drink? Then you can tell me all about your plans for your dress, because I know you have them, even if you haven't started yet."

"You read my mind."

My heart spun, a thousand fireworks bursting in my chest. If this was where we were headed, I loved the look of the road ahead.

CHAPTER SIXTEEN

West

I TOUCHED MY SORE, swollen cheekbone, conscious of the bruise forming there as I ducked into The Court, a bouquet of roses clutched in my other hand.

At least the fucker had managed to miss my nose when he'd kneed me in the face during this afternoon's match. I wasn't sure how many times my nose could be re-set without ending up permanently inflamed and crooked. I knew it was all part and parcel of being a rugby player but having to explain to people that my bruised face or busted nose had happened at work had led to more than one awkward conversation in the past.

My fingers felt around the edge of my eye, hoping the inflammation hadn't spread far because the last thing I wanted was another black eye.

Maybe I should ask Rory to teach me how to use concealer.

I pulled my phone out of my pocket as I wandered through into the theatre, toying with the idea of letting Rory know I was here. It had been a spontaneous decision on my part—I'd been sitting in the medical suite after the match with an ice pack on my face while one of the staff had prodded my cheek and checked for a concussion, and my mind had drifted to what Rory might be doing with his afternoon.

He'd sent me some pictures of the designs he'd sketched for his story hour outfit, with long notes about finding patterns and the perfect material. When we'd first discussed it over drinks, I'd asked whether he was going to repurpose something from his wardrobe, which from his Instagram seemed pretty extensive. But Rory had shaken his head and insisted it needed to be something completely new, if only because he wanted the full princess effect and nothing he had went far enough in his eyes.

I knew next to nothing about sewing, so the fact he was even considering tailor-making something from scratch was enough to melt my mind.

The closest I'd ever come to sewing was when I'd been a kid and my mum had taught me how to sew on some of my Scout patches. I'd found that hard enough and it had been a simple running stitch around the edge under close supervision, not making a whole fucking dress.

Once I'd thought about Rory, my mind had made itself up about seeing him.

A quick check of The Court's Instagram had told me he was performing this evening, so I'd bought a ticket and taken myself home to eat the enormous post-match meal I'd been craving and clean up. The flowers had been another spontaneous decision. I'd passed M&S on my way home and seen them through the sliding door, their bright petals reflecting off the glass.

In my experience, men liked getting flowers just as much as women, maybe more since they weren't used to getting them in the first place. So I'd ducked in and bought the biggest bouquet in the bucket without a second thought.

I must have been noticeably dithering on the spot because the same bartender who'd served me the first time I was here waved at me, beckoning me over.

"Hey," he said. "I know you. Are you okay? You look a bit lost."

"Yeah," I said. "I, er, I'm here for the show but also for Bubblegum Galaxy. She's my… I'm her boyfriend." It was the first time I'd used the word and I felt bad for saying it without asking Rory whether he was comfortable with it since we hadn't had any type of conversation about what we were to each other. But saying *I'm Bubblegum's friend and hook-up* to the barman sounded weird and might've even made me sound like a creep lingering around in the hope of ambushing her.

The barman grinned. "Want me to let her know you're here?"

"Er, yeah… if that's okay?"

"Sure. Give me a minute. What's your name?"

"West."

He nodded and ducked out from behind the bar, disappearing into a black door beside the stage that I assumed led to the backstage area.

A flurry of nerves collected in my chest and I wondered if coming here, especially with the flowers, was a bad idea. I guessed the barman had left me waiting so he could verify my identity with Rory and see whether he actually wanted to see me. If not, I assumed the bouncers on the front door would swiftly escort me from the building.

The stage door swung open again and Bubblegum burst out, bouncing towards me with a beaming smile on her beautiful face. She was half-dressed with a hairband pushing her caramel brown hair out of her face and fluffy slippers on her feet, but her make-up was already perfectly in place. "West! I didn't know you were coming tonight."

"Surprise," I said, suddenly aware people were watching us. I wasn't sure if I cared, though. Bubblegum flung herself into my arms and I did my best not to wince. There was a bruise forming on my ribs but where that one had come from I didn't know. When she stepped back, I held the flowers out awkwardly, like a teenager trying to impress his first crush. "These are for you."

"Oh my fucking God! You got me flowers," Bubblegum said, melting against me. "You're so fucking cute."

"You're welcome."

She leant up to kiss my cheek, her eyes widening as she saw the bruise. "Fucking hell, baby, what happened to your face? Are you okay?"

"Yeah, I'm fine. Perils of the job, unfortunately. Some wanker managed to knee me in the face during a tackle."

"Does it hurt?" She brushed her fingers across it. Her

touch was featherlight but it still stung. "I'm going to take that as a yes."

"A bit," I said. "I've had worse, though. At least I didn't get a broken bone out of this one."

"You say that so casually, like it's not a big fucking deal," she said, raising a perfectly drawn-on eyebrow at me.

"It's not. At least, it's not to me."

"Rugby players." She sighed dramatically and then laughed brightly. It was a breath of fresh air whipping around me. "Want to come backstage? I still need to get dressed and I want to introduce you to everyone."

"Is that okay?"

"I wouldn't have offered if it wasn't," she said as she reached out to take my hand. "Fair warning, they're all mad as a box of frogs, probably half-naked, and there'll be at least one inappropriate joke at my expense."

"Who knew drag dressing rooms and rugby locker rooms had so much in common," I said with a dry chuckle. I didn't add that at least here nobody was going to question my sexuality and tell me to pick a side or ask me the ins and outs of gay sex.

Bubblegum led me through the stage door and up a set of wooden steps that creaked underfoot to the side of the stage, and then we kept walking until we reached a narrow corridor with various doors leading off it and another set of stairs.

"I'm just up here," Bubblegum said as we climbed, our footsteps echoing on the painted concrete. "There are a few dressing rooms downstairs and a few up. We tend to keep the downstairs ones for visiting performers and anyone with mobility issues since we don't have a lift because the building is so old. And I'll apologise now because our room is a mess—none of us are very tidy and the room isn't very big, so we tend to just throw our shit everywhere."

"It's fine," I said, trying to watch my feet while glancing at the photos on the walls, which showed various performers and special events across the years. "Besides, I can guarantee it'll smell better than the locker room at least. That just stinks of old sweat, mud, and occasionally blood."

"Delicious," Bubblegum said with a laugh as she stopped outside a wooden door with a faded brass number three in the middle. "Okay, give me a second to make sure the others are at least wearing underwear." She let go of my hand and opened the door, sticking her head around it. "What are both of you wearing? I've got West with me and I don't want to scar him for life."

There was some laughter and a couple of responses I couldn't hear. My stomach bubbled strangely.

Bubblegum turned back to me. "Ready?"

"That sounds like I'm about to do something dangerous," I said. "Like getting in a shark cage."

"I mean, Bitch is here. But she's more of a rabid raccoon than anything else, and easily pacified with snacks."

"I heard that!" called a voice from behind the door. "Stop loitering, Sparkles, and bring your man in."

Bubblegum flushed but opened the door, and as we stepped inside, I realised neither of us had mentioned the boyfriend thing. But it was too late to bring it up now.

The dressing room was small and cluttered, with a rack

of clothes against one wall and more clothes strewn across various chairs. The wall opposite had a long wooden counter running along it with a huge mirror above it surrounded by bright lights. There was make-up spilling out of various bags scattered across the counter alongside stacks of palettes, sponges, and brushes, and three chairs sat in front of it. Two of them were occupied, one by a queen I recognised as a half-made-up Bitch Fit and one I didn't know.

"West, this is Bitch Fit and Eva Nessence," Bubblegum said, pointing to each of the queens in turn. "Girls, this is my boyfriend, West."

My head tried to pivot sharply to look at Bubblegum, but I forced it to remain vaguely in place. To the others, it probably looked like I'd done a very strange head wiggle.

Bitch Fit grinned at me with a knowing look in her eyes. "I see Sparkles throwing cocktails at you didn't put you off then."

"Oh God," Bubblegum muttered. "I fucking knew it."

"Cocktails?" Eva asked, picking up a make-up brush and a large palette filled with varying shades of black, white, and grey. "I think I've missed something."

"You know the last drag brunch at Fox & Taylor?"

"No, but I know what you mean."

"Well, our adorable Sparkles managed to get a member of staff to dump an entire jug of cocktails into West's lap during her routine. Definitely a unique way to get a man's attention," Bitch said, shooting me a wink.

"You're leaving out that it was a total accident," Bubblegum said as she walked over and gently put the flowers onto the counter, running a finger slowly across one of the rose petals.

"But it's more fun if it sounds deliberate."

"Don't be a cow," Eva said, reaching out to lightly jab Bitch in the face with the pointed end of her make-up brush. She smiled at Bubblegum sympathetically. "Sorry, hun, that must've been awful. We've all had disasters during shows, and they never get any easier."

"Speak for yourself," Bitch said, playfully returning the jab with a make-up brush of her own.

"That's because your entire routine is a disaster to begin with, so it can't get any worse."

Bitch laughed. "Oooh, someone's feeling snarky today. Who put salt in your coffee?"

"It's being around you," Eva said with a withering smile. "It's naturally draining."

Bubblegum snorted and Bitch looked at me, sighing dramatically. "You see what I have to put up with? Dealing with these two on a regular basis is a cruel and unusual punishment."

"One you bring upon yourself," Eva said.

"I do, but it's because I secretly love you very much." Bitch leant over and pressed a loud, smacking kiss to Eva's face. "Sparkles, find your poor man somewhere to sit down so he doesn't have to loiter."

"God, you're bossy," Bubblegum said, gently pushing me over to the spare chair and grabbing a load of clothes off it, throwing them into a heap in the corner.

"Don't you need it?" I asked.

"Nah, I can stand. Or I'll steal one of theirs." She

gestured at the other two. "Do you need something for your face? It looks really swollen."

I shook my head as I lowered myself into the chair. My muscles were starting to ache but no more than usual after a match. I'd be sore tomorrow, though, and would probably need to spend most of the morning gently stretching myself out and going for a walk to loosen everything off. "Nope. Although, I might have to get you to teach me how to use concealer at some point. I get so many funny looks walking round Sainsbury's when I'm like this."

"How often does this happen?"

I shrugged. "I don't keep track. Every couple of months? Depends really."

Eva looked at me studiously. "At least they missed your eye. And your lip. And the bruising suggests they didn't break your cheekbone or your nose."

"No, I just took a hard knock," I said.

"Since when do you know so much about bruising?" Bitch asked.

"I'm a paramedic, remember, dipshit?"

"Oh… that explains a lot," Bitch said, nodding to herself before turning back to me. "You should meet my boyfriend at some point. I think you'd like him. He played rugby at university and I'm sure he's dying to talk to someone who actually understands the rules. Apparently, my commentary about the length of people's shorts or their hairstyles is not helpful. I thought he was going to throttle me during the World Cup."

"How Tristan doesn't throttle you on a daily basis is

beyond me," Eva said dryly. "Any man who willingly decides to live with you has to be slightly unhinged."

"I'll have you know I'm a delightful roommate," Bitch said. "Ask Orlando next time he's around. He'll tell you just how wonderful living with me was."

Bubblegum giggled. "Oh, don't worry, babe, I'm definitely getting all the tea. I need to message him anyway to see if he's got room for a last-minute wig styling for story hour."

"He'll squeeze you in because he loves you," Bitch said. "He's doing mine too but only because apparently I'm not allowed to style my own fucking wigs these days unless I'm deliberately trying to look like I've been dragged backwards through a hedge."

"Even that's a step up from normal," Eva said with a wink.

Bitch laughed boldly. "Seriously, you are full of it today. What's going on, babe?"

"Honestly, I'm fucking exhausted." Eva put the palette down and yawned. "I've been working nights and my new neighbour is some fitness freak who listens to fucking drum and bass at nine in the fucking morning. One of these days I'm going to fucking murder the Welsh bastard!"

Bubblegum smiled softly at me as Bitch began casually interrogating Eva for details about her infuriating new neighbour and I watched everything with comfortable fascination. I'd never been in an environment that felt so safe. I had a couple of friends I was happy being open around, but they were few and far between. But being here sent a feeling of comfort and belonging down into my bones.

It was like nothing I'd ever experienced before, and I didn't know how to fully describe it.

Was this what other queer people meant when they talked about safe spaces? Was this how those places made them feel?

"Are you okay?" Bubblegum asked, sliding into my lap. I put my arm around her waist to hold her steady, feeling her comfortable weight on my thighs anchoring me to the here and now.

"Never better." I didn't want to distract her with my internal musings, so I simply smiled and said, "This is fun. I like them."

"Yeah." She looked at her friends fondly. "I guess they'll do."

CHAPTER SEVENTEEN

Bubblegum Galaxy

THE FIRST TIME I saw the negative comments, I was lying on West's bed on Sunday afternoon.

I'd ended up back at his after the show on Saturday night, and I still hadn't gone home. Neither of us had said anything about it, but after we'd fucked, West had held me until we'd fallen asleep and this morning he'd insisted on making me breakfast before asking if I wanted to chill for a bit.

I'd spent all day either naked or in a borrowed pair of boxers and an oversized T-shirt, and it was all so fucking perfect I didn't want the bubble to burst.

At some point I'd have to head home, if only because I had work in the morning and didn't have any clothes, but I was going to leave it until the last possible minute and enjoy every second until then.

We hadn't talked about me introducing West as my

boyfriend last night, but the idea of calling him a friend didn't sit right in my stomach and I didn't fancy explaining the ins and outs of my sex life to Bitch and Eva. So boyfriend it was.

West hadn't freaked out, which was a good sign, but he hadn't mentioned it either. I knew I needed to say something but I didn't want to ruin the day with a heavy, emotional conversation that might not end the way I wanted. Because the more I thought about it, the more my heart attached itself to the idea of being West's boyfriend. And while there were signs he felt the same, like showing up unannounced with flowers, not batting an eyelid at meeting my friends, and bringing me back here and spending hours kissing every inch of my body until I was nothing but a melted puddle of need in the middle of his bed, I didn't want to assume.

There were the breakfast sandwiches too, and the way he'd asked about my story hour outfit with genuine interest and had me explain the very basics of dressmaking. The way he'd put his arm around me and pulled me close as we'd watched old episodes of *Made in Chelsea*, laughing at the scripted pretentiousness of it all.

If we were only hooking up, I doubted he'd have wanted to spend the day hanging out with me like this—lounging in bed without a care in the world.

I was lying there scrolling through my phone while West sat on the floor with a foam roller, gently stretching out his muscles. My eyes kept roaming across to him, silently taking in the gorgeous expanses of skin and muscle. He was currently shirtless, in nothing but a small pair of shorts, and I kept focusing on his broad shoulders and thick thighs. There was a dark bruise blossoming across his ribs that he had no idea where it'd come from, but it didn't look as bad as the one on his face, which was now varying shades of purple and yellow.

"You're watching me," West said as he adjusted his seat and leant forward, stretching out his thigh.

"Have you seen you? Of course I'm going to watch," I said, rolling onto my stomach and wiggling down to the end of the bed, phone still in hand. "How're you feeling?"

"A bit sore, but no more than usual."

I didn't know if I'd ever understand how he could spend eighty minutes charging up and down a pitch, throwing himself into other men and repeatedly being slammed into the ground, and only be *a bit sore*, but maybe it was something you got used to. Like how my feet had started to give up protesting wearing Pleasers and decided the pain was nominal instead of excruciating.

West looked up at me and gestured with his head at my phone. "I thought you were supposed to be posting stuff from last night?"

"I am. I'm just taking a break." I grinned. "There's a half-naked man right in front of me. It's very distracting."

West laughed softly, then winced as he stretched a bit further. "Do your stuff while I stretch and then you can do whatever you want to me."

"Whatever I want?"

"Within reason. I don't know if I've got the energy to suddenly go skydiving."

"Damn, there go my plans," I said. "How about a gentle

massage instead? It has a ninety-nine point nine percent chance of ending in a blow job."

"If you're offering, I'm not going to say no," he said, giving a little groan of pain as his muscles protested. I'd always thought about stretching after my routines but watching West wasn't convincing me. The outcome was probably worth it, but I didn't fancy putting myself through the whole palaver for *probably*.

Tearing my gaze away from West, I pulled up Instagram and my list of notifications. The new Lincoln Drag Story Hour account had tagged me in a promo post, as had a couple of businesses as they advertised their participation. It all looked perfectly fine. Until I opened the fucking comments.

This is absolutely unacceptable. Why are you advertising explicit adult entertainment for kids?!!

Fuck off with this gay bullshit.

Oh great, just what we need, weirdos in dresses turning our kids gay.

And those were the tamest ones. My stomach roiled at the sheer hatred and disgust in these people's words and the vile implications they were throwing at us. Bile rose up in my throat and panic clawed at my chest. I knew anti-LGBTQ+ sentiments were getting worse—it was all over the media and fuelled by their support for anti-trans rhetoric—but to see it so clearly directed at my friends and me frightened me.

The UK had a long, proud history of drag. Lily Savage had presented prime time fucking television, for God's sake, and every year thousands of people went to see pantomimes with a man in drag playing the dame or the ugly sisters in *Cinderella*. And yet here we were, in 2023, with hideous anti-drag sentiment imported straight from the depths of right-wing America fuelling the flames of hatred right here on my doorstep.

It revolted, terrified, and angered me all at once.

Drag queens needed pretty thick skin and I could cope with a lot, but some of these allegations—like the idea we were only doing this to abuse children—made me want to vomit.

Part of me wanted to message Peaches and pull out, because I knew it was only going to get worse as we got closer to the event, and another part of me wanted to add more rhinestones and glitter to my dress. Because fuck anyone who wanted to bring us down with their small-minded hate. The queer community had been through enough bullshit, and backing down wasn't an option.

I exhaled deeply, trying to let the comments roll off me like water off a duck's back.

"Rory?" West's voice was laced with concern. "What's wrong?"

"It's nothing," I said, wondering how he could tell.

"It's obviously not. You look like you want to kill someone and you're breathing funny."

"I made the mistake of looking at the comments." I held out my phone for him to see, watching his face as he scrolled through them.

"What the fuck?" He looked up at me and then back at the screen, his confusion and anger evident. "That's bollocks. Who the hell are these people?"

"No fucking clue," I said with a shrug. "Half of them probably aren't even local. They're just jumping on the bandwagon. I wonder if Peaches has seen them—I should let her know so she or Ink can limit comments."

"I'm sure they know," West said, climbing up off the floor and coming to sit next to me on the bed. He was still only wearing shorts. "Leave them to sort it and try to ignore all the bullshit." He reached out for me, looping his arm around my waist and pulling me into him. His skin was hot against mine, and he smelt of sex and sweat in a way that was almost delicious. We fell backwards into a tangled heap, and I rested my head against his chest.

For a few minutes there was nothing filling the room but the sound of our breathing and the steady beating of West's heart in my ear.

"I wish I could ignore it," I said finally. "I know I should."

"Then why can't you?"

"Because... even though they're just words on a screen, someone still typed them. There are people out there who really believe this shit and who actively want to hurt me and people I love. They get to be vile because they have anonymity to protect them, but that's the scary part because they could be anyone. And there's a real chance they could turn up to one of my shows or one of these events and try and hurt someone." It was hard putting it all into words, acknowledging my fears and giving shape to them. But ignoring them was worse to me. I'd be haunted by their shadows.

"Do you think they would?" West asked. "Turn up, I

mean."

"Maybe? Other drag queen story hours have been protested before," I said. "Sometimes they've even been cancelled or moved to protect the queens and families. I think a couple even got bomb threats."

"Fucking hell. But that's… that's not going to happen here, right?"

"I don't know." I sighed and traced my finger lazily over his chest. "Maybe I shouldn't have signed up for this. I mean, I've had enough hate thrown at me for being a queen and visibly queer, but this feels different."

"Did you just ignore it then?" West asked. There was something in his tone I couldn't place and it unsettled me. I wondered if he was still asking about me, or if there was something bigger here. "Isn't that the best thing to do?"

"Sometimes," I said slowly, letting myself get lost in tracing patterns in his chest hair. "It depends. I mean, if your safety is at risk then yes, but also we didn't get the rights we've got by asking nicely and politely and deferring to people who treat us like shit."

West hummed and his hand tightened slightly around my waist. "Just don't put yourself at risk, okay? Please?"

"I won't," I said. "But I want to do this. I'm not going to let these wankers win. Fuck that bullshit."

I rolled in West's arms so I could look at his face, studying his expression. He was obviously concerned, but there was more to it than that. I didn't know if poking it would help, though. If it was something personal, which I'd have put my most expensive wig on it being, there was every chance he'd clam up or lash out.

A lot of men, queer and straight, struggled to be open about their emotions. The patriarchy got to us all in some way or another, and admitting any kind of vulnerability was always seen as weakness. And that was without throwing in the fact West was a sportsman.

Rugby, like most sports, had a reputation for being a shitty boys' club, especially at the top level. I didn't know the sport well enough to know if there were many out players, but I knew football only had a handful.

I fucking hated that sport chucked all the shittiest, most toxic aspects of masculinity into a blender and ground them into a sludgy pulp it forced down the throats of everyone involved, from players, to coaches, to the fans themselves. I'd seen the way it tore people apart and the damage that shit could cause.

And I didn't want it to hurt West.

But it sounded like it might be a bit late for that.

"Please," he said quietly, reaching up to brush the hair out of my face. "I don't want to see you get hurt."

"I won't," I said. It wasn't technically a promise I could make, because if someone chose to do something unbelievably wank there was no guaranteeing anything, but I wasn't going to go out looking for a fight. I wasn't my dad. "I'm not going to back down, but I promise I'll do whatever I can to stay safe."

West gave me a tight smile, but he didn't say anything. Instead he pulled me into a deep kiss, wrapping his arms around me and holding me close.

Like he didn't want to let me go.

CHAPTER EIGHTEEN

West

I TWISTED my phone in my hand, trying and failing to focus on the highlights of the Las Vegas Grand Prix. This year's championship had been really tight and gone all the way to the wire between the two Cadigan drivers, Mateo Llorente and Dean Williams. I'd seen the results online and knew that Mateo won, both the race and the championship, but I'd have been happy for it to go either way since both of them were talented and ridiculously hot. They seemed to be really good mates too, which was nice. You didn't always see that between teammates.

But even though the race had been a good one, my mind was still occupied with all the shit that had happened with Rory on Sunday afternoon.

The comments had been playing on a loop through my mind for two days straight, and it hadn't helped that I'd gone and read some of them on Facebook. It had been a stupid move on my part and I'd known it at the time, but that still hadn't stopped me.

The comments on a post by a local newspaper had been the worst, especially since most of the commenters didn't appear to be from anywhere near Lincoln.

I just didn't understand the level of vitriol.

The thing that frightened me most, though, was Rory's attitude.

It was obvious the comments had upset and scared him, but he was still determined to take part and stand up for himself. I didn't know what to say beyond to try to ignore them, because that was all I'd ever done. Making a fuss had always made things worse in my experience, and I didn't want to be labelled as difficult or a troublemaker or some dick who took everything too seriously.

Biting my lip, I paused the highlights and looked down at my phone. Talking through all of this with someone would be helpful, but my options felt limited. I didn't have many queer friends, and while Mason might get it, he never understood why I didn't push back, so he'd probably side with Rory on principle.

There was only one option, really.

Theo picked up after only three rings. "Hey! This is so spooky. Laurie and I were just talking about you!"

"About me?" I asked with a weak chuckle.

"Yes! What are your plans for Christmas? I know it's only November, but since you don't talk to our sperm and egg donors anymore, I wasn't sure what you were doing."

"I'm not sure." After I'd stopped talking to our parents, I'd spent a couple of Christmases alone. Until last year when Mason had realised I'd be by myself and had insisted on taking me home to his family where I'd spent three days being fed enough to satisfy an army with leftovers.

"Well, if you have no plans, you should come to ours," Theo said. "It'll just be low-key, but we'll have yummy food and presents and alcohol. Oh, and we can play games together too! And we all meet up on Christmas Day for a beach walk, which usually ends up with at least one person going in the sea. Usually Spencer, but last year he dragged Alex in with him. Then we all have hot chocolate and biscuits together and do presents. Normally, we do Secret Santa because it's easier than trying to buy presents for everyone."

That did sound appealing, and I liked the idea of meeting all of Theo and Laurie's friends in person. I hadn't had a chance to when I'd gone up for my very brief visit in October. I didn't know what Rory's plans were, but I didn't want to assume I'd be part of them since our relationship was so new.

"You don't have to decide now," Theo continued. "But give it a think and let me know. We've got plenty of space and I'd love to have you. I do have to warn you, though, that our tree topper is a taxidermy mouse dressed as an angel. And there's a lot of skulls too."

I chuckled as I tried to imagine what their decorations might look like. Theo was very femme and loved both bright kitsch and taxidermy, while Laurie was the ultimate gothic gentleman. I assumed at least half of their Christmas skulls were pink and covered in glitter.

"That sounds fun," I said, my chest filling with warmth.

"I'll let you know."

"Good! Now, I'm assuming you didn't call because you got a spooky feeling we were talking about you?"

"Er, no, not really."

"I didn't think so," he said. "What's wrong? Did something happen with Rory? You did take him out for dinner, right?"

"Yeah, I did. That was a couple of weeks ago actually." I stretched out on the bed, trying to put my thoughts in order. "It was something that happened at the weekend. And I… I don't know if I'm doing something wrong."

"Whatever it is, we can fix it," Theo said soothingly. "Is it more of a sex problem? Or a dispose-of-a-dead-body type problem? Because I can help with both of those."

"It's neither," I said, a smile playing across my lips.

"Darn, those are my areas of expertise! Oh well, what's up?"

I told Theo about the drag story hour, the comments that had started popping up on social media, and how much they'd shaken Rory. I didn't mention that they'd worried me too. But I did tell Theo how Rory seemed determined to continue and what he'd said about not giving in to hate even when I'd told him to ignore everything and be safe. I didn't tell him all the details about our relationship, but I knew Theo would put the pieces together. He was a smart cookie.

"I know he's not going to engage with the comments," I said. "But I wish he'd ignore them and let it slide. It's not like these people are going to do anything."

"What if they did?" Theo asked. His question threw me

and a stunned silence echoed between us. "What if some of these dickweeds turned up and protested? What if they confronted him?"

"I don't know… I'd still want him to ignore them. I don't want him putting himself at risk of getting hurt."

"Okay," Theo said. "I understand that, I suppose."

"I'm guessing you'd start throwing words back?"

"Maybe." He laughed, and there was an undercurrent of menace that made me think of a creepy doll in a horror movie. "I don't think Laurie would let me, but I'm a bit more used to trolls and haters than most. And sometimes, I can't ignore it. Or I don't want to."

"Why…"

"Why am I used to it? Or why don't I ignore it?"

"Both, I guess."

"Firstly, I'm femme as fuck and a lot of people get very upset about someone assigned male at birth wearing very feminine clothing on a daily basis," Theo said. "Apparently, me liking pink and ruffled skirts has a massive impact on everyone else's lives despite the fact that it's fuck all to do with them and none of their fucking business." He sighed exasperatedly. "And yes, mostly I do ignore it, especially online. The block button is a fabulous tool. But sometimes, it's harder to shut it out and I will call people out on their shit. I'm not always expecting to change their mind, but I might convince someone else, or I'll show other queer people that I won't let the haters get to me. I deserve to take up space, and I'm not going to let some right-wing wanker take that away from me."

"I'm sorry," I said as a surge of emotion rushed through

me. "You shouldn't have to deal with that."

"I know, I shouldn't. But I'm very visibly queer, online and in public, and it's the fucked-up price I have to pay for existing in my own skin."

"Have you ever considered… I don't know…" I didn't know how to ask the question on the tip of my tongue. It felt wrong but I needed to know the answer anyway. Because I had a sinking suspicion it had roots in how I'd reacted to things over the years.

"You can ask it," Theo said gently.

"I don't think I can."

"But you should. I'm guessing visible queerness is a new-ish thing for you? And this is a conversation you've never had before? Or something you've not really considered, at least consciously."

"Not really," I admitted. "I mean, I'm aware I can be pretty imposing and I don't exactly look queer. I've been six foot three since I was sixteen and rugby just helped me put on muscle, and I guess spending a lot of time playing sport… it made me more masculine? Is that the right way to say it?"

"Yes, you're not exactly camp, but that's okay. There's nothing wrong with being a masculine queer man," Theo said. "I know tons of masc guys. It's just not being a dick about it and expecting all queer people to fall in line and follow social gender binaries."

I thought for a second. "Do guys do that?"

"Yes, and you're doing it too, although I don't think you realise it," Theo said, but his words weren't unkind. "It's like… some queer men, and women too, seem to believe that if they act 'normal', you know, like the way society expects them to, that they'll fit in better and be accepted. It's why you still see queer people voting for the Conservatives or Republicans, because they think that if they're 'acceptably queer', aka they're just straight guys who suck dick, that people will like them. But it doesn't work like that."

I nodded. I'd seen that before but never understood it. Theo's words made something settle uncomfortably in my chest, because while I'd never intentionally acted like that, I'd definitely found myself conforming over the years to be like all the men I'd played with.

Even if I'd hated it.

And it had never worked anyway.

"No," I said quietly. "It doesn't."

"And it never will," Theo said, a simmering note of anger in his tone. "Once those conservative assholes have finished picking on whatever minority group they're currently targeting, they'll come after gay people next. And there's nothing wrong with being a masculine man or feminine woman and having traditionally accepted interests or desires, like marriage and babies, but you can't punish or ostracise other queer people for not wanting those things. Does that make sense? I've said this to people before and they've called me a preachy bitch. Not that I care about their opinion."

He laughed sarcastically, and once again I was reminded that while my brother might look adorable on the surface, he probably knew a hundred different ways to murder someone and get away with it given that he was a mortician.

"No, you're fine," I said. "I appreciate it. I guess I've been aware of it but not really thought about it before. Fuck, that makes me sound awful."

"It doesn't. You're just going through something a lot of us go through at some point or another."

My stomach bubbled and twisted. It was hard realising this was something Theo had dealt with all his life, and yet it had barely affected mine. I wondered if Rory had experienced it too. My gut feeling was it'd happened more often than I wanted to think about.

"West," Theo said. "Can I ask you something?"

"Yeah."

"Have you ever tried to make yourself smaller so people would like you? Like letting them make comments or jokes about being bisexual because you want to fit in?"

"Yes," I said quietly. I couldn't deny it, not after everything Theo had said. "Of course I have. I play a team sport, Theo, and I can't do that if people think I'm an uptight asshole who can't take a joke."

"Okay… but why should they be allowed to harass and bully you because you're bi?"

"It's not… they're not… it's only banter."

"Banter is still bullying," Theo said. It sounded like he was working hard to keep his anger in check. "And you deserve to exist as yourself as much as anyone else."

"I guess," I said. This whole conversation had made my chest tight, a deeply uncomfortable feeling worming its way inside me and sitting there, slowly crushing the air out of my lungs.

"There's no guessing about it. You matter, West, and

you're allowed to be openly bi without people being dicks. Every LGBTQ+ person is allowed to decide how open and visibly queer they are and how much they share with other people, but it should always be up to them to decide, not anyone else."

I nodded, then realised I hadn't said anything. "Do you think that's why Rory still wants to do the story hour?"

"Probably," Theo said. "But as much as I'd like to be able to have awesome mind-reading powers, I don't think Laurie would let me have them. You'll unfortunately have to ask him yourself!"

"Yeah… I will. Thanks, Theo."

"You're welcome!"

We chatted for a little bit longer, and before we hung up, Theo made me promise to let him know about Christmas in the next few weeks.

Afterwards, I stared up at the ceiling, all of my brother's words running round in my head in flashing neon letters. My chest still felt like it was being crushed, and I didn't know whether I was ready to talk about any of this with Rory. Especially because my whole inexperience with this kinda shit might make me look like a complete wanker.

When I'd come out, I'd naively assumed it would make a difference. And maybe it did.

Or maybe it wouldn't until I actually began to exist in the space I'd tried to create for myself instead of lingering like a ghost.

Either way, recent events had opened a door I couldn't close. Now I had to decide whether to charge through or pretend I couldn't see it.

CHAPTER NINETEEN

Bubblegum Galaxy

"Can you slags get a fucking move on, please? I'm freezing my bloody arse off out here," Eva yelled, leaning in through The Court's stage door and gesturing to Bitch and me as we finalised some details with Moxxie and Peaches. It was nearly midnight and I was fucking shattered because I'd been up since the arse-crack of dawn on an emergency call-out and my caffeine high was finally wearing off.

Drinking back-to-back cans of Monster had sounded like a good plan at lunchtime, but the sickening wave of nausea and exhaustion was proving me very wrong.

"Sorry!" Moxxie called. They were on a quick break from their DJ set, which they'd be doing until at least two. I didn't know how Moxxie could do a show and then DJ in full drag, but more power to them. Bitch used to do the same until she'd given up the DJ slot at the start of the year when she'd gone on tour with a big drag show run by a former *Drag Stars* contestant. To say I was jealous was an understatement, but I'd done my best to be happy for her. "We're done."

"Good! Get your arses over here. It's colder than a witch's tit out here and I want to go home."

"All right, keep your tits on. We're coming," Bitch said. She turned to me and grinned. "Ready, Sparkles?"

"God yes, I'm so fucking tired." I yawned and followed her over to the door, pulling my coat around me. The three of us were still half-made-up and dressed in drag because The Court's central heating system had thrown a temper tantrum and half the dressing rooms had no heat, although the bar and stage were fine, which meant the show went on. I'd grumblingly given Phil the name and number of a good emergency plumber I'd worked with in the past and made him promise to call first thing tomorrow.

"I'm starving," Bitch said, linking her arm through mine. "Do you fancy walking to McDonald's? I'm craving fries and an apple pie."

"Oh… yeah, that sounds really good."

"Eva," Bitch said as we reached the door. "Fancy a Maccy's? It'll be warm in there at least."

Eva thought for a second as we stepped out into the freezing November air, the stage door thudding shut behind us with a loud clang that echoed around the street. The stage door was at the side of the building, so we could hear the sound of people queuing up to get in and the strains of cheesy dance pop, but the three of us were completely alone.

"Sure," Eva said. "I could go for a Maccy's."

"Excellent," Bitch said. "Let's go." She linked her other arm through Eva's and the three of us set off along the dark road lit only by a couple of streetlights. The nearest McDonald's wasn't far, no more than a five- or ten-minute walk depending on how much we dawdled.

The side road we'd been on soon joined up with one of the main roads leading into the centre of town and we followed it onto one of the wide pedestrianised streets packed with bars and restaurants and the odd shop that had been long since locked up for the night. There were quite a few people around, mostly dashing from one bar to another or from taxis into nightclubs, chatting and laughing and dragging each other along, filling the street with noise. Pairs of black-clad bouncers stood either side of the doors to all the bars, tucked slightly in from the cold.

Most people ignored us, although I noticed a few pointing and staring. It was something I expected, given that I was still in a wig and full-glam make-up, a puffy coat thrown on over my dress, and my usual heels replaced by a battered pair of Nikes. Normally I'd have ignored it, but there was something about the looks that set my teeth on edge and made my blood run cold.

There was a sinister feel to it that I'd never experienced before, and my heart rate picked up as my steps quickened. I didn't know if it was the comments I'd seen online playing tricks on me or if there was a cold, cruel edge to people's looks, but it made me wish West was with me.

Eva and Bitch didn't seem to have noticed because the two of them were lost in conversation. Or maybe they had and were trying to pretend it wasn't happening.

My eyes fixed on the pavement ahead of me and I focused on putting one foot in front of the other, my breath clouding in the air like puffs of smoke from a steam train. My footsteps sounded heavy, like the stomp of a giant, and I wished I could float through the city like a ghost, silent and unnoticeable.

"Oi!" The sharp cry snapped me to attention and I twisted my head, looking for who'd yelled. Bitch and Eva stopped beside me, and I felt the tension radiating off of them.

A group of guys sauntered towards us, dressed for a night out in the tightest trousers and shirts they'd been able to squeeze themselves into. They were obviously smashed off their faces from the way a couple of them staggered across the wide, flat paving stones, and I guessed they'd been on their way to another bar or club.

Except they'd now spotted the three of us.

"What the fuck are you supposed to be?" the guy at the front yelled, gesturing wildly at us. "Halloween's fucking gone, man."

Bitch sighed, squaring her shoulders as she turned to face them. "Aren't you observant?"

"You fucking what?"

"I said, aren't you observant," she said acerbically. "It means, well done, you have eyes and can use them. Congratulations, you have the intelligence of a toddler."

"Eli," I said quietly, his real name slipping out as I tried to get him to back down. "Don't."

"It's fine, babe," Eli said. "They're all hanging out their arses."

"I know but—"

"Are you fucking talking about us?" the guy asked, clearly agitated. "I'll fucking have you. Fucking fags!"

"That's enough," Eli snapped, all pretence of nonchalance gone as he drew himself up to his full height and glared at the group. At least a couple of the men looked nervous, like they'd suddenly realised their friend was getting them deeper and deeper into the shit. Their shouting was going to have drawn attention since we weren't far from at least half a dozen pubs and bars, and out of the corner of my eye I noticed Eva tapping away on her phone.

In boy mode, Eva was a paramedic, I remembered. Maybe she knew someone who could help.

Were we supposed to ring the police? I'd grown up in a household where the phrase "all coppers are bastards" was regularly used by my dad, and I'd actively avoided any police wherever possible, especially since it was often hard to tell who was queer friendly.

Fuck, I wished my dad was here.

"We've not done anything to you," Eli continued, his voice deathly cold and calm in a way I'd never heard. "I'd suggest you fuck off to the nearest bar, and we'll go to McDonald's."

"No fucking way, mate," the guy slurred, lurching towards us. I took half a step back. "We don't want any of you fucking faggots round here."

He sprang forward, hand outstretched as he tried to take a swing at Eli. His mates yelled and tried to grab him. There was a slap of his hand on Eli's face, then a gasp and a sickening crunch of bone, and the man crumpled to the ground, howling and shrieking.

When he finally looked up, there was blood trickling out of his nose.

It was only then I realised that Eli had punched him.

Everything had happened so fast I could barely process it, and the world was starting to spin at the edges. I couldn't remember how to breathe. Why couldn't I remember how to breathe?

"Anyone else?" Eli asked, shaking his hand out and wiggling his fingers. "Or will all you now fuck off?"

My heart was pounding in my ears and my lungs were desperate for air. I wanted to tell Eli to stop because he was waving a red flag in front of them and this was how people got mobbed. Sure, they were drunk, but there were six of them and only three of us. And I couldn't feel my hands well enough to throw a punch. I could barely feel my body at all.

A couple of them took a step towards us and one pulled their mate to his feet. Blood was still oozing from his nose and dripping down to his lip.

It felt like being surrounded by wolves, only wolves didn't have eyes full of cold, drunken calculation. Alcohol and hatred had given these men more confidence than they deserved. It chilled me to my core, and I didn't think I'd ever be warm again.

"You've fucking done it now," the man said, spitting blood and phlegm onto the ground. "I'm gonna fucking kill you."

He lurched forward again, this time accompanied by his

cronies, and I stepped back. Fear flooded my body, screaming at me to run. But I couldn't leave Eli and Eva. They'd stepped in front of me, a protective wall of queer fury, but I knew it wouldn't be enough.

I wanted my dad.

I wanted West.

I wanted someone, anyone, to help us before it was too late.

"Hey!" A sharp woman's voice cut through the air and there was the sound of boots on stone. "Stop right now!"

Through hazy eyes I saw reflective jackets and light glinting off badges. Bouncers? No, community support officers. At the sight of them, the drunk men tried to scatter, two of them tripping over each other and landing in a heap on the ground. It would have been comical at any other time but I felt like I was watching everything through a telescope. Or one of those kids' kaleidoscopes with blurry plastic and cheap coloured crystals floating around in front of my eyes.

The two community officers, a man and a woman, were saying something to Eli, and the woman broke off to speak into her radio.

"Rory..." Eva's voice was soft and I felt her arm around my shoulder. But it somehow felt far away, like my body wasn't mine anymore. "Are you okay?"

"No," I said. "I don't think I am." I shook my head and felt myself shiver, even though I didn't actually feel cold. But my breath was clouding in front of me, so it must have been freezing.

"Do you want me to call someone?"

"I... I can do it."

"It's okay, just tell me who to call."

I glanced over at Eli, who was talking to the officers, gesturing firmly. His words eluded me but I could hear his calm, collected tone. He'd once told me something about studying law... he wasn't a lawyer, though. He'd been a receptionist before his drag tour...

"What's going on?" I asked as I tried to dig in the pocket of my coat for my phone, but my fingers shook so much I couldn't control them.

"Eli's giving a statement," Eva said, gently taking my phone out of my pocket and using my thumb to unlock it. "They might need to talk to you as well."

"Will Eli get in trouble?"

"No, I don't think so. You and I both witnessed them harassing us and clearly saw that guy hit first. Eli's actions were self-defence."

"Okay." I nodded, not really sure what else to say.

"Here," Eva said as she pushed something into my hand. It was a slightly squashed Double Decker. "Eat that. It'll be good for your blood sugar. I'm just going to make a phone call."

"Can... can you call my dad, please?" I asked, slowly peeling back the wrapper of the bar. "He'll come and get me." I half wondered if it was silly to want my dad at twenty-two, but I didn't care. He was my dad and the one man I trusted more than anyone else in the world.

No... he wasn't.

He was one of two.

"Eva," I said softly but insistently as she turned away. "Can you call West too, please?"

Eva nodded and a tiny bubble of relief burst in my chest.

I lifted the bar of chocolate to my lips.

It tasted like blood and fear.

CHAPTER TWENTY

West

"Hey, sweetheart, I didn't expect to hear from you tonight," I said sleepily as I swiped the screen to answer Rory's call. I shouldn't have even been awake since we had a match tomorrow, but I'd gotten suckered into playing *Call of Duty* with Jonny and Mason and when I'd finally come to bed, I'd ended up scrolling through TikTok instead of going to sleep.

"Sorry, it's not Rory," said a male voice I vaguely recognised. "My name is Evan—Eva Nessence. I'm sorry to disturb you but Rory asked me to give you a call."

"Is everything okay?"

"Rory is fine," Evan said. "We've just had a bit of a nasty scare. We were all heading to McDonald's after tonight's show but on the way we... encountered a group of drunk lads who thought they'd try and pick a fight since we're all in drag. Anyway, long story short, we're all fine, nobody's been hurt, but Rory's in shock. His dad is coming to pick him up but he's asking for you. Do you think you'd be able to come and see him?"

"Yeah… shit, yeah. I'll be right there." I was already climbing out of bed, phone tucked between my ear and my shoulder as I tried to find some fucking clothes. Where the hell were my joggers? And my hoodie? Shit, I needed boxers as well. My heart was thudding in my chest and I could barely string any thoughts together. "Where are you?"

"We're in town, but Alan's just arrived," Evan said. I assumed that was Rory's dad. Fuck, I didn't know where Rory lived. We'd always come to mine.

"Stupid question, but what's Rory's address? He's only ever been to mine." I didn't care what judgements Evan made from that statement, but I needed to know.

"I'm not sure, but I'll have to give him his phone back in a second, so I'll get him to message you. Or I'll get his address and send it along."

"Cheers. Can you tell him I'll be right there? And that…" I didn't know what to say. "Just tell him I'll be there."

"Will do," Evan said and hung up.

I swore violently as I grabbed whatever clothes I could find, not caring if I woke the whole fucking city as I clattered around. I'd probably get an earful from everyone tomorrow, but I didn't give a shit. The only thing that mattered was getting to Rory.

My feet thundered on the stairs as I took them at a breakneck pace, grabbing my keys off the side in the kitchen and heading for the door. It slammed shut behind me and the security light above it threw golden light onto the step as I hopped down and into the street, jogging over to my car.

My breath fogged in front of me, the cold air needling my skin as I slid into the driver's seat and glanced down at my phone to see if Evan had sent me the address. He had and I quickly threw it into Google Maps, cursing as my fingers kept hitting the wrong button and deleting things. I knew it was stress and if I slowed down, it would be easier, but all that did was make me angrier. I just wanted to be there, not sitting in my freezing cold car on the other side of the city.

The journey only took me twenty minutes since it was nearly half one and the roads were dark and empty, but every one of those minutes felt like a lifetime. When I arrived, I could barely remember how I'd gotten there, and if anyone had asked me the route, I wouldn't have been able to tell them a damn thing.

Rory's house was a semi-detached set back from the road with a couple of vans parked in a front drive that looked like it had been converted from the garden. I could tell there were lights on downstairs because I could see hints of light behind the blinds covering the windows.

I didn't know if his family was expecting me or if they even knew who I was, but neither of those things mattered. All that mattered was Rory.

The street was silent as I walked up the path to the door, not even the noise from a car in the distance. I knocked firmly and waited, listening for the sound of voices or feet.

But I didn't hear anything before the door swung sharply open, revealing a shorter man, probably in his mid-fifties, with a bald head and fading tattoos along his arms. He had similar grey eyes to Rory's that were fixing me with a suspicious look.

"Can I help you?" he asked, his hard London accent clear as he spoke.

"Hi," I said. "I'm West Russell, Rory's boyfriend. Evan called me."

The man, who I had to assume was Rory's dad, nodded. "You better come in then," he said, stepping back and gesturing for me to enter. "He's in the front room. Poor lad's had a nasty shock. I swear, if I'd have been there…"

"Yeah, me too…"

He nodded. "I'm Alan." He pointed at a door on the right where another man was standing. He looked younger than Rory, with scruffy light brown hair and stubble dusting his cheeks. Alan signed something and I realised that had to be Christopher, Rory's younger brother.

"*Hello*," I signed, drawing on the tiny amount of British Sign Language I'd managed to teach myself from YouTube over the past few weeks. "*Nice to meet you.*"

Christopher grinned and signed something in return, but his hands moved too fast. Behind me, Alan sighed.

"Give over, you daft bastard, and let him in," he said and when I glanced over my shoulder, I realised he was speaking as he signed. I assumed it was so I knew what he was saying. "Then go and put the kettle on."

Christopher frowned but didn't sign anything as he moved slightly to one side to let me in. I nodded and stepped past him into the living room where I saw a police officer sitting in a floral armchair talking to a woman sat opposite on a floral sofa. And next to her, still in drag with a fluffy blanket over his knees, was my Rory.

The three of them looked at me as I entered, their conversation drifting into nothingness.

"West…" Rory's voice wavered as he said my name and my heart cracked like someone had stamped on the top of a frozen puddle.

"Hey, sweetheart," I said, crossing the distance between us in barely three strides and crouching down in front of him, taking his hands in mine. His skin was cold to the touch and I squeezed his hands gently, trying to force some warmth into them. I knew the two women were still looking at me, so I turned my head and nodded at both of them. "Sorry, I'm West. I'm Rory's boyfriend."

The woman beside me on the sofa smiled, a softened version of one I'd seen on Rory's face a hundred times. "Thank you for coming," she said. "I'm Louise."

"Nice to meet you."

"This is Officer Jennings," Louise said. "She was just getting all the details sorted."

"Can I ask when you found out about the incident?" the officer asked. "Did anyone try and contact you while it was taking place?"

"No." I shook my head. "I've been at home all evening with my roommates. The first I knew about it was when Evan called me on Rory's phone asking me to come round. That was… I don't know, maybe half an hour ago."

Jennings nodded. "Thank you."

Louise asked something about next steps and I heard Alan chime in with another question from the door, but I wasn't really listening. I was too busy looking at Rory, who was staring off into space in front of me. His make-up was still in place but his eyes were slightly red and puffy, like he'd been crying. Or maybe he'd wanted to cry but hadn't because it would make everything run. Although I didn't think Rory would care about that because it wasn't like it would matter if it did.

I slowly rubbed my thumbs over his hands, pressing just firmly enough that he'd realise I was there. "Are you still with me, sweetheart?" I murmured, keeping my voice low so I wouldn't disturb the conversation going on around us.

Rory hummed but didn't say anything.

"I'm here for you," I said as I continued to massage his hands. "You're safe and I'm here."

A sense of utter powerlessness began to seep into my bones, draining my strength and smothering the simmering anger I'd felt ever since I'd answered the phone. What could I do except sit here with him? I wasn't Batman. I couldn't wreak vigilante vengeance on those who'd wronged Rory. I didn't even know everything that'd happened. Evan had said nobody had gotten hurt but that didn't mean much. Emotional wounds hurt just as much as physical ones but weren't as easy to see and couldn't exactly be healed with a plaster or some stitches.

"West," Alan said, calling my name loud enough to catch my attention. I glanced over and saw him wearing a grim smile. "How'd you take your tea?"

"Er... milk, please, two sugars," I said. "Thanks." It felt rude to turn down the gesture even though it was so early in the morning any caffeine would fuck with my sleeping patterns. I was supposed to be playing a match that afternoon too. I'd have to give our head coach, Clive, a ring as soon as I could and explain.

"Here," Alan said a minute later, handing me a mug patterned with cats and full to the brim with tea. He had another in his hands that he held out to Rory. "Roo-Bear, this is for you."

"Thanks," Rory mumbled as he slid his hands out of mine and reached for the mug, taking a small sip of tea. He glanced down at me and a tiny smile nudged at the corner of his lip. "Why are you sitting on the floor?"

"Because I like being different," I said and Rory let out the smallest laugh. It was the most beautiful and welcome sound I'd ever heard.

"Here," he said, scooting slightly to his left so there was a bigger gap next to him. "You can sit down now."

I stood, my thigh and calf muscles complaining at the sudden change of position, and gently eased myself down onto the cushion. As soon as I did, Rory leant against me, drawing his legs up and snuggling into my side, clutching his mug to his chest. I put my arm around him, holding my tea in my other hand, and squeezed his shoulder.

Everyone else was still talking but it all blurred into noise, leaving only Rory and me.

I wished things could have been different, but no matter how much I wanted them to be, nothing would change what had happened. The feeling of powerlessness pulled me under, filling my lungs and drowning me in guilt.

But this wasn't about me, and I couldn't make it about me. This was about Rory, and I had to be strong, for him at least.

I squeezed him a little bit tighter, trying not to let my fingers tremble.

CHAPTER TWENTY-ONE

Bubblegum Galaxy

Even pressed against West's solid body, the world was still slightly fuzzy around the edges. My heart rate had slowed from its earlier racing pace, but now every beat felt like a clap of thunder echoing through my chest. Nausea bubbled in my stomach and it was clear my body hadn't yet decided whether I was going to throw up or if it was just going to simmer and stew.

I didn't know which was worse, because while vomiting sucked, at least it would get it over with. The bubbling could go on for hours, gnawing away at my stomach until it felt like I was dissolving from the inside out.

Dad had made me tea, but every sip repulsed me. The warmth of the mug was nice, though, almost like a hot water bottle, and sitting with it pressed against my stomach seemed to help.

I'd lost track of the conversation going on around me.

Mum was chatting to the police officer who'd arrived not long after Dad and I had gotten home. I'd given them my statement, forcing myself to remember as many details as possible, but I didn't know why they were still here. Maybe it was out of politeness.

"Do you want to go to bed?" West asked, his voice sounding far away. I registered his words but didn't react. It was like my body was working in slow motion and everything took twice as long to process. "Sweetheart? Can you hear me?"

"Yeah." I nodded a couple of times, then stopped because it made my head spin.

"Do you want to go to bed?"

I didn't know why West had repeated himself. I thought I'd answered his question. Or maybe he'd thought I was responding to the second part about me hearing him. Although the answer was yes to both, so did I need to respond twice?

"Yeah," I said again. "I need to take my make-up off, though. I think…" I looked around for my bag because I had a nagging suspicion I'd put my wipes, micellar water, cleaning pads, moisturisers, and the box for my lashes in my bag before I'd left. I often took most of my make-up off before I left The Court simply because I felt guilty crashing around at home when everyone else was in bed.

Or at least, Mum was in bed. Dad was usually asleep in front of the TV pretending he was watching *Match of the Day* and the *English Football League Highlights* with Beans stretched out on his lap.

"Where's my bag?" I asked, glancing up at West and then around at everyone else.

"*In your room,*" Christopher signed from the door. He was leaning against the frame like a bouncer. "*I took it up earlier.*"

"Thanks."

Christopher shrugged like it was no big deal. Then he grinned and nodded at West with his chin. "*Is your boyfriend staying?*"

"I don't know. I haven't asked him."

"You should. Then tell Dad."

I tried to raise an eyebrow but I was too tired. Dad had never made a fuss about us bringing people home because he'd always said he'd rather know where we were and who we were with, but that hadn't stopped him glowering at people. Dad said it was just his face, that he was naturally scowly, but I thought it was because he didn't trust anyone within five feet of us but knew he didn't have a choice, so his expression had become one of permanent distrust.

"Do you want to stay?" I asked West, deliberately not signing and turning away from my brother so he couldn't read my lips. I didn't want him to think this was all his idea and gloat.

"Is that okay? I don't want to intrude."

I slipped my hand into his and squeezed it tightly. "Stay. Please."

"Sure." He leant forward and kissed my forehead. "I have a match this afternoon, so I'll need to ring Clive when I can."

"Why?"

"To let him know I've been up all night. In case he wants to swap me out." He said it casually, like it wasn't a big deal, but it sent an icy chill down my spine. I must have reacted somehow because West added, "It's not your fault and it's not an issue. I just need to let him know."

"It feels like my fault," I said quietly.

"No, sweetheart, it's not."

I didn't believe him but I was too tired to argue. The longer I'd sat here, the more my muscles had started to wind down from the adrenaline and now my body felt like a dead weight.

"Come on," West said, gently prizing the nearly full mug of cold tea out of my hands and setting it on the end table. "You need sleep." He slowly helped me to my feet and I realised everyone had stopped talking. "Rory needs to go to bed. Where's his room?"

"Upstairs, first door on the left," Mum said. She was smiling fondly at me. "Do you need a hand?"

"I've got him," West said. "Do you mind if I stay?"

"Not at all," Mum said before Dad or Christopher could chime in. "Do you need anything?"

"No, thank you." I felt West's body turn where I was leaning against him. He was about the only thing keeping me standing. "Do you need anything else, Officer?"

"No, I've got everything. I'll be in touch if I need anything else."

"Good," West said. "Goodnight."

I mumbled goodnight and tried to step forward, but as I did, I felt two strong arms around me, scooping me up and lifting me off the floor. I tried to squeak and protest, but all that came out was a mumbled groan that sounded more like the old man noise Sausage made first thing in the morning when he got out of his nest and stretched.

"I'm not putting you down," West said as he carried me out of the room. "You look about ready to drop."

I buried my head against his shoulder, not wanting to look at anyone because I was sure I'd never live this down. But I also loved that West had done it. He didn't care what anyone else thought; he only cared about me.

His footsteps were muffled on the carpeted stairs. I counted them in my head but must have lost track because soon we reached the landing and I heard my bedroom door squeak open.

It was only then I remembered how much of a fucking tip my bedroom was.

Of all the days for West to finally see it, it had to be the day I'd left clean washing all over the place, not made my bed, emptied half my wardrobe looking for a pair of shoes that had been in my bag all along, hadn't emptied my bedroom bin, and had left a collection of random glasses and mugs festering on my bedside table, dressing table, and chest of drawers.

If he was still attracted to me after seeing that, it would be a damn miracle.

And I was pretty sure I'd left the drawer of the bedside table nearest the window open, which meant my dildo collection would be on display as soon as he walked around the bed.

Fuck my life.

"I'm going to put you down," West said before slowly

lowering down and setting me on the end of the bed like I was made of glass. He gently brushed the hair off my face, tucking it behind my ear. I was still wearing my wig, and I didn't know if West knew how to take it off. I'd glued it down with hairspray, so it would need gently peeling off or the lace front would get ripped.

"Where's your bag?" West asked, smiling at me before glancing around the room. "Is it the pink one?"

"Yeah." I followed his gaze to the large pink dance bag resting just inside the door. "I need to take my wig off too."

"Okay, let me get your stuff." West covered the gap between the bed and the door in two quick steps, returning a second later with my bag in one hand as if it weighed no more than a feather. I guessed to him it didn't. "What do you need? Do you want me to do it?"

"It's fine," I said, unzipping the bag and digging around inside to find what I needed. My lashes were starting to irritate me, so they were the first thing to go, even if peeling them off with stiletto press-on nails was a pain in the ass. I wanted to pop my nails off too, but even though they were only fixed on with little glue tabs, I still needed to soak them and I didn't have the patience for that right now.

I grabbed my various cleansers out and then remembered I'd put a ton of fucking face gems on and hadn't taken them off. I reached up, trying to scrape them off with my nails, but instead I jabbed myself in the corner of my left eye. "Fuck! Mother... fuck, that hurt!"

Stinging tears slid down my cheeks as my eye tried to expel its unseen intruder, and to make matters worse, my right eye started leaking in sympathy. Fuck, why did it burn so much?

"Here," West said softly, his fingers lightly brushing across my cheek. "Let me."

"You just… fuck, they should just peel off," I said as I tried to dab my eyes with the back of my hand.

"I've got it. Do you want to keep them?"

"No, they can go in the bin."

The tip of West's finger gently caught the edge of one of the gem bursts beside my eye, slowly peeling it off. The glue pulled at my skin, but it didn't hurt as much as pulling off a plaster. "There's one," he said, putting the gem cluster in my hand. "Only four more to go."

"This is making me never want to apply them again," I said as West peeled another off my temple.

"They look beautiful, though."

"Beauty can suck it." I tried to make it sound like a joke, but my words came out shaking. "I'm sorry."

"Why are you apologising? You've got nothing to be sorry for."

"I don't know… for this? For everything that happened tonight."

"Fucking hell, sweetheart. That was not your fault," West said. He'd knelt down in front of me and now he sat back on his heels to fix me with a firm look. "Those cunts started this. Not you."

"I know." I sighed. In my head I knew that, but my body was still processing everything and the whole thing still felt raw and red. It was like the back of my heels when they'd been rubbed bloody by new shoes, except the feeling was everywhere. "I'm glad Eli was there. Did Eva tell you what he did?"

"No."

"One of them, the leader I guess, took a swing at Eli… so Eli punched him. Gave him a bloody nose and everything."

West whistled under his breath. "Remind me not to get on his bad side."

I laughed softly, but it was more from disbelief. "I still can't believe it. I mean… I know Eli's been in scraps before. He and his oldest brother got into a punch-up over Tristan, but I wasn't sure if he was being dramatic or not. But now… yeah… I don't think it would've gone well for them if they'd kept going." Yeah, there'd been more of them, but now I thought about it, I wouldn't have been surprised if Eli had grabbed his shoes out of his bag and used the heels as a weapon.

"I'm glad it didn't get worse," West said as he removed the last of my gems. "I wouldn't have wanted you fighting."

"Do you know the worst thing?" I asked, reaching for a pack of make-up wipes and pulling a couple out. That would hopefully be enough to take most of my face off.

"What?"

"I was frightened… really fucking frightened… but also, not surprised."

West frowned, a glimmer of anger flickering in his eyes. "Why not?"

"Because it's not the first time." I swiped a wipe across my face, smearing it with foundation, contour, and blush.

"It's the first time someone's ever hit, or tried to hit, me or someone I was with, but… it's not the first time I've been yelled at or threatened."

"You're not serious, are you?" His naive disbelief would have been sweet at any other time, but now it just felt like the ground was cracking between us.

"Of course I'm serious."

"But that's…"

"Fucked up? I know, but I'm visibly queer out of drag, and in drag… well, I'm pretty fucking noticeable. I don't even know why I'm surprised it happened." Part of me wished I'd gotten changed at The Court, even though it had been cold. Because then none of this would have happened.

Then again, if they'd been looking for a fight, Eli, Eva, and I would've looked different enough they'd have started something anyway. We weren't the problem here—those dickheads were. But we were the ones who everyone would blame.

It was times like this that I started to understand what women meant when they talked about their experiences with men, both in private and public.

West was still watching me. "I'm sorry," he said. "I… I know I've been lucky. That's never happened to me."

"It shouldn't happen to anyone," I said, snappier than I'd intended.

"You're right. It shouldn't. And I'm sorry, I shouldn't have assumed. It's not an excuse that this is new to me. Maybe next time…" He sighed. "Fuck, I'm making a mess of this." He picked up another make-up wipe and gently wiped the edge of my face. "You missed a spot."

"Thanks."

West handed me another wipe, a little smile on his lips. He leant forward and kissed me. "I'm glad you're safe."

His mouth was soft and warm. It was sweetness and safety and something more I couldn't place. But I didn't know if it was a good thing. I was glad West was here, but there was something about his words that hurt. Out of everyone I knew, I shouldn't have to explain things to him.

As I sat back, it looked like he was thinking about saying something, but he didn't. Depending on what that was, that might have been wise. I wasn't in the mood for West to tell me it was a one-off, or a rarity, or suggest I should change the way I looked.

I didn't know if he would, but I felt my guard coming up because those were *always* the reactions I got.

If I didn't want to be picked on for being queer, I shouldn't look queer. Or act queer. Or *be* queer.

I should just be normal.

Fuck that. I was going to be Rory. And Bubblegum.

Because bigots were just that, bigots. And I was never going to let them beat me, no matter what happened.

Even if I was afraid, I was going to keep on being me.

There was no other option. Not to me.

CHAPTER TWENTY-TWO

West

I LOVED WATCHING RORY SLEEPING. There was something so peaceful about his face, a different kind of beauty to the one I saw when he was awake or in drag. It almost looked like someone had carved it out of marble.

It'd been five days since Rory had been harassed and Evan had called me, and ever since then everything had felt vaguely off-kilter. It was as if the ground underneath us had shifted slightly and while neither of us had said anything, it felt like Rory was slowly sliding away from me.

I didn't know what had caused it and I didn't know how to fix it either.

Maybe it had been something I'd said, but every time I thought through our conversations from that night, I couldn't see any obvious mistakes. Except maybe my surprise that this was a regular sort of thing. It made me think of my conversation with Theo. I'd wondered then if harassment and bigotry had been something he'd experienced regularly, but I'd never asked because it felt... well, wrong.

Now I had my answer.

I'd fucked it up by asking if Rory was serious and going on about how lucky I was.

Rory was right—it shouldn't happen to anyone.

I'd tried my hardest not to blame him, intentionally or not, because it wasn't his fault. A tiny insidious voice in the back of my head whispered maybe things would've been different if Rory and co. hadn't been in drag, but I shooed it away. Rory shouldn't have to make himself smaller to fit in, shouldn't have to change who he was or how he dressed because some people were cunts.

Rory shifted in his sleep, wiggling closer to me and throwing an arm across my chest, burying into my side. My arm was pinned at an awkward angle underneath him that couldn't have been comfortable to lie on, but when I tried to move it, he grumbled under his breath. "Stop moving. I'm sleeping."

I chuckled quietly. "Then why are you talking?"

"I'm not."

"Sounds like you are."

Rory lifted his head. "You're hearing things."

I tilted my head down and kissed him softly. "Your mouth is moving."

"You're seeing things," he said, and I could hear him smiling. I rolled him gently over, landing between his thighs and bracing myself on my hands either side of his shoulders. Rory looked up at me with tired eyes, new bags forming underneath them. I tried not to frown because now wasn't the time to bring it up.

"Maybe I am," I said.

"Maybe you should kiss me again. Then I might wake up properly."

A smile played across my mouth as I lowered my head and kissed him again, deeper this time. Rory groaned, wrapping his arms around my neck and pulling me closer. "More."

I caressed the seam of his lips with my tongue, pressing inside and making him melt further into the bed. I'd always loved kissing. There was something so heady and perfect about it as a gesture. You could say so much with a kiss: I need you, I appreciate you, I want you. *I'm sorry for being a dick. For not believing you.*

We kissed slowly, taking our time and revelling in the moment. It was Wednesday morning, so we both had places to be, but those could wait until we were ready.

Rory's hands tangled in the back of my hair, tugging on the fine strands. A little shiver of pleasure ran across my skin, making the hair on my arms stand up. That was… new.

"Do you like that, baby?" Rory asked, leaning back into the pillows, a playful smile dancing across his face and gleaming in his eyes.

"Yes," I said, slightly hesitantly. Rory smirked and gently pulled my hair again, kissing me and nipping my bottom lip as he did. Another shiver shot down my spine and I groaned into his mouth.

"Mmm, I like making you moan," Rory said. His foot

slid up the back of my calf, hooking around my thigh and pulling my body against his. He moaned happily as our cocks ground together, both of us already hard and desperate for more. We'd both slept naked because Rory turned into a fucking furnace at night and I liked the idea of potentially being cold, even though it wouldn't happen with my boyfriend sprawling across me.

"What do you want, sweetheart?"

Rory thrust his hips up, using his foot around my thigh to rub against me. "I want you to fuck me. I want you to send me home dripping with sweat and full of cum. I need, fuck, I need to spend the day thinking about you. Every time I move, I want to be reminded of your cock."

His kisses were hungry and desperate, like he was chasing something.

Or running from something.

Either way, I wanted to protect him. And bring him enough pleasure to make him forget, at least for a few minutes.

Making my partners feel good had always been something I'd loved. There was something heady about knowing I could bring them exquisite bliss with the flick of my tongue, the curl of my fingers, or a thrust of my cock. And tasting their release was better than any hundred-year-old whiskey or fine vintage of wine.

I trailed my mouth down his body, leaving marks across his tanned skin so he wouldn't forget this moment. He groaned, his back arching off the bed as I sucked his nipples into my mouth one after the other. I smirked around the dusky, hardened nub. His moans were music to my ears, making my body hum in anticipation.

My mouth moved lower as I shuffled down the bed until I could trail my mouth down the dips in his hips. Rory's legs were still around me, only now they were virtually resting on my shoulders as I laved my tongue over his inner thigh, leaving a hickey on the soft, sensitive skin.

His hard cock jumped as I ran my tongue over his taint, slowly using it to caress his balls. Precum dripped onto his abdomen and I was tempted to lean forward and lick it up, but I was having too much fun sucking his balls into my mouth and hearing Rory gasp. His fingers tightened in my hair, tugging my head forward in the universal sign for more.

Saliva slicked my lips as I released his sac and teasingly slid the tip of my tongue along his shaft, barely touching his burning skin.

"Oh fuck," Rory said with a groan, pushing his hips up and thrusting his cock against my jaw. "More... I need, fuck... I need you to fucking suck my cock."

"Is that a request?"

"No. It's a demand."

I wanted to tell him demands wouldn't work, but we both knew Rory had me wrapped around his little finger. I'd give him anything he wanted.

I wrapped my lips around the head of his cock and sucked slowly, running my tongue along his slit. I teased the silky skin, tasting the drops of precum and savouring every one of them. Rory moaned as I sucked him deeper into my mouth, letting his shaft slide into my throat as I buried my nose in the trimmed dark hair at the base of his cock, the scent of him filling my senses.

Rory's hips stuttered like he didn't know whether to fuck my mouth or let me take him apart.

Tightening my lips around him, I started to work his cock slowly, drawing out every move until he was buried in my throat or balancing on the tip of my tongue. I wiggled a hand free underneath me, rolling his balls between my fingers and letting the saliva dripping from my lips slick the sensitive skin.

Rory gasped, his fingers tightening in my hair like it was an anchor.

I ran my fingers down his taint, rubbing the skin firmly, knowing that it would send little pulses of pleasure to his prostate. The lube was still on my bedside table, but Rory's hole was soft from last night when he'd pinned me to the bed and ridden me hard, using my body to take what he'd needed while I'd held on to his hips and watched him with awe.

Last night had also been the first time we'd gone without condoms, since our STI tests had both returned negative results, and I'd been unable to resist watching my cum drip from Rory's hole, catching it on my fingers and pushing it back inside while he gasped and moaned my name.

I pulled off his cock for a second, spitting saliva onto my fingers before taking his shaft back into my mouth. I slid the wet pads of my fingers over the furled skin of his hole, tapping it gently and circling his entrance. Then I sucked him deep into my throat as I slowly pressed a finger inside him.

"Y-yes," Rory said, bearing down on my finger and allowing me to slide deeper into the tight heat of his ass. "Fuck, I love your fingers. They're so fucking thick."

I smiled around his cock, a pleased rumble emanating from my throat. Rory whined and moaned, clearly desperate for more but unsure what he wanted. Slowly, I pumped my finger in and out of him, curling it so I could stroke and tease his prostate before sliding another finger into him. He gasped at the stretch, and I stopped moving my hand to let his body adjust.

I didn't stop sucking his cock, though.

It felt far too good in my mouth.

Rory's body relaxed, and I pushed both fingers deeper, stretching him open for me. My fingertips rubbed over his sweet spot, making him gasp out my name and pull my hair, and I smirked around his cock as heat slid down my spine.

"West…" Rory muttered. "I… I'm close…"

I pulled off his cock with a slick pop that echoed in my ears. The head was red and swollen, and his shaft looked almost painfully hard. I'd have felt bad for him if this wasn't my own doing. I'd be the source of his release too, and my dick throbbed at the thought of Rory coming on my cock, his ass squeezing me tightly.

"You're not going to come, sweetheart," I said, my voice rough. "Not yet."

"But I want to. I need it."

"I thought you wanted my cock?"

Rory hesitated, releasing my hair and lifting his head, looking at me with an amusing mix of pleading and annoyance. He wanted both but knew there wasn't time, not this morning at least. We might only be in our twenties, but neither of us had an instant recovery time.

And, annoyingly, I had training this morning, which I couldn't be late to. I could take the shit from the guys because I could easily give it back—after all, how many of them had gotten laid this morning?—but Clive didn't tolerate lateness and I didn't fancy doing burpees as punishment. Burpees were the spawn of the devil, or whatever foul fitness freak had invented them.

"Yeah, I do," he said. "But next time I see you, I want a blow job because your mouth…" His eyes rolled back and he smiled wantonly. "Fuck, I could write songs about your mouth."

"I'm glad you appreciate my talents."

"Mmm, you are very talented!" He propped himself up on his hands and looked down at me. "Are you going to fuck me then?"

"Of course," I said, carefully sliding my fingers out of him to give him more room to move. "But you need to pass me the lube."

Rory shuffled across to retrieve the small bottle and chucked it at me with so little finesse that I almost laughed. "What?"

"Nothing," I said, sliding my hand up his leg and gently pulling him back into the middle of the bed. His thighs were either side of me and he looked so fucking beautiful like this, all stretched out and wanting. I trickled lube onto my fingers and drizzled some onto his skin, watching as it slowly ran down towards his waiting hole.

"If you're going to say I can't throw for shit, it's true." He grinned at me, a lightness that I hadn't seen in days sparkling in his eyes. It seemed like sex as a distraction was working. "But also, you're a fucking professional rugby player and I'm a spark who moonlights as a gay clown."

I did laugh that time and had to bury my head in his stomach to stop the sound from booming around the room.

"You laugh, but it's the truth. All drag queens are just clowns with better wigs. And make-up. And shoes. Although I will admit I can't make balloon animals for shit. I tried once and the fucking thing burst in my face."

"I hate balloon animals," I said, pressing kisses across his stomach. My cock was painfully hard against the bed, but I wasn't going to rush us back on track if Rory was happy for the first time since everything had happened. My dick could wait. "They're creepy and weird. A balloon dog looks like someone just blew up a bunch of condoms and tried to pass it off as cute. Also, why the fuck do we give fragile balloon things to kids, knowing they'll probably burst them in two minutes and scream? It's a fucking recipe for disaster."

Rory giggled and sighed, relaxing back onto the bed. "Okay, less chatting. More fucking."

"You're the one who brought up clowns."

"You distracted me."

I leant down and kissed the inside of his thigh again, where the hickey I'd left earlier was blossoming in dark purple. "I'll distract you again."

Rory moaned as I peppered kisses on his skin and ran my fingers down his taint to his slick, waiting hole. I pressed two straight into him, making him gasp. I scissored and stretched him open, teasing his prostate before slowly adding a third. Rory had said recently he didn't need three because he was getting used to the size of my cock, but I always erred on the side of caution. It was better to be careful than risk hurting him. And while I was happy for it to burn if that was what he wanted, there was a difference between sexy, pleasurable pain and excruciating agony where nothing felt good and you just wanted it to stop. And I was never, ever going to let Rory experience the second.

"Please," Rory said, his breath coming in pants as my fingers stroked over his prostate. "West, I need…"

"What do you need?" I asked, leaning over him and brushing my lips across his. "Tell me."

"You. I need your cock inside me. Want to feel you. Want…"

I stole the rest of his words with a kiss, pulling his bottom lip between my teeth as I gently slid my fingers out of him. I ran my hand down his thigh, lifting it and tilting his hips up, never letting my eyes leave his face as I lined my cock up and began to press inside his greedy, waiting hole.

There were some men who thought any kind of missionary sex was dull as fuck but, in my opinion, that was because all they did was hammer their partner with their dick for two minutes before having the audacity to ask if their partner had come too.

Being face-to-face with someone, with Rory, gave me a window into his soul. I could see every moment of pleasure written in his expression, from the twitch of his lips to a breathless moan, to the way his eyes fluttered closed and his chin tipped back when my cock filled him so perfectly he thought he couldn't breathe.

Seeing that was everything to me, knowing I'd brought him that bliss. It was a heady feeling and more intoxicating than any liquor I'd ever tasted.

Rory groaned, arching into my touch as I lifted both his legs off the bed, resting them on my shoulders and leaning over him so I could press my cock deep inside, filling him with every inch until my balls brushed against his ass. I gripped the front of his thighs and pushed my knees underneath me, giving myself the balance and leverage to drive into Rory over and over, hitting his prostate with every hard, slow thrust.

His eyes were closed, mouth hanging open in ecstasy, his hands gripping the pillow beside his head. Sweet moans and desperate groans filled the room, mixed with the slap of skin on skin and the creak of my bedsprings. Heat bubbled under my skin, rolling through my body like I'd sunk into a hot bath. A familiar pressure began to build in my balls, and I knew I wouldn't last much longer.

Rory felt too good, his channel hot and tight, squeezing around me and wringing every drop of pleasure from each thrust. He looked so fucking perfect spread out beneath me, like every one of my wildest dreams come to life. How I'd convinced him to be here with me was a mystery, and my only worry was convincing him to stick around, even though I'd never be good enough for him.

"W-West…" Rory looked up at me with pleading eyes. "I'm… fuck, that feels…"

"Yeah? You like my thick cock, sweetheart?"

He groaned and nodded. "Yes! Feels… God, I feel so fucking full. Love the way it stretches me wide… fuck, I'm going to be thinking about you all day."

I leant down and captured his mouth in a biting kiss. "Good. I don't want you to think about anything else. Just me. Just this moment." I sat back and ran a hand down his thigh so I could grip his cock.

"Yes! Just like that!" Rory gasped, bucking up into my touch. I stroked him hard and fast as I pounded my cock into him, using my other hand to hold one thigh against my chest, using it as leverage to pull him onto my dick.

The heat, the pressure, the sheer perfection of this moment, it was all too much and I felt my orgasm barrelling towards me with the speed and intensity of a million fireworks. But I needed Rory to come first.

I twisted my hand across the head of his dick, collecting his precum on my skin and using it to slick my fist as I pumped his shaft. "I know you're close," I said, my voice a low, needy growl. "I know you want to come all over my cock."

"I… I do."

I smirked, driving deep inside him. "Then come for me, sweetheart."

Rory's body went tense and he cried out my name as his cock stiffened in my hand, shooting thick ribbons of cum across my fingers, his stomach, and all the way up to his chest. His ass tightened around me, squeezing me impossibly tight. And that was all it took for my orgasm to slam into me, harder than any tackle I'd ever experienced on the rugby pitch, knocking the breath from my lungs.

I growled out his name as I pulled him towards me, burying my cock as deep as I could and filling him with my release.

Sweat beaded on my chest, which rose and fell like a great barrel, and my muscles twitched and trembled from the rush of endorphins and adrenaline. Rory smiled up at me, looking ridiculously pleased with himself, and it made my chest purr with satisfaction.

Slowly, I released his legs and lowered them to the bed before bending down to kiss him sweetly, savouring the moment. My cock still filled him and when I tried to pull out, Rory stopped me.

"No," he said quietly. "I want you to stay inside me. Just for a minute." His hands carded through my hair as he kissed my lips and peppered my face with tiny pecks.

"Whatever you want," I said, kissing him again. "When it comes to me, you can have whatever you want."

Rory bit his lip, an earnest look in his eyes I'd never seen before. "Do you promise that?"

"Of course. I will give you everything, Rory. I promise."

I kissed him again, hoping he could feel how much I meant it.

Now, all I had to do was prove it.

CHAPTER TWENTY-THREE

Bubblegum Galaxy

I KNEW MAKING West promise he'd give me everything was stupid, but I couldn't stop myself. Because more than anything, I wanted it to be true.

I'd felt so out of sorts since the weekend, and even though it was totally understandable, I was kind of annoyed I'd let the whole thing get to me as much as it had. I should have been able to shrug it off, but it felt like it'd wedged itself under my skin like a nasty splinter that stung whenever I thought about it and wouldn't come out no matter what I tried.

It wasn't just the harassment that was getting to me either.

I loved that West had come straight to my house as soon as Eva had called him, and I loved that he'd taken care of me without a second thought. But the way he'd talked about my experience, like it was a one-off or bad luck, was still bugging me. He hadn't come out and said I should've made sure I'd gotten changed or anything, but it felt like those words were hanging unspoken between us.

I knew I needed to actually talk to him rather than stewing and chasing ghostly thoughts around my head, but finding the words to even ask the question felt like wading through wet cement. I was afraid once I'd opened that can of worms, things would never go back to the way they were. Because if West truly believed it was my fault, or that I was making a big deal about nothing, or that it happened to everyone, so I should put up and shut up and change myself to lower the chances, then I'd have to end what we had. And tear my own heart out in the process.

But there was no way I could be with someone who wanted me to change or give up who I was.

That was how hatred won.

We didn't really talk much as we got up and dressed, both of us seemingly lost in our own little worlds. I threw my stuff into my bag and slung it over my shoulder before we headed downstairs.

"Do you want some breakfast before you go?" West asked as we reached the bottom of the stairs. "Or a drink?"

I hesitated because I really needed to go home and shower before I started for the day, but my stomach was rumbling and my throat was achingly dry. "Yeah, a drink would be great, thanks. And maybe some toast? Or a cereal bar? Whatever you've got, really. I don't want to put you out."

West's forehead wrinkled, and then he smiled. "You're not putting me out. And I can definitely do you some toast.

I'm going to make scrambled eggs too and some smashed avocado. And a smoothie. Probably need a bit more protein too." He shook his head and muttered to himself. "Fuck it, I'll just stick some powder in the smoothie."

I smiled to myself, my chest warming. Sometimes I forgot he was a professional athlete and his diet consisted of more than energy drinks, sandwiches, sweets, and chocolate Hobnobs. I still hadn't been to one of his matches, and that was shitty of me because he'd been to three of my shows. I'd have to ask him if I could get some tickets and either drag Dad and Christopher along or some people from the club. I didn't know if any of them knew anything about rugby, but I figured either way we'd have a good time.

"What smoothie are you making?" I asked as I followed him towards the kitchen.

"I don't know, maybe peanut butter and banana. Why?"

"Can I have some too, please?"

West grinned at me, then leant down and kissed me. "Of course. I'll make you a proper breakfast too."

"Thanks." I kissed him again, wrapping one hand around the back of his neck and leisurely brushing my tongue across the seam of his mouth.

Someone coughed pointedly behind us. My face prickled as we broke apart and I saw two other men standing in the kitchen. One of them was Mason, who I vaguely knew because I'd seen him at The Court with West. He'd been at Fox & Taylor too, handing West napkins. The other was a man I didn't know, and all I could assume was it was one of West's other roommates.

There was a pinched expression on his face of barely concealed disapproval and I felt my face settle into the best resting bitch face I could manage at this time of day.

"Morning," West said nonchalantly, walking into the room and over to the fridge like he couldn't sense the icy chill emanating from his housemate.

"Morning, sunshine," Mason said with a grin, leaning against the counter with a giant mug in his hand. He watched West for a second, then turned to me and added, "Since Westley has forgotten his manners, I'm Mason and that's Guy." He gestured at the third man, who rolled his eyes and continued chopping the tomatoes on the board in front of him.

"Hi, I'm Rory."

"Nice to meet you," Mason said. "I've seen you perform a few times. You're amazing!"

"Thank you! And thanks for coming along."

"Of course. It's nice to do something different instead of kicking all their butts at *Call of Duty*."

Guy muttered something under his breath and Mason frowned but didn't respond. West had finished getting things out of the fridge but was now busy pulling things out of a nearby cupboard, including what could only be described as a bucket of peanut butter. I walked across to stand next to him and put my bag on the floor. West smiled when he saw me and it soothed some of the strange discomfort buzzing around in my chest.

"Do you need a hand?" I asked.

"Not at the moment," he said. "I'm just going to chuck a load of stuff in a blender first. Are you okay if I put protein powder and Greek yoghurt in the smoothie? Then I can make us one big one to share."

"Sounds good," I said. "It'll be better for me than my usual breakfast of crunchy nut and black coffee."

"You can still have the coffee." He glanced at Mason. "Can Rory have some of your coffee, please? I don't have any."

"Yeah," Mason said. "Knock yourself out." He picked up the kettle, which was on the counter beside him, and weighed it in his hand, clearly checking to see if there was enough water in it. He saw me watching as he put it down and flicked it on. "West said you're doing a drag story hour in a couple of weeks? I think I saw a few posts about it popping up."

"Yeah, there's a few of us doing them over December," I said. "There's two at the library and then a couple at various shops. Mine's up at The Lost World on the top of Steep Hill."

"They should be good," West said. "Have you sold many tickets?"

"I think so, but I'd have to check with Peaches." The tickets were fairly low cost, enough to cover a small fee for each of us, some of the venues, and a little bit of money for Legs for all the marketing and graphics. Any profit was being donated to a local LGBTQ+ youth charity. "I'm hoping we get a good turnout, though. Although…"

"What?" West asked, a look of concern flashing in his eyes.

"It's nothing." I shook my head. Now was not the time or place to bring up what Moxxie had put in the group chat yesterday. I'd been trying to ignore it, and I'd succeeded until now, when my brain had decided to wave the headline in front of my eyes in flashing neon lettering.

"Tell me, please." West's voice was quiet, almost pleading, as he put down the spoon he'd been holding.

"Apparently, there might be people planning protests for some of the events. Just because… I don't know. They think we're a danger to children or some bollocks." I sighed, hoping I could trick myself into thinking it was nothing. "It's stupid and it's probably nothing. I mean, there was that anti-trans protest organised earlier this year and I think about three people turned up, and the counter-protest was, like, several hundred."

"I remember," West said. The worry was clear on his face now, etched into it like someone had carved it there. "Do you think… you know, with everything that happened… do you think…"

I stared at him. "Are you seriously telling me I should step down?"

"No, I'm not. I just don't want you to get hurt."

"What are you asking then?"

"I… I don't know…" West looked back at the food in front of him, and I was suddenly painfully aware we were having this conversation in the middle of his kitchen. But now he'd started it, I wasn't going to let it end until he'd finally admitted what he truly thought.

"You must know or you wouldn't have said it."

West shook his head. "It's nothing. Forget it."

"No," I said. "I need you to tell me."

West opened his mouth, but before he could speak,

another voice spat, "Oh for fuck's sake, can you stop whining and shut up?"

The question was stinging and exasperated, thrown into the middle of our conversation like a hand grenade. We both turned to see Guy staring at us, his face contorted with irritation.

"Excuse me?" I asked. "Do you have a problem?"

"Yes," he said, glaring at me. "Yes, I have a bloody problem. You."

I pursed my lips, anger flaring in my chest like a volcano waiting to erupt. "Can I ask why? Considering we've never met each other before."

"You're such a fucking drama queen," he said coldly. "All of you."

"All of us?"

"Yeah, gay people. You're all such fucking drama queens. Like boo-fucking-hoo, people don't like me. Grow the fuck up, nobody cares! Maybe if you all weren't so fucking over the top and acted like normal people and didn't try and get everyone involved in your gay shit, then people would like you. Like, why the fuck do you need a drag story hour? What the fuck is that? Don't try and get the rest of us involved in your shit. It's just weird. Like, why the fuck do you want to dress up for kids? It's gross." He pointed the knife he was holding at West. "Why the fuck can't you all just be normal, like West? I mean, sure, he sucks dick but at least he doesn't flaunt it or throw it in our faces like the rest of you."

My mouth hung open in shock at the sheer stupidity and cruelty of his words. It was like Friday night and the online comments section all at once, and while my heart was racing with fear, my anger was stronger.

West and Mason were both stood there, looking just as shocked as me. But the fact that neither of them had said anything, hadn't tried to cut Guy off or come to my defence, spoke louder than anything. Especially from West.

He looked so helpless, like he was torn between saying something and keeping quiet.

But the time for keeping quiet had long since passed.

"Do you want me to apologise?" I asked. "Because I'm not going to. Queer people have always been here and we always will be, and it's because of assholes like you that we have to stand up and be counted. Nothing we do hurts you in any way. We just want to fucking exist. And if being normal means being like you, then I can't think of anything worse. So just fuck off to whatever hole you crawled out of and stay there. Because I may be a drama queen, but that still makes me a queen. And I'm going to fucking own that."

I turned and grabbed my bag off the floor, trying to stop myself from shaking. I levelled a look at West. "Thanks for defending me. I'll see myself out."

I walked towards the door, praying it was open, and luckily it was.

It was only when I got to my car and was alone that I allowed myself to let out a howl of despair.

CHAPTER TWENTY-FOUR

West

As soon as the door slammed shut behind Rory, it was like the world snapped back into focus, time catching up with itself in a painful split second that rammed a thousand knives into my heart.

"What the fuck was that?" I exploded, rounding on Guy, who looked so fucking smug I wanted to smack him. My hand balled into a fist around the spoon I'd been holding, and I felt the metal bend in my grip. "Seriously? What the hell?"

"I was just being honest," Guy said. "You know I've always said what I think, and if people don't like it when I tell the truth, then that's on them, not me."

"You're a fucking wanker and you know it." I stepped towards him, my fists clenched painfully tight. "You being 'honest' is not being honest at all. It's you being an inconsiderate twat who never learnt to hold his fucking tongue. Well, let me be honest with you." I grabbed the front of his shirt, not caring that he was still holding a knife. "You are a slimy weasel of a man and a shitty rugby player. And if you have to go around insulting other people to make yourself feel better, then you're going to end up sad and alone, which is what you deserve. And don't you ever, *ever* say that I'm normal. I'm nothing like you."

"Come on, you know what I mean… you're gay, but you're not, like f—"

"That's enough!" Mason snapped, his voice as clear as one of the booming cathedral bells. "West, put him down." I growled and then smirked when I realised I'd lifted Guy six inches off the floor. I lowered him slowly but didn't release him. "Guy," Mason continued. "You're a fucking dickhead and West's right."

"Trust you to side with him," Guy said. "You're probably a bit gay too."

"Oh, fuck off," I said. "Put a fucking sock in it for once in your fucking life. What the fuck does Mason's or Rory's or my sexuality have to do with you? Fuck all. Sod off with your bullshit. Yeah, I like sucking dick, and I like eating pussy. I'm bisexual, dipshit, and that has absolutely nothing to do with you."

Guy rolled his eyes and my fingers itched to wipe the expression off his face. "God, now you're being the dramatic one."

"No," I said. "For the first time, I'm being myself. And I'm going to stand up for my community because I've let people like you walk all over me for far too long." I let Guy go and the bent spoon I'd still been holding clattered to the floor. All my stuff was still on the side but I wasn't hungry.

I wanted to follow Rory out of the door, drive round Lincoln for hours until I found him wherever he was working and hope he'd talk to me. Because he and Theo had been right about everything, and I realised, more painfully than ever, that if I wanted to be with Rory, I had to stand alongside him and support him.

Blaming him, even unintentionally, or telling him to change, placing the onus on him rather than those who questioned his life, his job, his happiness, even his very existence, was never going to cut it. And doing that or, even worse, keeping silent, made me complicit.

It was more than that, though. For the first time in my life, I felt real anger and hurt at the way some of my teammates had treated me. Deep down, it felt like some of it might have been my fault for never pushing back despite Mason's and Theo's encouragement, but at the same time, I shouldn't have had to call them out on their shitty behaviour and ask them to treat me like a real person. There was a difference between banter and biphobia, and I'd been letting them skirt the wrong side of the line for too long.

I'd told myself several weeks ago I was going to start carving out a place for myself, but it was only now, when things had spilled over and affected someone I cared about, that I actually wanted to do something about it.

Enough was enough.

I knew I couldn't change things overnight, but without

taking steps forward, nothing would change at all. I had to start somewhere, and if that was just putting one foot in front of the other, then it would do for now.

"You should learn to let people live their own damn lives," I said, half to Guy and half getting the words out for the first time. "Joking about me getting laid, yeah, maybe that's okay. But joking about my sexual preferences or asking me questions about what I like, or even worse, cornering, questioning, and bullying my partners is fucking harassment. And I'm not going to take it lying down. For too long, I've kept quiet because I didn't want to be the one who makes a fuss. But now... I have to make a fucking fuss. Or people like you won't change." I looked at him. He seemed less sure of himself now, like he hadn't expected me to stand up for myself or argue back. "I'm not expecting you to change, but I am expecting you to act like less of a wanker. And... I will be mentioning this to Clive. Just so he knows to keep us apart. Because I still haven't decided if I'm going to punch you."

Mason made a soft, spluttering noise like he was trying to choke back laughter. When I looked at him, he was smiling and there was a new sense of pride there.

"I'm going to have breakfast at the club," I said, grabbing my car keys off the side. My training bag was already on the small kitchen table because I'd repacked it yesterday afternoon before Rory had arrived. "Leave my shit. I'll clean it up later."

I walked out of the house and took a deep breath of the freezing morning air. The sense of accomplishment I felt at finally standing up for myself was tainted by the knowledge it was very well too little, too late.

I couldn't see Rory now, but there was tonight. He'd be at The Court hosting their fortnightly karaoke night, and while I wasn't going to get up on the stage and sing, I could find him and apologise. On my knees if I had to. Because I didn't want to imagine what my life would look like without him.

The drive to the club's small training ground was short and the car park was only half-full. Grabbing my bag off the back seat, I headed for the door, aiming to dump my stuff in the changing room and head to the canteen for breakfast, but as soon as I stepped inside, I saw Clive waiting for me.

He was a shorter man in his mid-fifties, with thinning grey hair, a neatly trimmed grey beard, and a thick Australian accent. In his youth, he'd played for the Australian national team and had a reputation for being both lightning fast and a mouthy little shit. I remembered watching him play against England as a kid, where he'd run virtually the whole length of the pitch to score a try and nearly picked a fight with the entire England back row.

Age seemed to have mellowed him out, but he had no problem calling any of us out on our bullshit and there'd been a couple of times when he'd been warned for verbal altercations with opposition coaching staff. He was the best coach I'd ever had, and he and his team pushed me to become a better player every day. It made me hopeful that, one day, I might finally achieve my dream of an England call-up.

"Morning, mate," he said warmly. "Got a minute?"

"Sure," I said, slightly confused. "Is something wrong?"

"Nah, just wanted to chat about a couple of things. You're not in trouble." He beckoned me to follow him and as soon as I started walking, a thought popped into my mind.

"Did Mason message you? Or Guy?"

Clive smiled slightly. "Mason might've dropped Tommy and me a message, and I might've given him a quick call."

"That was fast," I muttered under my breath as we climbed the stairs to the first floor, turning left down a corridor of offices. I'd not been to this part of the building very much since the gym, canteen, changing rooms, physio and medical facilities, and training pitch were all downstairs. The Knights training facilities weren't the biggest or most glamorous, but they got the job done.

Clive opened the door to a small office that I assumed was his and ushered me inside. There was a desk in the middle of the room, two large windows on the far wall that overlooked the training pitch, and several IKEA Kallax units on the wall to the left, which were packed with books, awards, folders, and photos. There was even a cuddly toy kangaroo wedged into one.

He gestured for me to grab the seat in front of the desk, which had clearly been acquired with rugby players in mind since it was broad and padded. I didn't feel like I was going to break it the moment I sat down.

Clive didn't beat around the bush, because as soon as my butt hit the seat, he said, "Mason said you had a bust-up with Guy this morning. Want to tell me what happened?"

"He was rude to my boyfriend," I said. Clive knew I was bi, everyone at the club did, and they'd been supportive—at least to some extent. "Telling Rory that he's a drama queen because Rory doesn't want to be harassed in the street or have protesters turn up at the drag story hour he's doing. And he said Rory should be normal... like me. Because apparently me letting them all talk shit about my sexual preferences and calling it banter means I'm acceptable to them."

"Do they do that?" Clive asked sharply. He'd taken the seat behind the desk and was resting his hands on the surface, his eyes fixed on me.

"Yeah. Sometimes. It's not everyone and I know it's because they just... fuck, I'm doing it again." I shook my head. "Look, maybe it's because they don't know where the line between banter and harassment is, or maybe it's because they're dicks who want to make me react, but either way, I'm done with letting them talk to me like that. I'm sorry if that's going to cause problems."

"Fucking Christ, West," Clive said. "Why didn't you say anything?"

I shrugged. "I didn't want to be the problem. I've played long enough to know that nobody wants to work with the guy who can't take a joke. And you're fine with me being bisexual, so I didn't want to push my luck."

Clive muttered something under his breath as he pushed away from the desk and walked over to the Kallax unit, grabbing a photo out of one of the alcoves. He handed it to me and I looked at it carefully. It showed a young Clive, his grey hair thick and dark blond, his eyes glinting with mischief, and a wide smile on his face. He was shirtless and wearing a pair of salmon pink shorts, with bare feet and tanned skin and sitting on the shoulders of a tall, handsome man with long, dark curls and burnished dark skin. He was wearing a ripped Metallica T-shirt, denim shorts, and flip-flops, aviator sunglasses perched on his head, and his hands linked with Clive's.

It had clearly been taken in the summer because golden light surrounded them and the landscape around them looked dry and dusty. But I'd never seen two people looking so happy. Or in love.

"That was taken of Alan and me in… I wanna say ninety-two. A mate of mine took it when we were having a barbecue at theirs." He chuckled fondly. "I'd forgotten how long his hair was. He shaved it off as soon as he started going bald."

I stared at the photo, then up at Clive. "You're gay?"

"Bisexual," Clive said, taking his seat again. "Alan's gay. We kept it quiet for a long time 'cos I was playing and then coaching and then just because we'd not talked about it for so long we kept it that way. Felt odd, finally being able to tell people." He crossed one leg over the other, his chair twisting slightly as he looked out the window. "That's why I never said anything when you wanted to come out. I figured… I hoped it was different now. And it is, but it's also not. But that's on me. You should've always known you had someone in your corner, and I should've been better at stamping this shit out from the start."

"It's fine," I said, still looking at the picture. Clive's smile reminded me of Rory's. It made me want to take a picture with him that I'd still be looking at fondly in thirty-odd years' time.

"It's bloody not. I'm sorry, West, I should've been more open with you and laid down some more rules. Because you're right, a lot of them don't know when they go too far. Or they do, and nobody calls them on their shit."

"Mason does," I said. "He's been encouraging me to do the same."

"Smart man."

"Do I need to apologise to Guy?"

"Sounds like he needs to apologise to you," Clive said. "And if you want me to look at the housing situation, I can."

"Maybe," I said. "Mason and I get on well, and Jonny's a good guy. I don't even know where he was this morning…" I frowned. I hadn't seen Jonny or heard a peep from him.

"He's in the canteen," Clive said with a wry smile. "Muttered something about people and their partners not respecting his sleep."

I felt my face flush. "I'll apologise to him. Maybe get him some earplugs."

Clive laughed then swung back to the desk. "I'll have a word with Guy and the boys in general. Maybe even the board. It's about time we start putting our money where our mouth is when it comes to inclusion."

"We're not playing on the ninth of December, are we?" I

asked, a new idea percolating in my mind like gathering clouds.

"No, it's a break week."

"I have an idea… optional obviously, but I could do with a hand…"

CHAPTER TWENTY-FIVE

Bubblegum Galaxy

I FINALLY EMERGED from my room about four that afternoon, having sacked off work and instead spent the whole day lying on my bed with a sharing bag of sweet chilli crisps, two sharing bags of chocolate buttons, and a packet of Hobnobs, catching up on the new season of *Drag Stars Legends* and rewatching my favourite older episodes.

Basically, doing everything in my power to forget about the shitshow that was today. And my relationship.

And my life in general.

It worked for a while, but eventually I realised I needed a drink and a shower because I was supposed to be working at The Court later and I couldn't show up still smelling like morning sex, sweat, and despair.

I slouched downstairs, ninety percent sure I was home alone, but then I heard the TV and Dad's quiet voice as he chatted to Beans. It was unusual for him to be home at this time of day, and I wondered if something was wrong.

"That you, Roo?" he called as my feet hit the bottom stair, which always squeaked. Not that I'd been trying to be quiet. I'd been stomping around like a herd of salty elephants since I'd dragged myself out of bed.

"Yeah."

"You feeling all right? How's your head?"

"Better." I'd lied to Dad and Christopher this morning and told them I couldn't work because I had a shit headache. Since I very rarely took sick days, neither of them had questioned it, but I didn't know if they actually believed me. "You okay? Didn't think you'd be home yet."

I stuck my head around the sitting room door and my heart caught in my throat.

Dad was sitting in his chair watching an old episode of *The Repair Shop* with his glasses perched on the end of his nose. In his lap was the bodice of my story hour dress, which Mum and I were still constructing, in his hand was a needle and thread, and on the arm of the chair next to a very interested Beans was a small plastic dish filled with sequins and rhinestones.

"Wanted to make sure you were okay," Dad said, pausing the TV and looking up at me. "And your mum's on lates at the hospital, so I thought I'd make dinner. Sausage and mash alright? Are you still going to work?"

"Yeah… yeah, that's great."

He lowered the needle and peered at me over his glasses. "You sure you're all right, Roo? You don't look well."

"Just been a shit day."

"Come sit down," Dad said. "I'd make you a cuppa tea, but I don't trust Beans not to eat the sequins as soon as I get up."

"I can make one."

"Are you sure?"

"Yeah," I said with a nod. "I think I need one. Do you want one too?"

"Please, mate." Beans chirruped beside him, waving her front paw in the air as she tried to get Dad's attention. He chuckled and gently tickled her under the chin with his free hand. "No, you don't get one. It's too late for you to have caffeine."

I smiled to myself as I turned and walked out to the kitchen, quickly flicking the kettle on and grabbing two mugs out. Sausage stirred from his nest on the windowsill and purred quietly when I rubbed his ears.

At least I could rely on the cats to always be there for me.

When I took the tea back to the sitting room, Dad was sewing again and Beans was lying across the back of the armchair like a fluffy cushion.

"Cheers," Dad said as I put the mug down on the small table next to his chair, twisting it so the handle was in easy reach. I sat on the end of the sofa, curling my legs up next to me, watching as Dad carefully put the needle into the sequin dish and slid it onto the table before putting my dress over the arm of the chair. "You want to tell me what's going on?"

"Not really," I said. Sharing would probably have made

me feel better, or at least lifted some of the weight off my chest, but I didn't know where to begin or if Dad would understand. Instead, I asked the question I was desperate to. "Why are you sequinning my dress?"

"Your mum's on lates all week and you know how tired she gets, so I thought I'd give her a hand since it ain't long to go until the big day. Don't worry, she gave me very strict instructions. I won't get it wrong."

My chest ached and I wished I was close enough to give him a hug. "Thank you. You're the best."

"I know." He winked at me. "Just remember that when I'm old and you're choosing my nursing home."

"I will." I sipped my tea again, the warmth rolling through me. "Although I could've done it."

"You're busy," Dad said, picking up his own mug. "We're very proud of you, Roo-Bear, and I hope you know that."

"I do."

"Good, because it's the truth. I've always been proud of you and everything you do."

"Thanks," I said, trying to ignore the lump in my throat. It wasn't the first time I'd heard Dad say that, but with everything that had happened, I needed to hear it more than ever.

"Roo, what happened?" Dad asked and I knew he'd heard my voice wobble. "I can't help if you don't tell me."

"It's nothing. I'm just being silly."

"Doesn't sound like nothing. And if it's making you upset, it's definitely not nothing."

"It's just stuff with West… something his roommate

said, and there was a post Moxxie shared yesterday about people maybe protesting the story hours and I'm… I'm exhausted and I'm sad and I'm just done. I'm so done."

"What did they say? This roommate."

I sighed and shuffled in my seat. "That I'm a drama queen. And if I don't want people to harass me or protest my job… if I want them to take me seriously, then I should just be normal. You know, not visibly gay. I shouldn't do anything remotely gay in public because then people would like me, or at least would ignore me, and I should stop shoving being queer in people's faces by existing as myself and be like all the straight men who hate me. And themselves. Because God forbid I make anyone feel vaguely insecure and threatened. I mean, if anyone attacks me, that's my own bloody fault."

"Who is this man?" Dad asked darkly, and I giggled. It was impossible to think of him as scary or intimidating when he had tiny glasses perched on his nose with a gold chain looped onto each arm of the glasses and around his neck so he didn't lose them. "Don't laugh. I just want to have a word with him. Let him know the error of his ways."

"You can't do that," I said. "For one, he's a professional rugby player."

"I don't see what that has to do with anything."

"And two, Mum would kill you if she thought you were picking fights."

"Hmm, you might be right there," Dad said, grumbling under his breath. "But that still doesn't mean he should get away with saying shit."

"I know. And I told him that."

"Good." Dad nodded and took a satisfied slurp of his tea. "What about West? What did he say?"

"Bugger all," I said. "And that's the part that hurts the most. He just stood there and did nothing. I don't know if he was too shocked, if he didn't know what to do, but either way—"

"Either way he stood there and let his roommate hurl abuse at you," Dad said pointedly. "Maybe it's him I need to have a word with."

"Don't worry. I'm sure he won't be back." I sighed again and took a swig of my tea, hoping the heat would somehow dispel the horribly tight lump in my chest. I didn't want my relationship with West to be over, but I'd not heard from him since and I wasn't sure I could trust him. I knew he'd probably never expected that to happen, and I wasn't saying I wanted a knight in shining armour to jump in and protect me. But standing up for me would have been nice.

"Do you want him to come back? If he apologised."

"Yes," I said quietly, looking down at the carpet. "Is that bad?"

"No," Dad said. "It's not. It's okay to want to give people a second chance, but it's not okay to let people walk all over you and take advantage of you. Relationships are tricky, even the right ones. Your mum and I have had our fair share of arguments over the years, big and small, but we've always worked through them 'cos we love each other and even on the days we're driving each other crackers, we want to be here."

He paused for a second and when I glanced across at him, he was deep in thought. "I did a lot of learning those first few years with your mum. About myself mostly, but also about other people. I didn't like all of it—I mean, a lot of people are bastards—but I also realised most people aren't malicious. They just don't get it. And I'm not saying it's your job to teach people. It's on the other person to learn shit themselves, but it sounds like West's suddenly realising that a lot of gay men's experiences are different from his. And he's gotta choose whether to play ostrich and bury his head in the sand or start figuring out what he wants to do. And… I don't know about his life, but there's probably experiences he's had that you haven't. That doesn't excuse it, but maybe you'll have to learn something too.

"You've always been out and proud, Roo, and I love that you've been able to do that, 'cos I knew a lot of men that couldn't be and I saw plenty of men die needlessly because the government would do fuck all to help them," he continued. "But West… he's a sportsman. That comes with baggage, and maybe he's never had your experiences because he's had to force himself to conform. It's one thing to be out; it's another to be accepted, you know that. And maybe… maybe the poor bloke's had to put up with a lot in the hope people will accept him. And you can say he should've said something until you're blue in the face, but you and I both know it ain't that easy. So, I'm not saying he's right, and I'm not saying you're wrong. I'm saying you're two men from different places and maybe you need to meet each other somewhere in the middle. There isn't a map for this shit, so nobody can help you but you, but sometimes life ain't about the destination. It's about how you get there. Do you understand?"

I'd never heard Dad speak so eloquently or so in depth about relationships and queerness, and it caught me off guard. But in a good way. He was right—West and I had different experiences, and I had no idea what being an out sportsman was like. We'd both spent our lives existing in separate bubbles, shaped by the lives we'd lived inside them.

Neither of our experiences was wrong, but neither was right either. Being queer wasn't a monolith and no queer person had the same experiences as another. And while sometimes we wanted and wished our experiences and opinions were the only ones, or the right ones, the world didn't work like that.

And yeah, there were still some opinions that, to me, would always be wrong—like the way some queer people tried to cosy up to right-wingers in the hope they wouldn't be targeted, when everyone knew it didn't work that way—but in a situation like this, where West and I were approaching it from our own experiences, I didn't think there was a right answer.

There was just the one we could come to together.

All I could do was hope the answer was one we were both happy with.

"Yeah," I said. "I understand. My experiences are mine, and his are his. And I can't apply my life to his, even if I want to. I mean, I've always had a supportive family around me who want me to succeed as me. But West... his family are different." I pursed my lips, wondering if I should tell Dad any of what West had told me. "His parents don't speak to him now because he's bi. He has a brother, though, Theo, and he sounds pretty awesome. They've only reconnected recently, though, so I think they're still figuring out the whole brotherly relationship thing."

"I'll never understand that," Dad said with a clucking noise of disapproval. "How people can throw their own kids away when they're not who they want them to be. Breaks my fucking heart." He shook his head, then slapped his knee with one hand. "Right, come on, you need food before you go out and your brother'll be back soon and he'll want feeding too. And then I need to get more of this dress done before I fall asleep."

"You know, Christopher is an adult. He can feed himself," I said, climbing off the sofa and stretching.

"I know, but watching him cook is like watching a hurricane go through the kitchen, and I'm not inflicting that on myself." Dad stood and put his arm out, pulling me into a hug and kissing my cheek. "Try not to worry too much tonight, Roo. Wait until tomorrow, then see if he wants to talk. I'm not giving up on him just yet."

CHAPTER TWENTY-SIX

Bubblegum Galaxy

Trying to draw eyebrows on while feeling like complete and utter shit was the single most annoying and frustrating moment of my day. The left one was passable, at least from a distance, but the right one could get fucked.

"Christ on a fucking bicycle," I muttered, grabbing a make-up wipe to scrub my eyebrow off and start again. This would be attempt number five and each one was getting worse, probably due to my own damn frustration.

"You okay, hun?" Moxxie asked from beside me. They were hosting tonight's karaoke with me and were already dressed up to the nines and ready to go. "Need a hand?"

"It's these fucking eyebrows. They won't behave."

"Want me to try?"

"Sure," I said, turning to face them and handing them the eyebrow pencil I used to sketch them in. Moxxie's attempt couldn't be any worse than mine. "Knock yourself out."

Moxxie steered me gently into a nearby chair and tilted my face up. Their nose wrinkled as they held my chin steady, examining my face like they were about to start a surgical procedure. I didn't know what Moxxie did outside of drag, but I was ninety-nine point nine percent sure they had no medical training.

"You want to tell me what's going on?" Moxxie asked as they slowly began to sweep the pencil across my skin.

"It's nothing."

"Nothing? Honey, I've seen you draw your eyebrows on using a compact mirror and your phone torch and they were perfect. Something is bothering you today. And you don't have to tell me if you don't want, but I'm here if you need me."

"Thanks," I said, a slight smile tugging at the corner of my mouth. "I remember that performance—where we had no mirrors or lighting. God, that was a shitshow." It'd been at some holiday club near Skegness during October half-term. A few of us had been booked to do a cabaret night, only when we'd turned up, the dressing rooms had been given to a group of kids' performers in giant costumes, so we'd had to get ready on the side of the stage using whatever shit we had on us. At the time it had been a nightmare, but hindsight made it funny.

And at least it'd taught me I could do passable make-up in virtually any circumstance.

Except, it seemed, dealing with an aching heart and

bone-deep anxiety that made me feel like my body was humming.

"Not as bad as the pub quiz Eva and I did where only three people showed up," Moxxie said. "That was just sad."

"Yeah, I think that might be worse. At least the holiday club had an audience, even if it was all drunk grannies."

"Hey, they gave it their all when it came to the singalong. I've never heard such a pitch-perfect rendition of 'Yellow Submarine'." I snorted and Moxxie gently squeezed my head, their tongue poking out between their teeth. "Keep still or you'll have wonky eyebrows again."

"Can't be any worse than my attempts."

"True. Yours made you look permanently shocked." They leant back for a moment to admire their handiwork and nodded. "Have you got any pomade?"

"Yeah, on the counter. There's a little pot of it somewhere, and a brush." I gestured vaguely and Moxxie shook their head as they went rummaging. They were just starting to fill my new brows in when there was a knock at the door.

"Yeah?" Moxxie called. "What's up? You can come in. I'm just doing Bubbles's eyebrows."

The door creaked open, and Moxxie and I turned to see the bright green head of Pierce poking through the gap. Moxxie grinned, a tiny flush covering their cheeks under their make-up. "Everything okay? I didn't think we were starting until half past?"

"You're not," Pierce said. "Bubblegum's got a visitor again."

"Oh?" Moxxie winked at me. "Has he brought more flowers? I heard last time he brought you roses."

"Mmm, he did," I said with a quiet hum. I felt Moxxie's eyes boring into me, undoubtedly putting two and two together from my inability to do my eyebrows and my less than enthusiastic response to West's arrival.

"Not telling," Pierce said. "But he seems a bit... I dunno, anxious? Want me to tell him to sod off?"

"No." I shook my head. It would be easier to get this over with now. "He can come up."

Pierce nodded and disappeared, the door squeaking shut behind him. The buzzing anxiety in my chest dialled itself up, almost making my teeth chatter and vibrate. I glanced at myself in the mirror, realising how unprepared I looked. My make-up wasn't done, my wig was still on the stand, and I was only half-dressed. For once, my insides totally matched my outsides and it made everything a million times worse.

But there wasn't time to change anything, so it would have to do.

"Want me to make myself scarce?" Moxxie asked. "I can finish getting ready downstairs."

"Would you mind? I don't want to kick you out."

"You're fine. Just let me finish your eyebrows first. You've got one and a half at the moment."

I chuckled then squeaked as Moxxie pounced, finishing my eyebrows with a swoop and a flick. And when I looked in the mirror, I realised they were better than mine on my good days. Maybe I'd have to get Moxxie to do them more often...

Moxxie slid the tiny tub of pomade back onto the counter, scooping the last of their stuff into their arms and grabbing their hat off a rack by the door. In true Moxxie Toxxic style, they had a midnight blue cowboy hat studded with rhinestones to match the rest of their fringed and bejewelled denim shirt and jeans. *Ryan Gosling, eat your heart out.*

My heart was thundering in my chest, doing its best impression of an EDM bass line, and my stomach churned like I'd decided to eat two greasy kebabs with a side of garlic cheesy chips. I didn't know what I was going to say or even where to start. I wasn't even sure I'd be able to construct a sentence without tripping over my own tongue.

"Can you grab the door please, hun?" Moxxie asked, looking over their shoulder at me.

"Sure." I pulled myself out of my chair and crossed the distance to the door. I was barely looking as I opened it, too busy thinking about what I'd say to West, but stood right outside, with his hand raised to knock, was the man I hadn't stopped thinking about since I'd left his house.

"West," I said, somehow shocked even though I'd known he was on his way up.

"Hey," he said. "I wondered… can I… can we?"

"Yeah… yeah, come in." I stepped back and Moxxie slid past me, smiling knowingly at the pair of us. They were now wearing their hat, which they tipped in our direction.

"I'll leave you two lovebirds to it," they said. "Just remember, Bubbles, you need to be downstairs and ready to start by half eight. And for every minute you're late, I'll roast you mercilessly to the audience."

"Got it," I said, grabbing West's hoodie to pull him inside. "Half eight or roasted to death."

"Good. And Bubbles? Don't smudge your eyebrows. I worked hard on those."

"Bye, Moxxie," I said dryly as I pushed the door closed behind them, shutting out the sound of their laughter. I turned and saw West staring at me quizzically from the middle of the dressing room.

"Eyebrows?"

"Yeah, Moxxie had to draw mine on tonight. It's a long story." I waved my hand vaguely dismissively. Silence hung in the air between us, heavy and oppressive like summer air when you knew a thunderstorm was on the horizon.

"Rory…" West took a step towards me, blue eyes brimming with emotion. "I'm so… I'm so fucking sorry. I should never have let Guy say those things. I should've stood up for you."

"Why didn't you?" It was my turn to take a step forward now, slowly closing the gap between us.

"I don't know," he said quietly. "And I know that sounds awful, but I don't. I wish I had. After you left I…" He shook his head. "It doesn't matter what I did afterwards. I didn't do it while you were there, and that's what matters."

"What did you do?"

West took another small step, the gap between us reduced to a couple feet. I could've reached out and touched him. A wry smile pulled at the corner of his mouth as he spoke. "I might've lifted him off the floor and told him to get fucked. And a few other choice things. I can't remember all of it. But I wanted him to know he can't treat you like that. Or me. Or anyone, for that matter. And I told him I won't let him or anyone else from the team walk all over me anymore. Because the reason they think I'm normal is because I've allowed them to push me around and make jokes about me… because I didn't want to be difficult."

"That's not being difficult," I said, closing the gap and reaching up to cradle his jaw. Two days of stubble prickled my skin and I thought it suited him. "That's just basic respect."

"I know," he said. "At least, I do now." He leant into my touch, his eyes soft and warm. "This isn't about me, though. Not about that part of me anyway. I'm here to apologise for everything, not just this morning but all the things I've said, or not said, lately. Like not believing your experiences, or suggesting you should step back from the story hour, or for saying you should be anyone but yourself. I don't want you to change, Rory, because you're the most amazing person I've ever met. I want you to always be yourself, sparkles and all. Fuck everyone else."

I smiled, tilting my head forward to brush my lips over his. I wanted to be angry with him, and maybe I was a little, but we were both fumbling our way through this from different angles, trying to apply our experiences and shoving things together to see if they fit. But the thing I wanted most of all was West. "Fuck everyone else," I whispered, my words ghosting over his lips. "And I'm sorry too."

"For what?"

"Expecting you to read my mind and know what I needed from you."

"You don't need to apologise for that," West said, resting his wide hand on my waist, holding me close to him. "I'm your boyfriend. I'm supposed to support you."

"I'm supposed to support you too," I said. "It's not a one-way street."

West huffed out a laugh. "Stop trying to one-up me and let me apologise."

"I am, but I'm apologising too."

"Nope."

"But I'm a drama queen, remember? I have to make everything about me." I snorted and winked at him. West rolled his eyes fondly before kissing me soundly and stealing the breath from my lungs.

"You're not a drama queen," West said. "Guy's just a dick."

"Oh, I don't know. I kind of like it. Bubblegum Galaxy: Drama Queen—it's got a nice ring to it. I should get it on a T-shirt."

"I'll get you one for Christmas," West said, kissing me again. "Can you forgive me, Rory? I promise I'll do better. I don't want to lose you, and I'll do whatever it takes for you to forgive me."

"You're not going to lose me," I said. "Not over this. If anything, I thought I was going to lose you."

West frowned. "Why? That doesn't make any sense."

"Because I'm dramatic, and bossy, and I won't take any shit," I said, shrugging one shoulder casually. "I have a job people hate me for, for no reason other than their own bigotry, and I refuse to back down. And I wear a lot of glitter, which you'll never, ever be free from because it gets everywhere."

West's expression melted and he pulled me closer. "Those things you just listed? They're the reason I want you. Yeah, I might get worried sometimes, but I promise I'll be there to support you. And I'm big and ugly enough that I can take a few punches. It can't be any worse than getting flattened by some bastard weighing twenty-two stone and built like a tank."

"I can't imagine anyone flattening you."

"You'll have to come and watch one day."

"I will," I said. "But you'll have to explain the rules. Although… if you're running around wearing tiny shorts that ride up your thighs, I don't think it'll matter. I'm not sure I'll be paying attention to anything else."

CHAPTER TWENTY-SEVEN

West

I HELD RORY CLOSE, the heat from his body radiating through me. I hadn't expected our conversation to be as straightforward as it had been and there was a nagging feeling in my stomach it couldn't be that easy. Although I wasn't sure easy was the right word for it.

We'd both struggled, misstepped, and forgotten to communicate, automatically expecting things of the other without telling them what we were thinking.

But the thing that mattered most was our willingness to forgive, to move on, and to not hold it against each other in some invisible grudge match that we'd throw in each other's face whenever we were pissed.

I didn't have enough experience with long-term relationships to know what the path ahead would look like for us, but all I could do was keep holding Rory's hand while we put one foot in front of the other. We might not have a map, but we had each other, and I hoped that would be enough.

Rory looked up at me, bright eyes dancing with playfulness. He was mostly made-up for the night, with his hair pushed back by a wide hairband. He wasn't fully dressed, wearing a loose tank top that I could feel something underneath, probably his waist shaper, and what looked like several pairs of pants and some sparkling nude tights.

The only time I'd seen him like this was the night he'd been harassed and I'd helped him undress in his room, but I hadn't really paid much attention to what he'd been wearing. I'd been too focused on getting him out of it and into something more comfortable.

"What are you thinking?" I asked, letting my hand slide further around his body to rest on his ass, which felt slightly more padded than usual.

"Not much," he said, too sweetly for it to be the truth. "Mostly about you in shorts."

"Maybe if you ask nicely, I'll put them on for you later."

"Mmm, that is tempting." He kissed me deeply. "But I do want to see you play, though. You've been to my shows, so I need to come to your matches."

"You don't have to," I said. "Not if it's not your sort of thing."

"Firstly, I'm coming whether you like it or not because I'm your boyfriend and I want to support you." Another kiss and a wicked smile. "Secondly, contrary to popular opinion, I actually know a bit about sport. Mostly because Dad and Christopher are football mad, but I can tell you the basics. I even know the offside rule."

"Impressive."

"I know. And I know rugby is basically lots of large men grappling each other, which sounds pretty fun, not going to lie."

"Apart from when they steamroller you or tackle you to the floor with the force of a truck."

"True, I prefer sexy tackling," Rory said, pressing close against me, one hand sliding around the back of my neck and one thumbing the waistband of my jeans. "I know how the scoring works, though—five for a try, seven if it's converted, three for a penalty or a drop kick."

"Very impressive," I said, grinning as Rory's fingers popped the button on my jeans.

"I'm a very impressive person." He kissed me, swallowing my groan as his hand dipped into my underwear, teasing the base of my cock.

"Don't you have to be on stage soon?" I asked. There was a clock on the wall above the door that read five past eight. Moxxie had said something about being downstairs at some point and something about Rory's eyebrows, but I couldn't remember what it was.

"Yeah, at some point."

"What time?"

"Half past."

"Don't you… fuck!" I gasped as Rory wrapped his fingers around my shaft, squeezing it in his grip. "Don't you have to finish getting ready?"

"Mmm, that won't take me long," he said as he pressed his mouth against mine.

"And what about… your make-up? I don't want to smudge it."

Rory paused and quirked an eyebrow at me. "You know, most men wouldn't be so considerate when their boyfriend has his hand on their cock."

"I know, but I'm not most men. And I'm also not going to be the reason you're late and half-dressed with smudged make-up."

"Would it take you that long to come?"

"Probably not," I said with a laugh, gently reaching down to ease his hand out of my jeans. I mourned the loss and hated being the sensible one here. But that didn't mean we had to totally stop. I slipped Rory's hand in mine and led him towards the make-up counter with the mirror running across the top of it. "But you need to get ready."

"What are you going to do?" Rory asked, watching as I sank to my knees in front of him, scooting backwards so I was partially under the counter. I put my hand on his thigh and drew him closer.

"I'm going to help you de-stress." I reached for the waistband of his underwear but Rory put his hand on mine, stopping me.

"Let me lock the door first," he said, stepping back and darting across the room. "And then I'll take these off and rescue my dick. It's shoved so far back between my legs it's basically inside me."

"That sounds… painful."

"It could be worse. I used to tape it in place—I still do occasionally if I need a really tight, smooth tuck—and that's a bitch to get off, especially if your pubes get stuck in it.

These days I mostly wear several pairs of the tightest underwear I can find under my tights, sometimes with a pair of tucking panties if there's a chance I'll accidentally flash my crotch. Honestly, the things I do to look pretty."

"You do look gorgeous," I said as Rory reappeared in front of me, quickly shoving down his underwear and untucking his cock. "Whatever you're wearing."

"Thanks," he said. Any further words were stifled by a gasped exhale as I ran my hands up his thighs and grasped his soft cock, pumping it slowly.

"Don't forget to finish your make-up, sweetheart."

"It's… shit, it might be a little hard to concentrate."

"I can stop if you want," I said, releasing his cock and watching it quiver in the cool air, a drop of precum clinging to the slit.

Rory thrust his hips forward, chasing my touch. "Don't you fucking dare. I can't fucking tuck like this."

I couldn't have that. Teasing Rory was fun, but I didn't want to make his life miserable. And tucking sounded painful anyway, so doing it with an erection sounded like literal torture. I wrapped my hand around his shaft again, leaning forward to lick up his precum and suck his cockhead into my mouth.

Rory groaned, his hands slamming down on the counter above me. I grinned around his cock, sliding him deeper and letting saliva dribble out of the corner of my mouth to slick the movement of my hand at the bottom of his shaft.

My mouth and hand worked in tandem, pumping and sucking his cock. This wasn't the time to go slow and leisurely take him apart; speed and efficiency was the name of the game here, especially since Rory had to be on stage in about twenty minutes.

"Fuck," Rory said, his thigh trembling under my other hand. "Oh shit... West... I'm so close."

I hummed around him, sliding my hand to the back of his thigh and gently pressing it, encouraging him to fuck my face. Rory thrust forward and at the edges of my vision I could see his fingers curled around the countertop, gripping tightly as he chased his pleasure.

My lips and fingers squeezed around him, creating a perfect tunnel for him to fuck.

Rory whined desperately as he thrust into me and the sound sent ripples of delight running through me. He always made the sweetest noises when he was enjoying himself.

"West," Rory said. "I'm gonna... I'm gonna cum!" He let out a strangled cry, his cock pulsing as he filled my mouth with his cum, the salty liquid coating my tongue and running down my throat. I swallowed as much as I could, trying not to let it escape out the sides of my mouth.

Rory's thighs were still shaking and I ran my fingers up and down the back of one, the muscles trembling under my touch. It amazed me I could do that—bring someone so much pleasure so quickly. It was a heady feeling, almost as good as my own orgasms.

"Shit! Oh shit," Rory said, suddenly jumping to life and laughing wildly, grabbing his tights and underwear and starting to haul them up. "I've gotta be on stage in fifteen minutes!"

"Shit!" I tried to dart out from under the counter and

yelped as the top of my head connected with the edge. I folded over, rubbing my head and waving away Rory when he tried to help. "Ignore me. I'll live! Finish getting ready."

"Are you sure?"

"Yeah." I lifted my hand to check I wasn't bleeding. "I'll live."

"Good," Rory said. He was peering in the mirror, drawing his lips on with a bright pink pencil. "Can you grab my shoes? The pink glittery ones. You'll need to help me zip my dress up too."

"Whatever you need," I said, grabbing the shoes he'd pointed out. The buckles on the ankle straps were still fastened, so I undid them as quickly as I could. They were fiddly as fuck and I growled at least once.

Rory had just about finished his make-up. He'd thrown his breast plate on and was now putting a wig cap on. Then he grabbed a blonde wig with the hair in gentle curls, some of the ends dyed soft pink, and carefully slid it on, applying something around the edge that I assumed would help it stay in place. He fiddled with some of the loose strands, curling them around his fingers and using them to frame his face.

I didn't disturb him. Instead I stood to one side wishing there was more I could do to help. But I knew if I tried, I'd just get in the way and make a nuisance of myself.

Rory, who was now virtually all Bubblegum, picked up a sparkling pink dress that reminded me of something I'd seen pop stars wearing. Or Barbie. It definitely had Margot Robbie vibes. Mason and I had gone to see *Barbie* in the summer and loved every second of it. It was the reason that Mason had worn Lycra for Halloween.

"Can you zip me up, please?" Bubblegum asked, turning away from me and moving her wig out of the way. "And can you bring my shoes downstairs? I can't walk fast in them and I need to be down there in two minutes."

"I've got you," I said, zipping up the dress before folding to my knees and tapping her foot. "Lift your foot. We'll put your shoes on here and I'll carry you."

"You can't—"

"Yes, I can." I smiled up at Bubblegum, my beautiful Barbie-esque drag princess. "Now, give me your foot."

Bubblegum dutifully lifted one foot and I slid it into her shoe like my very own Cinderella. The buckles were easier to do up than undo, and less than a minute later, her shoes were securely on. I stood and strode across to the door, unlocking it and throwing it open. Then I turned and held out my arms.

"Ready, princess?"

Bubblegum rolled her eyes and grinned. "Call me that again and I'll kick you."

"Really?" I asked as I scooped her up bridal style, careful not to catch her wig. "You don't like it?"

"I'm a queen, remember?"

I laughed as I carried her to the door and into the corridor. "Apologies, Your Majesty. You can have me sent to the tower later."

"Nah," she said, trying not to giggle as I carried her down the stairs. "I'd rather have you taken to my chambers later, see what other tricks you've got up your sleeve."

Moxxie was waiting for us at the bottom, an amused expression of disbelief on their face. "Where's my hunky man to carry me everywhere?"

"Tough luck, Moxxie, this one is mine," Bubblegum said as I slowly lowered her to the ground and helped her stand. She smiled and pressed a kiss to my cheek that I knew would leave a distinct print. "And I'm keeping him."

CHAPTER TWENTY-EIGHT

Bubblegum Galaxy

"Do you need me to put anything else in your bag?" West asked, inspecting the contents of the pink bag resting on my bed. Technically, it was a dance bag that I'd bought from an online pole dance shop, but it was the perfect size for drag accessories, especially because it was sturdy enough to hold a pair of shoes.

"Remind me what I already packed?" I asked, turning back to my dressing table and resuming sticking gemstones to my face. We had thirty minutes before we had to leave to get to The Lost World for the story hour, which started at eleven. I wanted to get there by half ten at the latest so I had time to check all the set-up and pace nervously up and down. Plus, I was hoping *if* there were protesters, I could slip around them.

Although with both West and Mason coming to escort

me, I doubted anyone would be able to see me behind the wall of muscle.

"Water bottle, two books—*The Great Dragon Bake Off* and *All I Want For Christmas*—snacks including a bag of Haribo, some mini pretzels, and a large bar of Dairy Milk, shoes—I've put your trainers in, but did you want to wear them up or are you going to wear your boots?"

"I'll wear my boots," I said as I tried not to poke myself in the eye with tweezers. "The heel's not very big and hopefully the ice from this morning will have melted. Plus then I don't have to worry about changing them beforehand."

"Cool, sounds good. I'll leave your trainers in for after. I've also got plasters, paracetamol, tissues, travel sewing kit, and your mini make-up bag with your eyelash glue, spare gems, a mirror, and you can put that lipstick in before we leave so you've got a spare. Plus I've got the little business cards Legs did you and the thank-you card for Jay. Oh, and a phone charger. Did I miss anything?"

"No, I think you've got everything. You pack more than I do."

West chuckled and I heard him zip up the bag. "It's called being prepared. You never know when you'll need something."

"I bet you're the one who plans everything when you go on holiday, takes everyone's passports, insists you get there three hours early, and frogmarches everyone through security. You probably have a whistle too."

"If you mean I make sure we actually get to the airport, make it to our plane, and have a holiday to go on in the first place, then yes, I do." He walked over and pressed a kiss to the top of my head. "And I make sure everyone packs sun cream too, mostly because I'm not spending another holiday with someone whining about turning into a lobster on day one."

"Was that you?"

"No, Jonny. He said he'd be fine without it then turned into a crisp in two hours. And he was a bloody pain in the ass for the rest of the week."

I smiled, trying to picture West's reaction. He could be a bit of a mother hen, but I imagined it came with a heavy amount of exasperation and side-eye. But the thought of West stretched out on a sun lounger in nothing but a tiny pair of swimming trunks, body glistening in the summer sunshine while he sipped cocktails, or pulling himself out of a pool while water cascaded down his arms, drops of it clinging to his chest hair, was enough to give me heart palpitations.

Was it too early to consider planning a holiday together? We hadn't exactly been together long, but now that December was here and winter was setting in, the idea of sunshine and sand and holiday sex called to me. And I didn't think West would object to seeing me wander round in a teeny pair of shorts all day.

He could even help me put sun cream on.

"How long have I got left?" I asked, forcing myself to focus again. My make-up was virtually finished except for my lashes, which I always did last. Then I just needed to get dressed and put my wig and shoes on. Nerves bubbled in my stomach, casually threatening to resummon the large breakfast Mum had forced down me.

"Twenty-five minutes," West said, kissing the top of my head again. "Plenty of time."

"Cool, cool, okay."

"It's going to be great, I promise."

"I know. It's just… performance nerves," I said with a breathless laugh, shaking out my hands before they started trembling. "I've never done anything like this before. What if I'm really shit? What if I throw something at one of the kids? Or swear!"

"First of all, there's not going to be any jugs of Sex on the Beach around, so I think we're safe from flying cocktails," West said with a wry smile. He rested his hands on my shoulders and rubbed the bare skin, squeezing all the tension out of my muscles.

"You're never going to let me forget that, are you?"

"Nope, but your concern was touching and I'll always remember how beautiful you looked."

"Flatterer." I grinned. "You have to mention those bits too, otherwise people will think I targeted you or something."

West chuckled. "Okay, I will." He squeezed my shoulders again, the firmness of his grip grounding me. "And secondly, you're going to be amazing. You've practised this and you're a natural performer. Once you get out there, I don't think you'll even remember you were nervous. And if you do get nervous or stumble, look at me. I'll be there."

"Thank you," I said, emotion welling up in my chest. Why had I ever doubted this man? He cared so deeply that nothing would ever be too much for him. He wanted the best for me, and while he might have directed his worries in the wrong way, his heart had been in the right place.

Dad had been right when he'd said relationships were tricky, and there was no map to any of this. All we could do was walk forward together, side by side and hand in hand, trying to look out for traps and pitfalls and helping each other when we fell in.

"You're welcome." He kissed my temple and smiled at me through the mirror. "You need to put your lashes on. Want me to grab your wig?"

"Please. It's the one on the end."

"I know," West said. "You sent me a million pictures of it when you picked it up."

"That's because it's gorgeous and amazing and I fucking love it," I said, reaching for my tweezers and my lashes of choice. "Orlando smashed it out of the park. I couldn't have imagined it any better."

Orlando was Bitch's best friend and former roommate who'd moved into styling drag wigs at the start of the year, turning his years of expertise as a stylist, and putting up with Bitch, to a new art form. He had a gorgeous studio in the house he shared with his partners, Charles and Jude, on the edge of Lincoln and I never, ever wanted anyone else to style my wigs again.

Seriously, if Orlando couldn't do them, I wouldn't be wearing them.

This one had been a bit last minute, but he'd managed to squeeze me in and been delighted when I'd told him my plan. We were going full Christmas princess for today, inspired by Belle's Christmas dress from *Beauty and the*

Beast: The Enchanted Christmas, the book cover of *All I Want for Christmas*, and my own princess fantasies of fur-trimmed capes and sparkling gowns.

Orlando had taken a blonde wig and transformed it into a half-up, half-down look with soft curls and bangs that framed my face. It had some traditional Bubblegum sparkle sprinkled throughout too, as well as a red and gold bow at the back.

All my wigs were special, but this one even pipped my favourite white-blonde one at the post.

West brought it over to me, resting the wig head on the corner of my dressing table so it was in reach for when I'd finished my lashes. It only took me a few minutes to get the wig perfectly fitted and in place, and then it was time for my dress.

It had taken Mum and me hours, with some help from Dad and his excellent sequin skills, but it had turned out better than I'd ever expected. It was red, cream, and gold and sparkly as fuck, with a flowing full-length skirt that twirled as I moved, a nipped-in waist, a soft, sweetheart neckline, and off-the-shoulder sleeves.

It was the biggest dress I'd ever worn, since Bubblegum usually wore skirts no longer than knee-length, and I'd had to practice moving around in it so I didn't catch my foot on the hem and fall flat on my face. We'd also fitted it so I could sit down comfortably and the boning wouldn't dig into my ribs or compress my lungs so much that I'd do a full Elizabeth Swan and pass out.

"Beautiful," West said, his smile so full of warmth and

affection it stopped my heart for a second. "You look incredible, sweetheart. Truly incredible."

"Thank you," I said as I did a little twirl, smoothing out my skirt and admiring myself in the full-length mirror beside my wardrobe. "I think it came out quite nicely."

"That's an understatement. It's perfect. You look like a queen. My queen." He leant in and kissed me ever so gently, trying not to smudge my lipstick. "Do you want a hand putting your boots on?"

"Please."

"Sit on the edge of the bed. I'll do them for you."

I carefully sat on the edge of the bed, sweeping my skirt underneath me. To avoid damaging the dress and putting my heel through the fabric, it was better to put my shoes on after I was fully dressed, but by that point it was also a fucking pain in the ass to reach my feet. I was glad West was here or I'd be hopping around swearing and trying to contort myself in ways my body just wasn't meant to go.

West knelt down in front of me, one knee raised. He tapped it gently and reached out to take my foot when I lifted it off the floor, placing it carefully on his knee. Then he picked up one of the white boots I'd bought especially for the occasion.

They were styled after Victorian boots, with white buttons down the outside and kitten heels, but luckily they had a concealed zip down the inside so I didn't have to faff around doing the buttons up.

West held up the shoe and, gently holding my ankle, guided my foot inside it. He wiggled the boot into place, making sure it wasn't going to rub or make my tights bunch up around my feet, before carefully zipping it closed and lowering my foot to the floor. Then he did the same with the other foot.

It was one of the most romantic, intimate things someone had ever done for me.

He smiled up at me as he lowered my other foot to the floor and reached out to take my hands. He drew them to his mouth and kissed the back of both of them like a knight pledging allegiance to his queen.

West stood and helped me to my feet, still holding my hands in his. "You're going to be amazing today," he said. "I know it. Everyone is going to love you."

"Thanks," I said, my heart fluttering wildly like the wings of a hummingbird. Was it too early for this to be love? Did it even matter if it was? Dad had always told us that he knew within two hours of meeting my mum that she was the one, and they'd been together for nearly thirty years now.

"Your chariot awaits, Your Majesty," West said, picking up my bag off the bed and slinging it over his shoulder.

I grinned. "And by chariot, do you mean Dad's van?"

"Nope, I mean Mason's ridiculous 4x4." He shook his head fondly. "Why the fuck he needs a Land Rover in the city is beyond me, but at least your dress will fit in the front seat."

CHAPTER TWENTY-NINE

West

I TRIED NOT to let my nerves show as Mason drove us towards Bailgate, where he was going to drop us off before going to park his car. It would mean a short walk to The Lost World, but it was easier than trying to get the car down to it.

I was still worried we might arrive to hordes of protesters swarming the streets, because Lincoln was a small city in a very conservative area of the country, but I hoped if that was the case, someone would've given us a heads-up by now. Rory hadn't said anything when he'd last checked his phone, and while it was currently sitting on Bubblegum's lap, she and Mason were singing Christmas songs at the top of their lungs.

I'd have to drag Mason down to the Christmas drag karaoke The Court was hosting on the twentieth and get him up on stage. I might need to pour a few drinks into him first, but if Bubblegum was there, it wasn't like he'd be performing in front of complete strangers.

"Okay, I'm going to drop you off by the Magna Carta," Mason said as we trundled down Bailgate, which was festooned with Christmas lights and packed with shoppers. Lincoln Cathedral loomed over us on one side, its twin towers stretching into the bright, crisp December sky, while on the other the gates of Lincoln Castle beckoned people inside the grounds. Lincoln Christmas Market was being held around the Cathedral in the grounds of the Castle and across the two roads that connected them, and the roads were lined with stands and stalls selling everything from seasonal food and drink to Christmas decorations and trinkets, to one stand that apparently sold replica medieval weaponry.

Luckily, the market didn't open until noon, so while there were a lot of people around, we could still get the car through. Jay had also given us one of the special car passes the shop got to allow us past the temporary barricades, which I was grateful for because otherwise we would've had to walk quite a way and that would've been difficult with Bubblegum in heels and full drag.

"Ready?" Mason asked, pulling the car to a stop near the pub on the corner. "Got everything?"

"Yeah," I said. "Stay there, sweetheart. I'll come and help you out." I climbed out the car, shoving my phone into the pocket of my coat and slinging Bubblegum's bag over my shoulder. Opening the passenger door, I put my hand out to help Bubblegum down onto the cobbled street. Luckily, any frost we'd had overnight had already melted, so she only had to contend with the cobbles for a few feet until we got onto the pavement.

"Thank you," Bubblegum said with a nervous smile, clutching my hand tightly. "Cheers, Mason. We'll see you in a minute, right?"

"Of course," he said. "I wouldn't miss it. I've got my ticket and everything." He patted one of his front pockets and grinned at us. I closed the door and we stepped back to let him drive off. I still thought the car was ridiculous, but I had to admit it was comfortable.

"He's so sweet," Bubblegum said as we watched him drive off. "Is he single?"

"Yeah."

"Is he straight?"

"I'm… not sure," I said. "I'm not sure he knows either."

Bubblegum snorted. "If he wants to figure it out, I'm sure I know people who'd be willing to help. Sometimes you just have to stick a dick in your mouth and see if you like it."

I let out a bark of laughter so loud that other people stared at me. "I can't really disagree with that."

"Is that how you figured out you were bi?"

"Sort of," I said as we started walking. "That and I was a little too obsessed with Sam Warburton. He used to play for Wales."

"You definitely have to show me pictures later," Bubblegum said. Her boots clicked on the pavement as we made our way down the hill, past little shops and cafés decked out for Christmas, lights and decorations glittering in the windows.

We hadn't gone very far when I heard the noise of a crowd and my stomach sank faster than a lead balloon. Bubblegum clutched my hand tighter, both of us prepared for the worst.

I steeled myself, prepared to put all my tackling skills to use if I had to. I was six foot three and eighteen stone of solid muscle. There was no way any normal person was getting past me without extreme force. And if certain things had gone according to plan, I wouldn't be the only one of my size and skill on hand.

As we rounded the corner, I saw that the narrow street was full of people, all wrapped up in winter coats and waving pride flags. There were people dressed in bright colours, flags tied around their necks like capes or hanging off bags, and a couple were even sporting rainbow tinsel as scarves. There were signs being waved in the air, hand-painted-on bits of cardboard and wood, with brightly coloured messages of love and support. Quite a few of them were even covered in glitter.

The crowd was full of people of all ages, with everyone from students to parents with kids big and small, all the way through to a group of grannies in knitted rainbow hats with pompoms on. On one side, I saw Clive and a man who had to be Alan, Tommy and the rest of the coaching staff, and half the team, all decked out in Knights pride hoodies with rainbow laces on their trainers. There were a few notable exceptions, but I didn't want them here anyway. A few of the team even had their wives and girlfriends with them with their kids beside them, while Matty, one of the scrum halves, had his eight-month-old son strapped to his chest. Matty also had a lot of rainbow glitter stuck to his vast ginger beard.

Jonny saw me and waved, calling my name, and some of the crowd turned to look, cheering loudly when they saw Bubblegum beside me.

"What the fuck?" Bubblegum squeaked, staring at the swathes of people in front of us. "What is this?"

"Looks like your audience," I said. "And some extra fans too."

"But I… I'm not…" She burst out laughing, a beaming smile on her face. "I guess I am." She squeezed my hand one last time and then released me. "I better go and say hello."

"I'll be right behind you," I said. "And I'll see if I can see Peaches."

"He'll be in boy mode, so look out for someone tall, dark, and handsome. And if Ink is with them, she'll be in flannel and Doc Martens with pink hair and a nose ring. And Legs is bald, but he's probably wearing a hat."

I didn't tell Bubblegum that wasn't the most helpful set of descriptors. Instead I watched with pride as she walked towards the crowd with her normal bouncing gait, looking every inch the beautiful, sparkling princess she was. My chest felt hot and tight as if my ribcage was suddenly three sizes too small for my heart.

"Hello, my darlings," Bubblegum said as she greeted the people nearest to her. "Thank you so much for being here." There were a couple of families with children on the edge of the crowd, and I watched as she carefully bent down to talk to the kids, introducing herself and asking their names and answering any of their immediate questions. It really was like watching royalty.

I moved a little closer, craning to look over the heads of the crowd to see if I recognised anyone from The Court or if any of these so-called protesters had appeared. I couldn't see anyone I knew, bar the rugby crowd, but on the other side of the crowd, far away from everyone and being closely supervised by a couple of police officers, were three very sad, disappointed-looking protesters. They had signs and one of them kept trying to yell, but their voice was drowned out by the crowd.

It was almost comical, except for the fact that they were so deep in their hatred they'd decided they had nothing better to do with their Saturday morning than protest a children's story hour. I couldn't even find it in my heart to feel sorry for them.

"Hey, you must be West," said a voice to my left, and I turned to see a woman with bright pink hair that was shaved on one side, with a silver barbell through her eyebrow and a large decorative ring through her septum. She was wearing a large heavy-looking flannel shirt and dungarees, with battered Doc Martens laced with lesbian flag laces. "I'm Ink."

"Hey," I said, giving her a half wave, not sure if I was supposed to shake her hand or offer her a hug. Was there an etiquette here? I'd never had a lot of queer friends before. "Nice to meet you. Bubblegum said you'd be here."

"Me and the rest of the troublemakers," she said with a laugh, gesturing over her shoulder to two men now talking to Bubblegum. One had dark hair that softly curled around the base of his neck and stubble across his jaw and was wearing a peachy-coloured knitted jumper and black and gold boots patterned with flowers, while the other was slightly shorter with a neon green beanie and an astonishingly bright ugly Christmas jumper that almost hurt my eyes. I assumed this had to be Peaches and Legs. "You wouldn't happen to be responsible for the rugby boys, would you?"

"Yeah… I thought we might need a bit of physical support. And nobody's getting through them—doesn't matter if half of them are complete pushovers in reality. I hope it's okay, that they're here, I mean. I know they're a bit imposing."

"You're fine," Ink said. "They seem like a sweet bunch. My only worry is there definitely isn't enough room in The Lost World for everyone. And I know we sold out all the tickets."

I thought for a second. They'd spread the events out over December so there was one every Saturday and Sunday from now until Christmas Eve, when Peaches would do the final one at one of the large bookshops in the middle of town, so it wasn't like there was another event they could go to today. Unless…

"Could you do two today? Ask people to come back at… I don't know… two?" That'd give Bubblegum a chance to have a break in between the two, even if the first one ran long, and I could run out and find us some food.

"That could work," Ink said. "I'd have to check with Peaches if we're allowed to do that. And with Jay, obviously, since it's his shop. And Sparkles."

"Give me a second."

I broke away and hurried over to Bubblegum, who was now chatting to two women and their daughter. I hovered for a second, not wanting to interrupt, but Bubblegum saw me and grabbed my hand excitedly. "Oh my gosh, this is another fabulous small world thing. This"—she gestured at one of the women, who had dark blonde hair and a warm smile—"is Jules. Long-suffering sister of Bitch Fit. And this is her girlfriend, Chantelle, and her daughter Kelsey."

"Who said long-suffering? I'm a delight!" said the familiar voice of Bitch, popping up beside his sister and hugging her tightly. There was a gentle-looking man behind him who was watching Bitch fondly, so I had to assume that was his boyfriend, Tristan.

"Uncle Eli!" Kelsey squealed.

"Hello, gorgeous," Eli said, sweeping her off her feet and kissing her cheek loudly. "I say, Sparkles, don't you look smart? You scrub up nicely."

"She looks like a princess," Kelsey said in a loud whisper. "Can I have a dress like that?"

"Maybe," Eli said. "You'll have to ask your Uncle Edward very nicely and see what he's got in his magical dressing-up box."

"Nice to meet you," Jules said, stepping past her brother, who was plotting with Kelsey, and reaching out to shake my hand.

"You too," I said. "Thanks for coming out."

"We wouldn't have missed it," Chantelle said. "There's a lot more people than I thought there'd be."

"Yes," Bubblegum said with a soft laugh. "I'm not sure

how we're all going to fit inside, unless The Lost World is somehow bigger on the inside."

"About that," I said. "I was just chatting with Ink. A lot of these people only came along today, so they don't have tickets. And—"

"Can we do two readings?" Bubblegum asked instantly. "I don't mind, as long as it's okay with Jay. You will have to get me food in the middle, though. Maybe something off the market... Oooh, maybe one of those giant pretzels with brie and cranberry. And some doughnuts."

I smiled, desperately wishing I could kiss her but not wanting to smudge her lipstick. "Great minds think alike," I said. "Ink and I said the same thing. Although not about the doughnuts."

"Number one rule," Bubblegum said with a mischievous smile, leaning in close and brushing her lips across my cheek. "Always feed your drag queens."

CHAPTER THIRTY

Bubblegum Galaxy

"So, now we know what Princess Annette and Olive wanted for Christmas, I want to know, if you could have anything for Christmas, what would you want?" I asked, grinning at the sea of faces in front of me and watching various hands shoot into the air.

Despite my initial nerves, the story hour had gone much better than I'd expected because as soon as I'd introduced myself to the audience, it had felt like any other performance. And if there was anything I was good at, it was performing to a crowd.

My worries about being good with kids and staying family friendly had all melted away too, because they all asked the most wonderful, sweet, and random questions. Like if I ever wore my dresses to Tesco, what I liked about being a drag queen, why I was so pretty, how did I learn to walk in heels, who my favourite superhero was, and if I had a favourite Pokémon.

Which I did and it was obviously Tsareena because there was no other Pokémon that embodied such glorious drag queen vibes. She had thigh-high boots and lashes for days —she couldn't be anything else.

After the Christmas present question, which had some wonderful answers including new football boots, a Furby, and a pet dragon, someone asked me what I wanted and I thought for a second, looking out across the crowd. West was stood at the back of the room, right in my line of sight so I could always find him. His expression was full of pride and admiration, the same one he'd been wearing since we arrived. I'd never felt so loved or supported by anyone outside of my family before.

I grinned at him and looked back at my audience. "If I could have anything, I think I'd like a castle. Because all queens need a castle. And I'd also like a NERF gun so I can annoy my brother. Because I love him but he keeps eating all my chocolate biscuits!"

Some of the kids laughed and someone asked me a question about Christopher, so I ended up teaching them all how to sign Merry Christmas. My eyes caught West's as I did, and I couldn't resist signing the last demonstration at him, adoring the way he signed it back. By that point we were over time and Peaches stepped in to thank everyone for coming and reminding them of the rest of the events coming up in the run-up to Christmas.

"Finally, can we all give our beautiful Bubblegum Galaxy a round of applause, please, and show our appreciation for her being here today," Peaches said. He started to clap and everyone joined in, a few whistles and cheers mixing into the applause.

"Are you still okay if people want to take pictures?" Peaches asked, tilting his head towards me and lowering his voice.

"Sure," I said. "That's fine."

"Perfect, Ink and I can supervise."

"Thanks."

Peaches turned back to the crowd, a bright smile on his handsome face. "If anyone would like their picture taken with Bubblegum, we can do that now. Please form a queue on this side of the room." He pointed at the wall nearest the far wall of shelves, which meant anyone waiting wouldn't block the exit. "If not, thank you very much for coming. Please leave up the stairs. Have a wonderful rest of your weekend and a very Merry Christmas."

There was another round of applause and people started to filter out. I didn't expect anyone to want their picture or to come and talk to me, so I was wonderfully surprised by the number of people who came over to thank me, tell me how much fun they'd had, ask for a picture or a hug, and ask me questions. Ink and Peaches supervised carefully, although Peaches kept getting sidetracked when people stopped to ask him more in-depth questions about the events.

Throughout all of it, West waited patiently at the back of the room and whenever I looked across at him, he always smiled at me in a way that made me feel lighter than air and hotter than the sun. My skin tingled and my heart raced, like a crush but a thousand times more intense. I'd never felt this way about anyone before. And I couldn't imagine ever feeling this way about anyone else.

"I think that's the last of them," Peaches said as the final footsteps faded away on the stairs. He checked his watch. "Are you still okay to do another one at two?"

"Sure," I said, stretching my arms and rolling my head from side to side, trying to make my neck pop. "I need some food, though. I'm fucking starving."

"I'll go," West said, stepping forward from the back of the room where he'd been chatting to Mason.

"No, I'll go," Mason said. He pushed West towards me. "You two sit down and chill. I'll get food. What do you want?"

"Anything with cheese," I said. "Oh wait, actually, if they have those giant stuffed pretzels with brie and cranberry, I'd like one of those. If not, a cheeseburger, please, with chips. Or cheesy chips with gravy. Any of those, please. And maybe some doughnuts? And something to drink too, preferably with caffeine. Is that okay?" Now I'd thought about food, I wanted everything. I hadn't had a chance to get down to the Christmas market, and the food they did there was always amazing.

"Sure." Mason pulled out his phone and began to tap something out. "West?"

"Maybe a burger? Or one of the stuffed pretzels. Anything really."

"That's desperately unhelpful," Mason said with an unimpressed look at West. "If you don't like what I bring back, that's on you."

"As long as there's no mushrooms or pears, then I'm good." West reached into his pocket and pulled out his wallet, sliding a card out. "Take my card."

"Are you sure?" I asked, looking around for my bag. "You can take mine."

"Yes, I'm sure," West said.

Mason looked between us and grinned, shaking his head fondly. "Right, you two stay here. I'll be back in a bit."

"Want some company?" Legs asked. He'd been talking to Jay and Ink at the bottom of the stairs. "I was going to get something too."

"Er, yeah," Mason said, a rosy flush blossoming over his cheeks. "Sounds good."

"Anyone else?" Legs asked, grabbing his backpack off the floor. He looked at Ink and then around for Peaches, who'd already disappeared upstairs for something or other. In that split second, I stared at Ink and shook my head wildly, waving my hand back and forth in a desperate "no" motion. Luckily, Mason was stood between her and me, so he couldn't see me basically trying to set him up.

But West had said Mason was single and maybe not straight. And I'd seen the way he'd blushed when Legs had offered him company.

I might not be the best matchmaker in the world, but even I could read signs that were that bloody obvious.

Ink grinned and winked at me. "Nah, I'm good. You two go."

"I thought you were hungry?" Legs asked with a raised eyebrow. "You were just saying you'd kill for cheesy chips."

"Fine, can you bring me some cheesy chips, please? I'm

gonna stay here in case the mob descends early, plus Jay has a dog and I *need* puppy snuggles."

"Ohhh," I said. "How is Rupert? Is he okay?"

"He's fine," Jay said, stepping to the side as Legs and Mason ducked around him to head out. "There were just a lot more people than I anticipated and he gets a bit nervous around crowds, so he's snoozing in his bed behind the till. You're welcome to snuggle him before you go as long as you don't mind being sat on."

I laughed because that was more than okay. I wanted to get at least one picture too, because Rupert would hands down be the cutest member of my audience today.

Ink and Jay disappeared up the stairs, chatting together about dogs and Dungeons & Dragons, leaving West and me alone.

"Well done, sweetheart," West said as he closed the gap between us, wrapping me tightly in his arms and kissing the top of my head as I sagged against him. "You were amazing."

"Thanks," I said, mostly into his pecs because, damn, they were a nice pillow. Firm but the right amount of squishy. "It went a lot better than I expected. It was actually fun, which sounds weird because it should always have been fun, but with all the build-up and everything…" I sighed, suddenly completely drained. I'd built this whole thing up in my head until it resembled a mountain, and now I'd conquered it, I'd quite have liked a nap.

Except I still had a second show to do, which was a bit wild. Hopefully, Mason would bring back plenty of sustenance to get me through. And if not, I'd beg someone to go out and get me a Red Bull. Several Red Bulls. "Did anyone actually turn up to protest? I didn't see anyone."

"About three people," West said with amusement. "Apparently they tried to use a megaphone to yell things at the crowd, but that didn't last long. Clive told me it got taken off them, maybe for hate speech? Not sure. Anyway, they'd all pissed off by the time Mason managed to get in because he didn't see them at all."

I laughed into his chest. "Oh no, boo-hoo, poor them. Anyway, I'm amazing."

"You are." West kissed the top of my head again and ran his hand slowly up and down my back. "You're the most amazing person I've ever met, both as Bubblegum and Rory. And I… I think…"

"Yes?" I tilted my head to look up at him, certain the only thing keeping my heart in place was the boning on my corset.

"I love you," he said simply. Then he smiled. "I love you. There's no need to think about it. I love you as Bubblegum. I love you as Rory. I love you today and I'll love you tomorrow and I'll love you a hundred years from now. I know we haven't been doing this long, but when I think about you, it's like my heart is too fucking big for my chest. I don't want to imagine what my life would be like without you in it, because I know it's a million times better with you. You've changed my life, sweetheart. You're everything to me."

My eyes prickled with tears and I had to blink ridiculously hard and fast to stop myself crying because I knew it would fuck up my make-up and I didn't have time to fix it.

West loved me. All of me. Every sparkling, sassy, mouthy inch of me. He loved me in drag and out of it, because of who I was, not just how hot I looked in a dress and heels.

"Oh shit," he said, gently wiping my face with his thumb. "Don't cry. I'm sorry, shit… I shouldn't have—"

"I love you too," I said in a voice that was barely above a breathless gasp. "I love you so much it feels like I can't breathe. Like the only reason my chest is still in one piece is because of this fucking corset." I sniffed and blinked as West's hand cradled my face. "I fucking love you, West. Every single part of you. I can't even put into words what I feel like, but I know that I've never, ever felt this way before. And I don't think I'll ever stop feeling this way either." I leant into his touch, cherishing the heat and the roughness of his palm. "You're it for me. I'm keeping you. Forever."

"I'm not going anywhere," West said. "You can't get rid of me that easily."

I leant up and kissed him deeply, my hands fisting in his hoodie and holding him close to me. I almost wished I didn't have another show to do so we could get out of here and spend the rest of the afternoon getting lost in each other.

We broke apart slowly, and I giggled when I realised West's lips were painted red.

He grinned at me and brushed his finger across his bottom lip. "Am I wearing half your lipstick?"

"Maybe," I said, leaning in again. "Want to wear the rest of it?"

CHAPTER THIRTY-ONE

West

IT WAS late afternoon by the time Bubblegum and I finally made it back to mine. Despite everything that had happened with Guy, my house was still the place that offered us the most space and privacy. Funnily enough, none of us had seen much of Guy since that eventful morning, mostly because none of us would talk to him, and I'd heard on the grapevine he was looking for a new place to live.

Even Jonny, who hadn't been there, had been pissed when he'd found out because, as he'd so eloquently put it, "What the fuck is it to do with him anyway? If anyone's the drama queen, it's him."

Jonny had also apologised for his apathy too, because while he'd never said or done anything, he'd never stood up against the banter either and he'd admitted that was almost as bad. I'd noticed him recently prodding Danny into shutting up.

And by prodding, I meant kicking him hard in the shins. I'd had to try really hard not to laugh.

"Why am I so tired?" Bubblegum asked, flopping onto the bed, her skirt flaring out around her. She was still mostly in drag, except she'd swapped her boots for her trainers and peeled her face gems off in the car. "I'm fucking knackered."

"You did do two performances today," I said. "Two *excellent* performances."

"Hmm, I am pretty excellent."

"You are."

Bubblegum leant up on her elbows and smiled sweetly at me. "I know you're a professional athlete and you've already eaten a burger today, but do you have any objections to getting Chinese later? Or do you have a very strict eating plan to stick to?"

"Yes, I do have an eating plan, but... just this once, we can get Chinese. I can make it work as long as I don't eat anything too deep-fried."

"Don't worry, you can have sensible things like vegetables and rice. I'll eat the deep-fried chicken balls."

"We don't have to order them," I said teasingly, leaning over to kiss her.

"Yes, we do. Sorry, it's the rules."

"Is it?"

"Yes. All Chinese takeaway orders must include chicken balls and prawn toasts. And special fried rice." Bubblegum kissed me again, smiling against my mouth. "I have to ask, though, are you the sort of person who wants to order a dish or two for themself or are you happy to get several different things and share? So we get lots of delicious things. Except the chicken balls, obviously. Those are mine."

"We can share," I said. "And you can take any leftovers home with you."

"You really are the best boyfriend ever."

"I try."

Bubblegum smiled up at me. "I don't think you need to try; I think it's just who you are. You're the sweetest man I've ever met."

I felt my skin prickle with embarrassment and couldn't think of anything to say. Instead, I just kept kissing her. Bubblegum groaned against my mouth, her hand running down my chest. When she reached the bottom of my hoodie, she slid her fingers underneath it, running them around the waistband of my jeans. I was still leaning over the bed, standing between her legs with my hands planted either side of her head. I wanted to put my knee between her legs, but I was afraid of crushing her skirt and damaging it.

"I love you," Bubblegum whispered, her lips barely leaving mine.

"I love you too."

"And I want…" Another kiss. "Mmm, I really want to keep going."

"But?"

"But I need to take this dress off first. And my waist shaper. And my wig. Especially the wig." She chuckled and rested our foreheads together. "I really don't want to mess it up and have to explain to Orlando what happened. I don't want to get anything on the dress either, because it'll be a pain in the ass to clean."

I smirked and pushed myself into a standing position, offering her my hand. "Let's get you naked then."

Bubblegum snorted and took my hand, squealing with delight as I pulled her to her feet in one smooth movement. I'd helped her put the dress on earlier, so I knew how and where it was fastened.

Carefully, so I didn't pinch the skin, I undid the concealed zip on the side. Then I slid the small sleeves further down her arms and began to ease the dress down. Objectively, it wasn't the sexiest or easiest thing to remove, but there was something so intimate in undressing Bubblegum like this. Taking her from glittering drag queen into sweet, demanding Rory.

It was one of those moments I doubted many people got to experience, at least not in the same way I did.

Sure, Rory got undressed around his fellow queens all the time, but he was still Bubblegum to them. I got to see the person underneath the glitz and the glam, and that was special. And while Bubblegum was an extension of Rory, she was her own person in a way, just as Rory was his own person.

And I loved both of them with all my heart.

Rory stepped out of the dress and I lifted it off the floor. I dug a hanger out of the wardrobe to put it on, because I didn't have anything like a desk chair to drape it over, and hung it on the door. When I turned back to Rory, he'd removed his wig and breast plate and had laid them out on top of the chest of drawers. He was working off his tights and underwear, making small squeaking noises under his breath.

"Do you need a hand?" I asked, watching with amusement as Rory shimmied his tights down to his knees.

"No, I'm okay. I just got a bit sweaty, so they're stuck. I probably need to have a shower."

I walked over and knelt on the floor, helping him roll them down. "No point having a shower now, I'm just going to get you all sweaty again."

"Sure? I'm a bit gross."

"Not gross," I said, peeling off his underwear. "Sexy as fuck."

I pressed a kiss to his hip, tasting the salt of his sweat. It didn't bother me. There was something deeply sexy and attractive about it because this was Rory at his most open, most human. He wasn't first-date polished or all glammed up; he was sweaty and naked and real. It was why morning sex was one of my favourite things, when we were both half-awake, rumpled, and as unglamorous as we could be.

I trailed my lips across the bottom of his abdomen, pressing another kiss to his opposite hip. Rory sighed and I watched his body relax under my touch. My hands caressed his thighs and I slowly climbed to my feet. Rory kissed me, melting against me, and it was easy when we broke apart to reach around and scoop him up. He groaned and wrapped his legs around me, his hands tangling in my hair and pulling it tight.

"You should fuck me like this," he said. "Fucking use me."

A low growl of desire rumbled through my chest. "Yeah? Want to be my little fuck toy, sweetheart? Want me to fill your tight hole with my fat cock and use it for my pleasure?"

"God yes!" Rory kissed me fiercely, attacking my mouth with his desire. I took two steps forward until my shins bumped against the edge of the bed and then gently dropped Rory onto it. He yelped in surprise. "Hey! This isn't being fucked in your arms."

"I know," I said with a soft chuckle. "But I'm still dressed. And I'm not talented enough to undo my jeans while holding you." I reached for the lube and tossed it onto the bed next to him. "And you're not ready either. I'm not fucking you with no prep."

Rory grinned wickedly and spread his legs, showing off his dusty pink hole surrounded by trimmed soft brown hair. I watched as he sucked two fingers into his mouth, his eyes never leaving mine. He winked as he pulled his fingers out of his mouth with a wet pop that was so sexy it should have been illegal. Then he reached down between his legs and began to play with his hole, using his wet fingers to tease the sensitive skin.

He hummed with pleasure, hard cock twitching and dripping as he put on a show for me, and I could only stare as unbridled heat coiled in my gut. Rory spat on his fingers again and then sank one into his ass, a deep groan sliding from his lips.

"You can't fuck me if you're still dressed," he said, lifting his head to look at me as he began to pump his finger in and out, his other hand reaching for the lube.

I snapped into action, fumbling for my belt buckle and the button on my jeans. I'd never known undoing a pair of jeans to take so long and by the time I'd finally gotten them open and down to my feet, Rory had dripped lube down his taint and added a second finger to his hole.

"Fuck, sweetheart," I said, practically ripping off my underwear to get to my aching cock. "You look so good like that. I love watching you play with yourself."

"I want… want you to play with me," Rory said with a whimper that set my body on fire. "Please, West."

There was no way I could say no to that. I threw off the rest of my clothes and dropped to my knees in front of the bed, sliding my hands up the back of his thighs and lifting his legs, showing off more of that perfect ass. Rory had two fingers deep inside himself and I watched with hungry fascination as he slowly worked them in and out.

"Mmm, keep doing that, sweetheart," I said. "You look so fucking sexy."

"I… I… ah!" Whatever Rory was going to say was cut off as I leant forward and flicked my tongue around the edges of his fingers, and his words dissolved into a needy moan. Rory tasted like sweat and lube, deep and earthy with a slightly strange aftertaste from the lube that was easy to ignore. I'd spent more than half my life regularly getting a mouth full of mud on a rugby pitch, and that was far worse than a bit of lube, especially since I'd bought an expensive one that supposedly had very little taste to it.

"Keep fucking yourself," I said, lifting my head enough to look Rory in the eye. I wanted to see the effect my words had on him, and it made my cock throb as Rory moaned, his mouth hanging open.

I lowered my head back between his legs, licking around his fingers and pushing my tongue into his hole alongside them, sucking and teasing. Rory worked his fingers in and out of his ass, his rhythm sporadic and jerky as he lost himself to pleasure. I flicked my tongue around his rim, loving the way Rory groaned, and moved my hand to brush a finger across Rory's.

"Oh God," Rory said. "Yes!"

Gently, I began to work my finger in alongside Rory's two, the tight heat of his body pulling me in. I loved watching his hole stretch around our fingers; it was almost as sexy as watching him take my cock. I could have watched him for hours, listening to the moans and gasps dripping from his mouth like honey, but I'd promised to use him and fuck him hard on my cock. And I wasn't one to break my promises.

I pressed a final kiss to the edge of his hole, then slowly eased my finger out of him. "You can stop now, sweetheart," I said, reaching for the lube to drizzle some on my palm and slick up my aching cock. I eased to my feet and leant over him, lowering my head to brush my lips against his. "I promised to use you, so I'm going to fuck you so hard you see stars."

"Fuck," Rory said with a moan, his hand wrapping around the back of my neck. "You make the best promises."

"If I make a promise to you," I said before kissing him, "I'm always going to keep it." I nipped his bottom lip and pushed my tongue into his mouth, kissing him fiercely. "Are you ready?"

"I'm ready." Rory smirked coyly at me. "Show me what you've got."

I straightened slightly so I could slide my hands down his sides until I reached his ass. I lifted his hips and Rory spread his legs, wrapping them around me, one hand still on the back of my neck so he could hold on. With my hands holding him tightly, I bent my knees and stood, lifting Rory off the bed. His thighs squeezed my hips, his arms around my neck, and I moved one of my arms to his waist, holding him against me while I reached under his thigh with the other and used my hand to line my cock up with his waiting hole.

Rory groaned into my ear, the sound reverberating through me, as I slowly breached his rim and pushed inside him. His fingers dug into the back of my shoulders, his arms crossed behind my neck and his desperate breathing caressing my skin. A deep, rumbling sigh echoed in my throat as his channel pulled me in, squeezing tightly around my shaft as I sank deeper into him.

"Fuck, sweetheart," I said, easing him down onto my cock until virtually every inch of me was buried in his ass. "Your ass is so fucking perfect. Feels so good on my cock."

"S-shit," Rory said with a breathless laugh that morphed into a delighted moan. "I don't think I'll ever get over how good your cock feels."

He tilted his head down and kissed me softly as I started to fuck him, sliding his ass up and down my cock. He groaned into my mouth as I used him, working every inch of my fat cock in and out of his hole. He squeezed around me, milking my shaft and sending pleasure ricocheting through me like a pinball.

My senses were full of him: the taste of him on my lips, the scent of him flooding me as I buried my face in his neck, nipping his collarbone, the feel of him under my hands, the heat of his legs around my body and the perfect tightness of his hole, the little gasps and moans as I fucked him slowly, and the way pleasure was written across his expression when I tilted my head back to watch him, drinking in the sight of him.

My arms were starting to ache, a burn setting in across my shoulders, but I pushed it aside because there was no way I was stopping yet. Not when I could already feel my skin tingling and pressure sliding down my spine as my balls tightened.

"Can you reach your cock?" I asked. "I want you to come for me."

Rory gasped and nodded, wiggling his hand down between us and sitting back slightly so he had room to move his arm. The angle change pushed him deeper onto my cock, and our groans were so loud I was pretty sure the whole street had heard us. I hoped nobody else had come home or they'd be smirking at me all weekend.

"West," Rory said, gasping out my name as he spat into his palm and frantically jerked his cock. "I'm so close... I'm gonna... gonna come!"

He cried out and buried his head in my neck, panting against my skin as his body tensed. His ass tightened like a vice, intensely squeezing and pulsing around my cock as he painted our stomachs with his cum. I fucked him through his orgasm, barely slowing to let him breathe as I chased my own release. I was so fucking close.

"W-West," Rory said, his voice a decadent whimper, and that was all it took to send me crashing over the edge. I pulled him down onto my dick as I filled him with my load, our mouths meeting in a series of deep, panting kisses.

"I love you," Rory murmured. "I fucking love you. So much."

"I love you too, sweetheart."

I kissed him again, slowly staggering forward to the bed to lower the pair of us down, holding him in my arms with my cock still buried inside him as our hearts pounded like a thousand drums, all keeping time together.

CHAPTER THIRTY-TWO

Bubblegum Galaxy

WE ENDED up eating Chinese food in bed, stretched out in T-shirts and boxers, watching old episodes of *Friends* on Netflix. I'd pinched West's clothes since I didn't have much with me, and he hadn't complained about me stealing one of his Knights tees, even if it was long enough on me to be a dress.

"This is random," West said as the episode credits rolled across the screen. "But what are you doing around Christmas? Are you performing? Do you have a big family Christmas?"

I thought for a second as I dipped a deep-fried chicken ball into a pot of sweet and sour sauce. I'd technically finished eating, but I didn't want the chicken balls to go to waste because they were one thing that didn't reheat well. "The Court's final Christmas show is the twenty-third,

Christmas Eve I'm doing a drag brunch, then I'm off for a few days. I'm working New Year's Eve because we do a big New Year show. I hadn't really thought about the rest of it. I should probably buy some presents and see if everyone at the club wants to do Secret Santa—it's easier that way. But yeah, we usually have a bit of a family Christmas—my Uncle Ian and his family often come up, Mum makes too much food, Christopher cheats at board games, Dad and my uncle tell outrageous stories about their youth and fall asleep in front of the telly. Pretty standard stuff. Why? Have you got a match?"

"No, we're playing in Bath on the twenty-third," West said. "So we'll do some light recovery on Christmas Eve. Clive's giving us Christmas Day off and then training on Boxing Day in the afternoon. Then we're playing at home on New Year's Eve at three."

A thought suddenly clicked into place and I wanted to slap myself. Christmas wasn't a big deal for me because I always had people to celebrate it with. But West... "Do you have any Christmas plans? You're welcome to come to mine if you can put up with my lot. They're kinda loud but they mean well."

"Actually, Theo asked if I wanted to spend it with him and Laurie," West said. "And I wondered if you'd like to come with me? I know it's kinda soon, so you can totally say no, but I'd love them to meet you. I won't be going up for long, just Christmas Eve night and then back either the evening of Christmas Day or first thing Boxing Day. They live up in Yorkshire, so it's a couple of hours, but yeah... if you wanted, you could come with me."

"I'd love to," I said, leaning over to kiss him. "It'd be your first Christmas since you reconnected, right?"

"Yeah." He nodded and smiled. "They said they see all their friends, some of who I game with quite a bit, and walk on the beach and stuff. Theo said he cooks a lot too."

"I am very down for beach walks and food."

"Cool, awesome, I'll ask him." West suddenly flushed slightly and I saw him tense. "There's, er, there's just one thing I should warn you about. My brother is… he's got a MyFans…"

"Okay…" I said slowly, putting my hand on his arm. I wondered if he was worried that I'd react badly, and I supposed some people might have done given the general attitude of society to sex workers, even though most of the adult population consumed porn. Because hypocrisy. "That doesn't bother me. I think that's pretty cool, actually."

West brightened. "Awesome, I just wanted you to know."

"Can I ask who he is?" I laughed. "Oh God, is this where we find out I'm your brother's biggest fan or something? Shit, your brother isn't Austin Carter, is he?"

"No, but he knows him. He's Theo Foxx."

My heart stopped in shock and I stared. I wasn't sure whether to be embarrassed or awestruck. Would it weird West out to know that I'd wanked to his brother's videos more times than I wanted to count? "Cool," I said, knowing I sounded the furthest thing from it. "That's… really cool."

West laughed, the sound bouncing around the room and filling me with warmth. "I should've just waited to introduce you in person. Theo would have loved that."

"You're not, like, weirded out that I've watched your brother get..." I couldn't bring myself to say gangbanged.

West shrugged. "No, not really. I mean, it's his job. He likes it; his partner is supportive. It's not any of my business. I'm just not going to watch it with you."

"I wouldn't expect you to," I said. "Oh shit, did you know when you reconnected? I mean, his videos are everywhere."

"Yeah..." West flushed again, his face the same red as a Santa suit. "That's kind of how I found him again. Not going to lie, most horrific and uncomfortable realisation of my life."

"Fucking hell," I said, trying not to laugh. "Does Theo know?"

"I'm not sure. I think he thinks I found him through Twitch. Laurie knows, though, but he was very sweet about it." His face softened fondly. "They're a funny pair, but in the best way. I thought they were married when I first went to stay, because they've lived together for years, but apparently they've only recently gotten their act together. But for me, they're kind of goals. Like the way they look at each other? I always wanted something like that." He smiled at me and my heart soared. "I didn't think I'd find it, until I met you. That's why I want them to meet you, because you're everything I've been searching for. And I know we're young, but I know that I'll never find anyone like you as long as I live."

"I don't think age matters really," I said. "Not here at least. But I think sometimes you meet someone and you just know. My dad... he said he knew within a couple of hours of meeting her that he wanted to marry my mum."

"Yeah?"

"Yeah, they met in a pub in London. Some guy tried to hit on her and she said no. He persisted and my dad politely suggested he get lost. Apparently, he didn't like that, so he tried to argue back, which probably wasn't sensible since it ended up with them all getting chucked out for fighting." I chuckled softly. "Anyway, Dad offered to walk Mum home since it was so late and she said he could, but he had to know that she was a nurse and she was looking after her brother, my Uncle Stephen, who was dying of AIDS, and if Dad had a problem with that, then he could fuck off then and there."

"Shit, seriously?"

"Yeah, Mum wasn't fucking around. A lot of people didn't want to be around men with AIDS back then. It was like they were unclean or some shit. But Dad just asked if my uncle liked football and when they got back to my uncle's house, Dad went in to say hello. And that was it. Dad always said that he could see that my mum loved so fiercely that he'd give anything to be part of her life because that sort of love was powerful. And Mum said she knew she wanted to marry Dad because he kept coming round after work to keep Stephen company and watch football with him or read to him, especially right at the end. She said she'd never met anyone who cared so much."

"That's incredible," West said, putting his arm around me and pulling me close. "I like your parents. They're pretty cool."

"Yeah, they're not bad," I said with a grin. "They like you too, by the way. Mum wants you to come for Sunday dinner one day when you're not playing."

"I'll look at my diary," West said. He kissed my temple. "Will you consider teaching me a little bit of sign language? I want to be able to talk to Christopher. I've been watching some stuff on YouTube but I'm not picking it up very fast."

I twisted my head to stare at him. "You're learning BSL?"

"Well, yeah, I figured it would be pretty rude of me to ignore your brother. I thought it'd be common decency to at least learn the basics." He looked at me, lines appearing on his forehead. "Did I say something wrong?"

"No… no, it's just… I've never had a boyfriend who wanted to learn before," I said, trying to ignore the tears prickling at my eyes. "People usually think it's an inconvenience."

"People are assholes," West said. "It never occurred to me not to at least try. He's your brother."

I shoved the empty paper bag, which had had the chicken balls in, and the tub of sauce onto the bedside table before swinging my leg over West's thighs and climbing into his lap. I kissed him hard, holding the side of his face and trying to show him just what his gesture meant to me. Christopher was a pain in the ass, but he was my brother and I loved him, and I didn't ever want to be with someone who couldn't understand that.

"Thank you," I said when I finally let West breathe. "I love you so damn much."

"I love you too."

I stayed sitting in his lap, kissing him slowly over and over. I was too tired and full of food to do anything more, but sitting here and feeling the solid heat of West's body underneath mine was the best feeling in the world.

"I'm so proud of you," West said. He had his arms around my waist, hands resting on my spine. "I don't know if I've told you that enough today, but I'm so fucking proud of you and what you did. You're an amazing performer, Rory, and whether you get on *Drag Stars* or not, you'll always be the best drag queen I've ever met. You don't need that crown to be a star—you already are one."

"Thanks. And thank you for supporting me today, and well, throughout all of this. I know I'm a lot, that Bubblegum is a lot, but—"

"No, you're not. Don't apologise for being you, sweetheart. All those things you think are faults? They're some of the things I love most about you."

I swallowed and nodded, kissing him again because I couldn't think of anything to say. "I'm proud of you too," I said. "You've done a lot recently, and I don't think you realise it."

West shrugged. "Not really. I've just been me."

"You've been so much more than that. Mason told me more about your fight with Guy and some of the shit that used to happen at the club. He said you've been standing up for yourself more and that you're the reason half the team showed up today."

West glanced away. "When did he say that?"

"At lunch, when you were talking to Jay and his friend, the elven one in the fancy coat. He said he wanted me to know because he didn't think you'd say anything, but also I think... I think he's proud of you. And he wanted me to know that too."

West's lip curled into a half smile. "He's a good mate, even if he's messy as fuck."

"Are you very tidy then?"

"Not obsessively, but there's being tidy and there's basic hygiene and common sense. Like putting your shit in the dishwasher and not leaving mugs to grow mould in your bedroom."

I snorted. "I might be one of those people. But in my defence, I just forget to take them down."

West's smile widened and his eyes danced with amusement. "If we ever live together, am I going to constantly have to retrieve dirty mugs out our room?"

"For you, I'll make more of an effort," I said. "Also, I'll say now, I'm happy to clean the bathroom but I hate changing bins."

"I can do that. We could make a list."

"And I have a lot of shit. Drag doesn't exactly fit into a small suitcase. I mean, you've seen my room and that's only half of it. There's a whole wardrobe of it in the spare room. And another box in the attic."

West nudged his nose against mine and kissed me softly. "I guess we'll need somewhere with at least two bedrooms then, and plenty of storage."

"I guess we will," I said, my chest squeezing and stomach twisting. "Maybe... in the new year? Once we've gotten Christmas out of the way. When does your season finish?"

"May, but we're not playing for eight weeks between the end of January and the end of March so we're not clashing with the Six Nations. I'll have a couple of those weeks off unless I get a miracle call-up to the England squad."

"That would be amazing! Do you think you might?"

"I don't know," West said. "But who knows, maybe? We've just had the World Cup, so they might be looking at testing out some new players, give the squad a bit of a refresh or at least allow some of them to have a break and recover. I'm not holding my breath, but maybe…"

"I'll keep all my fingers and toes crossed," I said with another little kiss. "You'll definitely have to teach me the rules then."

"I'll try, but we both know you're going to spend most of it staring at my thighs."

"Not true! There's your butt and your shoulders as well."

West laughed and rolled me off him onto the bed, his hands resting either side of my head and his knee between my thighs. "Does this mean I can stare at your ass when you're in drag and wearing those tiny dresses?"

"Babe, I'd kind of be offended if you didn't."

West laughed again, leaning down to kiss me as I wrapped my hands around his neck and pulled him closer.

Whatever happened next, wherever life took us, I knew it would always be full of laughter and kisses.

And copious amounts of glitter.

EPILOGUE
THREE MONTHS LATER - MARCH

Bubblegum Galaxy

"Why are the seats so fucking small, I feel like I'm sitting in Eva's lap?" Bitch asked, pointedly nudging Eva's thigh with his knee as he took his seat. "We're at bloody Twickenham. I thought it would have better seats than this?"

"Stop bitching and sit down," Eva said as he sipped his enormous Baileys hot chocolate, glaring at Bitch from underneath his oversized sunglasses. It was strange seeing Eva out of drag in the real world, and it almost made me laugh because Evan and Eva were so different in appearance and exactly the same in personality. We'd gotten a little closer since last year, and it was nice to be one of a handful of people who knew Eva's boy name. "We're here to support Sparkles, not listen to you whine."

"New neighbour still keeping you up then?" Bitch asked with a smirk, patting Eva's thigh fondly. "Did you get his name yet?"

"It's Rhys, right?" I asked, unable to resist being nosy and teasing Eva. It was helping to distract me from the sickly feeling swirling around in my stomach. West had gotten his first England call-up during this year's Six Nations, and today he was making his debut in the starting lineup. He'd been on the bench for one match and a late substitute for the other two matches played so far, so this was a huge step and I'd insisted on being here to support him. It had been difficult to get tickets, but West had finally managed to get five for the family and friend's section, so Bitch, Eva, Theo, Laurie, and I had all made the journey down together. I'd been nervous about asking the two queens, but they'd insisted on coming to support me because, as Eva had said, "You'll be a fucking mess, babe."

She'd been right, especially since this was the first Six Nations match I'd been able to get to since one had been in France, one in Italy, and one at the exact same time I'd had a show. I kept twisting the match programme in my hand and then forcing myself to stop so I could take it home and keep it as a memento. Although at this rate, it would be easier to get a second one to keep since I doubted I'd be able to stop myself from destroying this one.

"Oooh, who's Rhys?" Theo, sporting his new England woolly hat alongside a white coat with a fur collar, asked from my other side, his head craning around me. I'd met him at Christmas and we'd clicked instantly, although I wasn't sure I'd have gotten much say in the matter either way since Theo had told me he'd decided we were going to be friends. He was so different from West, with a bubbling exuberance shining out of every pore, but they both had the same beautiful cornflower eyes and deep caring streak.

"My neighbour," Eva said dryly. "Some Welsh bastard with a fitness kink."

"Some *sexy* Welsh bastard," I said. "I saw him when we were at yours in January. He's really hot."

"He's a dickhead."

"He can be a dickhead and still be hot," I said.

"That's true," Theo said with a sage nod. "Most dickheads are hot in my experience."

"Agreed," Bitch said. "I've been called a dickhead many times and I'm pretty sexy." He winked at Eva, who grinned. "You smiled, I win."

"Yes, you're very clever. Now will you stop talking?"

"No, only when you agree to talk to the man instead of just stewing in your fortress of solitude."

"You should definitely talk to him," I said. "Or maybe just have really delicious hate sex over his choice of music."

"I think I filmed a scene like that once," Theo said. "The hate sex, not the music choice."

"You did," Bitch said, leaning across Eva. "It was hot."

"Thank you!" Theo beamed and behind him I heard Laurie sigh. He was very much the epitome of a gothic gentleman and it was obvious he adored Theo, but he refused to let him get away with much.

"Don't encourage him," Laurie said.

"He's not. He's just telling me he appreciates my work, and that should always be allowed!"

Laurie raised an eyebrow. "I know, but we are not here

to talk about you. We're here to support West and Rory. Behave."

Theo sighed. "Fine." Then he looked at me and put his hand on my arm, squeezing it gently. "Are you okay? You look very nervous."

"Yeah, I think so," I said with a nod, trying to ignore the nerves inside me. "I just want him to do well. And enjoy it."

This wasn't the first time I'd been to watch West play over the last few months, but this was the first time I'd felt nervous. I didn't doubt that West would be amazing. I already knew he'd give it a hundred and ten percent and would throw so much of himself at it that he'd spend the next two or three days battered, bruised, and sore as fuck.

He'd have to give in and have ice baths, even if he didn't like them.

And if West did well, there was a good chance he'd up with a regular place on the team, and I wanted that for him so badly. It was probably why I was nervous because it felt like this match had much higher stakes than any of the others, because there was a big difference between coming on as a late substitute and being part of the starting lineup.

Whatever happened, I was so proud of him I thought my heart would burst.

The past few months had been a whirlwind, but I wouldn't change a second. It had sometimes been hard to find time to see each other, with training and away matches and drag shows, especially since I'd started booking gigs a bit further afield with the help of some additional promotion from the drag story hour and Bitch introducing me to a few of the queens he'd met on one of his tours last year.

Sometimes all West and I could manage was a snatched evening together where we had dinner and then fell asleep in bed watching Netflix because we were both so tired.

I hoped that when we moved in together things would get a bit easier, because even if we were still ridiculously busy, we'd be able to fall asleep next to each other and wake up together every morning.

We'd decided at the end of January to look for somewhere to rent because that way we wouldn't be tied into anything. West wanted to stay with the Knights for a long time but it couldn't be guaranteed, although I'd already told him I'd move wherever he went, and if he did move, selling a house would be so much harder than ending a tenancy. And while there was a good chance we'd change our minds about buying in a year or two, at least this way we'd be able to figure out living together and what we wanted in a home of our own.

It had taken us a while to find something suitable and to actually get through the application process since it seemed like everyone and their dog was applying for every property that came on the market, but in just two weeks' time we'd *finally* get the keys to our new house.

Now all we needed to do was find some furniture, order essential things like a fridge and a washing machine, since this house didn't come with either, and a kettle—because I needed coffee and West needed tea—and sort all the admin shit like insurance and address changes.

I probably needed to start packing my shit too.

It was weird to think about finally moving out of my parents' house since I'd never lived anywhere else, but it wasn't like we were going far. And somehow I doubted my mum would let me go long without going round for dinner. Plus, I'd still see Dad and Christopher most days since we worked together.

I was going to miss the cats, though. I'd have to check our rental agreement and see if it let us have pets, because if so, I was going to rehome a cat as soon as possible.

"I think they're coming out for the warm-up," Theo said, giving me a gentle nudge and pointing at one of the tunnels. "I can't see West, though."

"There," I said, pointing to one of the tall figures jogging onto the pitch. "I'd know him anywhere." His perfect thighs were impossible to miss. And I was secretly pleased that even though he was wearing a long-sleeved training jacket, he was still wearing shorts. God, West's thighs in shorts should be illegal.

I couldn't wait until we went on holiday in July and I got to spend two weeks with him in the heat wearing as little as possible. It was going to be amazing.

"You know," Theo said with an amused smile, "I still think it's kind of ironic that West's a hooker. There's some sort of weird universal poetry in that."

I snorted. "Are you still telling everyone that?"

"Yes," Laurie said. "He is."

"Until you correct them," Theo said with a scoff. "The only person who actually knew what I meant was Fred—she's our local vicar—but that's only because she's on a crusade to teach me about rugby. Ohhh, if we see a camera, we should wave to Fred. I know she'll be watching. She's very jealous."

"Have you learnt any of the rules?" I asked, watching as West and the rest of the team began their warm-up. I pulled my phone out of my pocket and took a few quick photos so I could show him later.

"Yes, I can do the basics," Theo said. "What about you?"

"Same, I can do all the basics, but some of the more nuanced stuff I'm less sure on. Although… we were watching the Wales-Italy match last Sunday and I mentioned something about a scrum that the referee then called, so I think I've absorbed things subconsciously. I just can't tell you I know them."

"Makes sense," Eva said, still sipping his hot chocolate. "It happens with a lot of things. Sometimes you open your mouth and randomly know things."

"Don't say it like that, darling," Bitch said with a grin. "Or we'll all start thinking terrible things."

"You said it, not me."

I laughed. "I love you bananas, thanks for coming."

"Of course, babe," Bitch said. "We wouldn't miss it." He reached over and patted my leg fondly. "By the way, not to totally change the subject or anything, but what's this I heard about Legs moving in with Mason?"

"Wait, really?" Theo asked. "Hang on, who's Legs?"

"Legs Luthor," I said. "She's a drag queen we know. I think Mason's got a huge crush on her, and I think it might be reciprocated but… I don't know. Anyway, since West is moving in with me and Guy's already moved out, Mason and Jonny need at least one more roommate since the house has four bedrooms, because they can afford one being empty, but not two. And they were going to find someone else from the club, but Legs's tenancy was up, so the three of them just decided to move in together? I don't know."

"Okay, well, I'm definitely putting money on Legs getting with Mason at some point," Bitch said. "Mason is cute, Legs is cute, and two hot people can't live together for that long without fucking."

I grinned at Theo teasingly. "How long did you and Laurie live together before you got together?"

Theo rolled his eyes and stuck his tongue out. "This isn't about me! You're as bad as our friends at home! Two people can totally live together and be bestest best friends without banging or falling in love."

"True," Bitch said. "But what about if they're both really attracted to each other? Surely, then it'll happen."

I listened to them chat, slightly zoning out of the conversation as I watched West stretch, his shorts riding up around his broad thighs as he bent himself in half. I hoped he knew how much I loved him and how proud I was watching him. It would be a few hours before I saw him again, and when I did, I was going to kiss him senseless.

As I'd predicted, I didn't see him again until well after the match—after the interviews and recovery and all the other stuff that happened after an international rugby match.

And when I did see him, it wasn't some epic Hollywood-style moment where the music swept into a crescendo and we ran into each other's arms.

We were in an unremarkable corridor with laminate flooring and strip lighting, and West was walking towards me, freshly showered, in an England hoodie and jogging bottoms, bag slung over his shoulder.

"Hey, sweetheart," he said, a smile lighting up his face when he saw me. "You didn't have to wait for me."

"Of course I did," I said, putting my hand out for him to slide his fingers into mine. "You did amazingly today. I'm so fucking proud of you." I stood up on tiptoes to kiss him softly. "You were incredible."

"Thanks," he said. "I wish we'd won, though."

"I know but, horrifically cheesy as it sounds, you're still a winner to me." I kissed him again, squeezing his hand. "Want to get out of here? Maybe get some food?"

"Sounds perfect. I love you."

"I love you too," I said as we turned and began to walk towards the exit hand in hand, chatting quietly about the match.

We didn't stop talking until the early hours of the following morning when we finally fell asleep through sheer exhaustion, wrapped up in each other's arms.

If this was what the rest of our lives were going to be like, then every day was going to be perfect, no matter what happened.

Because I'd have West.

And that was all I needed to make my universe sparkle.

WHEN RORY MET THEO
BONUS SHORT

West

"Wow," Rory said as he peered out of the car window and down at the sweeping vista of Heather Bay spread out in front of us, all lit up with Christmas lights sparkling against the darkness, the castle picked out with spotlights on top of the cliff. "It's beautiful! Look at the castle! I think I can see the sea as well. Did you say there are beach huts?"

"Yeah, they're cute," I said, trying to focus on the narrow road in front of me and not Rory's beautiful smile. "I think Laurie and Theo bought one recently. Theo's been talking about his plans to do it up in the spring."

"Aww, I love that. Maybe we can see it tomorrow?"

"I don't think we'll be able to avoid it, Theo's desperate to show it off," I said with a soft chuckle. "He's also very excited to meet you." That was an understatement but I didn't want to freak Rory out by telling him Theo had been messaging me non-stop for the past week asking every question under the sun—from what Rory liked to eat, to if there were certain bath products he liked, to whether I wanted him to make sure he left lube in our room in case we wanted to have sex.

I loved my brother, and I knew his view of sex was probably a lot more liberal than most people's because of his work, but I still wasn't sure how I felt about him making sure I was able to get laid.

The questions had died down over the past day or two so I wondered if Laurie had said something.

I turned onto the street where Winchester & Sons funeral home was located, parking the car in the small car park attached to the side of it, making sure I left room in front of the garage doors in case Laurie suddenly needed to get one of the business's vehicles out.

Unfortunately, his business didn't stop at Christmas, even if people wished it would.

"They live in the flat up there," I said as we got out of the car, pointing to the second floor of the red brick building. "The door is round the back though. I'm pretty sure Theo will be watching for us."

"Do I look okay?" Rory asked, tugging at his Christmas jumper before reaching into the back seat to pull out his small suitcase. We were only here for two nights, but Rory had joked he'd never packed light in his life and wouldn't know how to even if his life depended on it.

I just had a large backpack and several giftbags of presents, one each for Theo and Laurie, and one for Rory. Since it was our first Christmas together, I'd wanted to make sure I got him some nice presents but I'd also tried not to go so overboard that I'd send him running for the hills.

Mason had helped with all of the wrapping, but mostly because he'd found me sat on my bedroom floor surrounded by tape and wrapping paper, and just sighed with despair. Apparently, my being a bisexual disaster wasn't just limited to interactions with people.

"You look gorgeous," I said with a soft smile. "I promise, they're going to love you. And if Theo gets too intense then just say and I'll distract him."

"I just... is it weird I want them to like me?"

"No." I walked around the car and kissed Rory gently. "It's because you care."

"They're your family," Rory said. Then he shook his head and chuckled. "God, I really hope I don't make myself look like a complete tit either. Especially because I've seen your brother naked."

"Trust me when I say that's not going to be an issue. Theo'll just take it as a compliment." I knew Theo wouldn't bring it up deliberately, but I doubted it would be something we'd be able to avoid since Theo was so open about it. And if I was honest, I loved how open he was about his work, and I was proud of him, not only for being himself but for everything that he did.

Theo had helped me so much over the past couple of months, I didn't think I'd be the person I was now without him, and it made me even happier that I'd plucked up the courage to send that first email all those months ago.

We walked around the edge of the building to the door

of the flat, which was flung open before I even got a chance to knock.

"West!" Theo yelled in delight as he slammed into my waist and squeezed me tightly. "You made it! I'm so glad you didn't get lost or hit any sheep. I was so worried."

"Sheep?" I asked with a confused smile and raised eyebrow.

"Yes, Will and Jamie let them go wandering around all over the place on the moors and I'm sure one day they'll hold you hostage," Theo said stepping back and beaming at me. He was wearing a dark blue, velvet dress patterned with silver stars and a pair of pink, fluffy slippers that had large bunny ears. He turned to Rory, his smile widening. "Oh my God, you must be Rory! It's so lovely to meet you. Can I please give you a hug?"

"Sure," Rory said, opening his arms as Theo darted into them and gave my beloved an equally tight squeeze. "It's so good to finally meet you. I've, er, West's talked a lot about you."

"That is because he is the sweetest baby brother ever," Theo said as he released Rory and winked at me. He turned and gestured to the tall, slim gentleman dressed in black stood in the doorway. "This is Laurie! Laurie, stop lurking and come and say hello."

"Or you could let them come inside where they won't freeze to death," Laurie said with a wry smile. I noticed he was wearing fluffy slippers too, except his were shaped like monster feet and I bit my lip to hide my grin because I'd never have pictured him wearing something like that. But they suited him.

"Hey Laurie," I said, walking over to him and giving him a half-hug, my hands full of bags. "Nice to see you again."

"You too. Here, let me give you a hand with those."

"It's fine, I can bring them."

"Nonsense," he said, reaching for the gift bags and taking them off me with a gentle but no-nonsense smile. "Come on in. Do you want a drink before we eat? Theo thought we could have dinner and then watch a Christmas movie. I know he's desperate to watch *The Muppet Christmas Carol*."

"It's tradition," Theo said, ushering Rory through the flat door behind me. We found ourselves in a little foyer, with coat hooks, a shoe rack, and a set of carpeted stairs leading up to the main body of the flat. "And then, if you fancy another one, we can watch *Die Hard*."

"My dad loves that film," Rory said as he toed off his shoes and tucked them neatly into place. He went to pick up his suitcase, but Theo had already swooped in and picked it up. "So does my brother. When he first learnt how to sign 'yippie-ki yay, motherfucker' he'd use it all the time and nobody knew what it meant until he had one teacher who knew BSL."

"Oh my God, you definitely have to teach me that," Theo said gleefully. "Come on, I'll show you the flat and your room. You're in my old room, which is now more like my gaming room, but it's all tidy and I made sure the PC won't light up randomly!"

He disappeared up the stairs to the flat and Rory

followed him, the two of them chatting easily, and I smiled as I watched them.

"After you," Laurie said, gesturing for me to go first. He was also smiling, a fondness in his expression that was impossible to miss. "He's been so excited, as I'm sure you've guessed, but… this means a lot to him. And I'll apologise now if he's overbearing, I've done my best but I don't want to force him to tone it down."

"I don't want him to either," I said. "This means a lot to me too. It's the first Christmas in a long time I've been excited for."

Laurie looked both startled and pleased, but all he said was, "then we'll do our best to make it memorable. In a good way."

I chuckled and headed up the stairs into the living room, which was a warm, cosy room with slightly old-fashioned décor… that looked like it had been hit by some kind of Christmas bomb. There was an enormous tree wedged into the corner, covered in so many lights it was probably a fire hazard, along with sparkling tinsel and a huge variety of ornaments from cute and kitsch, to vaguely creepy. As Theo had told me, the tree-topper was a taxidermy mouse dressed as an angel, complete with a little tutu and tinsel halo.

The bookshelves had little bauble clusters hanging off them, and the mantlepiece had a garland running along it, and I noticed the various taxidermy pieces on top of the mantlepiece all had some sort of Christmas decoration, including the stuffed raven, Lord Featherby, who seemed to be sporting a knitted scarf and a Santa hat stretched over the top hat he normally wore. There were sparkling skulls too, in pink, silver, and black, wedged onto the bookshelves and into corners, including next to the TV.

It was very over the top, and so very Theo that I had to love it.

"West? Where are you?" Theo called from around the corner, and I assumed he and Rory were still putting stuff in our bedroom.

"I'm here," I said as I walked through the living room and down the short corridor towards the spare room, Laurie following behind me with the gift bags still in hand. "I was just looking at your decorations."

"They're cute, right?" Theo asked. He'd put Rory's suitcase down at the end of the large double bed in the middle of the room, which was pink and white. He looked between me and Rory, smiling sweetly. "Okay, so, there are towels here,"—he pointed to the large stack of fluffy-looking towels on the bed—"in case you want a bath or a shower and help yourself to any products you want off the shelf. The bedroom door does lock but don't worry if you forget, neither of us will come in without knocking, and I left you some supplies in case you want to have some fun."

He gestured at the bedside table nearest the door, where there was a bottle of lube, a box of tissues, a box of condoms, and some foil packets that looked bulkier than condoms but weren't immediately recognisable.

"Don't worry, they're all unopened," Theo added casually, like this was a completely normal topic of conversation. Maybe for him it was. "And it's the really nice lube we use on set, so it's perfect if you have any allergies or sensitivities. I got you some condoms too because I wasn't sure whether you're using them or not. Oh, and the other packets are just some fun little surprises for you!"

He beamed at me and Rory, who was staring at my brother like he couldn't quite believe the words coming out of his mouth. Neither could I if I was honest.

"Also, tomorrow I thought we could all have breakfast together, then we're meeting everyone at eleven for our beach walk and afterwards we're going to Noah and Spencer's for hot chocolate and snacks—they're so sweet, you'll love them, and everyone's promised to be on their best behaviour—then I thought we could come back here, relax, maybe play some board games or something—I got some recommendations from Henry—and then we'll do dinner about six? Or do you want it earlier? You're leaving early on Boxing Day, right?"

"That sounds perfect," I said, my heart filling with warmth, because I couldn't believe all the effort Theo was going to. "And yeah, leaving about seven on Boxing Day because I've got training at eleven and that should get me back in plenty of time."

"Good, I'll pack you some snacks to go back with," Theo said. He bounced over and hugged me again. "I'm so happy you're here, this is going to be the best Christmas ever!" He stood on his tiptoes and kissed my cheek. "Come through whenever you want and we'll have drinks."

He practically skipped out of the room, closing the door carefully behind him, and leaving Rory and I alone. Rory still looked a bit shocked and for a moment, I wondered if I'd made a mistake.

Then Rory smiled and let out a little huff of laughter. "Wow," he said quietly "Your brother is… holy shit, I can't believe I met Theo Foxx! He's so sweet. Do you think it would be weird if I asked for a picture? I won't post it, but I maybe want one so the girls at The Court actually believe me. I'll ask Theo tomorrow, maybe when I've had a drink. And Laurie seems so lovely."

"He is," I said. "They're perfect for each other. And I'm sure Theo will take a picture with you." I chuckled softly. "If you're not careful, you'll end up with an autograph and everything." I wandered over to the bedside table and picked up one of the surprises, reading what was printed on the foil.

"What are they?" Rory asked, walking up behind me, and peering around my arm. "I can't believe Theo left us lube… and condoms."

"And sex toys. This is a vibrating cock ring."

"Ohh, that sounds fun." He grinned at me. "Is it weird that your brother is encouraging us to fuck in his house?"

"Not sure," I said. "I'm trying not to think about it. I guess with his job… maybe it's not a big deal to him?"

"I guess not." Rory picked up another of the packets, which was a different type of cock ring. He leant against my arm and sighed happily. "Thanks for bringing me, it's nice to get to meet your family."

"Thanks for coming," I said, putting the cock ring down and putting my arm around him. "I really appreciate it. Especially since we've not been together long and—"

"Baby, I was always going to be here with you," Rory said, sliding his arms around my waist and leaning up to kiss me. "It doesn't matter how long we've been together. I love you, you love me, and that's all that matters. Time isn't a thing and it's never going to be." He kissed me again and I felt everything in my body relax under his touch. "Besides, I can't imagine spending Christmas without you. I'd be so miserable and Christopher would make fun of me all day."

"I know that's what brothers do but still."

"It's because he's an immature bastard," Rory said fondly. "I hope he likes his present, I got him a new razor so he can finally deal with that shitty, dead-hamster style facial hair he keeps trying to grow."

I snorted and shook my head. I had to agree with Rory about Christopher's facial hair, but since he was only twenty, it'd probably get better as he aged. "Is it weird that I can't wait for it to be January so we can start looking at places to live?" I asked.

"No." He grinned, his cheeks flushing slightly. "I might've already started looking, just to see what's on the market. The answer is not much because it's Christmas and nobody wants to move."

I chuckled. "January it is then." It felt like forever away, but until then I'd try and spend as much time with Rory as possible.

We kissed again before heading back out into the flat, where Theo immediately ambushed us with drinks. Delicious smells wafted out of the kitchen and my stomach rumbled embarrassingly loudly.

We sat in the living room, casually catching up and chatting about random things, like how small the world was and all the friends we either had in common or who knew each other. Theo floated his desire for a local drag event past Rory, who promised to chat to some friends and see if they could arrange something in the New Year. He also offered to ask around, because he said there had to be some local queens who were probably desperate for something in Heather Bay, it was just finding them.

After dinner, which was a delicious Thai red curry, we all curled up with enormous mugs of hot chocolate and some of Spencer's mince pies to watch a couple of films. I hadn't met Spencer, but I knew he and Alex ran a local coffee shop where he did a lot of the baking. Based on how good the mince pies were, it was probably a good thing we didn't live locally because otherwise I'd be in there all the time. And half the team would be with me.

By the time Rory and I finally slid into bed, it was nearly midnight and both of us were so tired we couldn't stop yawning.

"I feel bad we're not putting any of Theo's presents to use," Rory said as he slid into my arms, resting his head on my chest. He could barely keep his eyes open. "Maybe in the morning… depending on when we wake up."

"Maybe." I yawned and pulled him closer. "Still not sure how I feel about having sex in my brother's house when he's literally on the other side of the corridor."

Rory chuckled quietly. "You don't have problem making me scream when we're at yours and poor Jonny is next door."

"Hey, I bought him those posh earplugs. I got some for Mason too."

Rory snorted. "See? How is this different?"

"I don't know, it just is. How would you feel if we had sex in your parent's house?"

"Depends," he said. "On who's at home and what time it is. If Dad's awake then no chance, if he's asleep…"

"See! It's different!"

He chuckled again and tilted his head up to kiss me. "Maybe. But if I decided to wake you up tomorrow with a Christmas blow job would you object? Because obviously you can't consent if you're sleeping."

"If you do that, I'm definitely not going to object," I said. The thought made my cock twitch in the loose pyjama shorts I was wearing and I made a mental note to explore more of that possibility in future.

Rory grinned. "I'll see what I can do. It'll depend if I wake up first though." It was my turn to laugh then because if Rory was comfy, his determination to stay asleep was usually pretty strong. "I can't wait for tomorrow," Rory added before yawning again. "I haven't felt this excited about Christmas in ages."

"Me neither," I said, kissing the top of his head as we snuggled down deeper, ready for sleep to claim both of us. "It's going to be fun."

And it was.

From Theo's Christmas French toast breakfast, to all the wonderful presents we exchanged, that included a very cosy pair of grey jogging bottoms and some fancy gaming headphones from Rory, to a walk on the beach under the winter sunshine with all of Theo and Laurie's friends, who adopted us into their group without a second thought. I even managed to convince Rory to paddle in the sea, even though it was freezing and after two minutes he'd wanted me to pick up him up and carry him.

There was delicious food, board games—which threatened to get contentious but ended with a lot of laughter instead—more films, more food, and a couple of bottles of wine. All accompanied by smiles and laughs and so many kisses from Rory I thought my heart might explode.

But maybe my favourite moment, apart from watching Rory introduce a wide-eyed Theo to the *Drag Stars Christmas Extravaganza*, had been late that night, when the four of us were sitting together, eating the last of a box of chocolates and drinking some homemade Baileys their friend Henry had gifted them, and I'd realised how at home I felt.

This was my life now, and this was my future. My family, in Theo and Laurie, and my best friend and love in Rory. Together, we'd had the perfect, cosy Christmas full of warmth and good food and wonderful people. I couldn't have imagined being anywhere else.

And if every future Christmas was like this then they'd all be perfect.

PRIDE

BONUS SHORT

This additional short was originally written for my Patreon to celebrate **Drama Queen**'s *release.*

Rory

"What do you think? Is it too much?" Dad asked, looking down at the new T-shirt I'd brought him before glancing in my floor-length mirror at the rainbow glitter and gemstones I'd plastered across his cheeks.

The T-shirt was black and had "Free Dad Hugs" written across it in enormous letters, with 'Dad' in rainbow font with a little heart in the gap in the 'A'. Getting it had been Dad's idea, based on something he'd seen on Facebook, and I'd helped him embellish it with a little bit of traditional Bubblegum sparkle, sewing a ton of sequins across the letters until it was so glittery you'd be able to see it from space.

He was going to get absolutely mobbed at pride. Everyone was going to love him, and I couldn't wait to see his reaction. Dad always believed wasn't anything or anyone special, but I didn't think he realised how much seeing someone like him offering supportive hugs would mean to people.

"Absolutely not, it's perfect," I said. "You look amazing!"

"Cheers." He grinned at me. "And you don't clean up bad yourself, Roo. Although... that skirt's a bit short, isn't it?"

I laughed and rolled my eyes, wiggling my hips and making the beading on my new pride dress rattle. It was inspired by 1920s flapper dresses and had taken me fucking forever to bead, but I was so proud of it I wanted to burst. "If you think this is short, wait until you see some of the others! And I'm twenty-three!"

"The others aren't my kids. And I don't care how old you are, I'll still be telling you your skirts are too short when you're forty."

"Be grateful I'm not just wearing a thong and a bodysuit."

"Who's wearing a thong and a bodysuit?" West asked, sticking his head around the door. He had bisexual flag stripes painted across his cheeks and a brand new Lincoln Knights pride shirt on. The team were also marching in the parade and I was so proud of my man for getting everyone from the Knights more involved.

"Not this one, I'm telling you now," Dad said as he

pointed at me. "I don't care how nice you think your bum is, I don't need to see that. If not I'll get one of those tiny speedos and come down The Court while you're working."

"If you think that'd embarrass me, you'll need to try harder." I winked at him and then totted over and put my arms around him, giving him the biggest squeeze while trying not to smudge either of our make-up. "Thank you."

Dad squeezed me back. "For what?"

"For this. You're the best."

"Yeah well... just doing my job. It's what Dads are for." He patted me on the shoulder and released me. Behind him, I saw West smiling softly. He and Dad had really grown closer over the past few months, and they chatted endlessly about sport and Dad's random DIY projects. I loved the way my family had folded West into it, like he'd been there all along, and given him the unconditional love and support he'd always deserved.

Dad had even gotten an England rugby shirt and made West sign it before hanging it up in the downstairs toilet at their house, which was pretty much the ultimate badge of honour. Mum said he'd already started telling people his son-in-law played for England, and the fact we hadn't even been together a year didn't seem to phase him.

Dad said he didn't think I could've met anyone better, and he was right.

"We should get going," West said. "You've got to be on your float at half-ten."

"Shit, okay, I'm ready," I said.

"Parade starts at eleven, right?" Dad asked as he

followed me and West downstairs to our kitchen, where Mum and Christopher were waiting. I'd attacked both of them with glitter as soon as they'd arrived.

"*Looking good,*" Christopher signed as he spotted us. "*But bloody hell that skirt's short. I don't want to see your bum!*"

"*Tough shit,*" I sighed, turning round and wiggling my bottom at him.

Christopher pulled a face, but his eyes were sparkling. He'd finally gotten rid of the terrible facial hair he'd tried to grow and he looked so much better for it.

"*Don't be rude,*" Mum signed. "*Your brother worked hard on that.*"

"*I'm not being rude! I'm being honest! I don't want to look at my brother's bum.*"

"Stop bickering and let's go," Dad said, waving us towards the front door. "I want to get a good spot for the parade. We'll meet you afterwards, and then you're on stage at three, right?"

"Yep." I had a slot on the main stage at three, followed by a couple of The Court's other performers. I'd been practising for months and it was going to be fabulous.

We all headed out, with my family going in Dad's van and West and I in his car. I'd got them family passes to park closer, so it was easy for us to all head into the centre of Lincoln together.

I'd done Lincoln Pride a few times, and my parents usually tried to come along with some sort of flags or rainbow shirts, but this was the first time Dad had worn a Free Hugs shirt. And copious amounts of glitter.

It never ceased to amaze me how much my parents

cared, and while I'd definitely taken it for granted in the past, I never would again.

I left my family to find a spot and West to find the team, and headed for The Court's float, which Phil and his husband had knocked up several years ago from an old lorry. They repainted it every year, and this year it had the Progress Pride flag lovingly painted across it along with a hell of a lot of spray glitter.

"You made it," Eva said as I climbed aboard. There were quite a few kings and queens already here, all milling around in their Pride finery. "I was starting to worry."

"I'm not the last, am I?"

She grinned. "Nope, Bitch is running late. I'm going to have fun with this for weeks."

I snorted. "You and me both. Maybe we should pretend we're leaving without her?"

"If she's not here in five, we will be anyway."

"Don't you fucking dare leave!" Bitch called, half-running, half-tottering across the cobbles towards us in huge boots, holding her wig on with one hand. "I'm here!"

"Aww, darn it," Moxxie said, their rainbow cowboy outfit glittering in the sun. They grinned at Bitch and dramatically checked their watch. "You're still late though."

"I'm not late, you're all just early," Bitch said as she hauled herself onto the float.

"Nope, you're still late," Eva said. Beneath us, the float roared into life and at the other end, I saw Ink fiddling with the buttons of the sound system, which suddenly began to blare Kylie's "Padam Padam".

I grinned, bouncing up and down as the parade started

to roll out. I loved Pride, and even though Lincoln's wasn't the biggest in the world, the crowd here was always enthusiastic and seemed to love every second.

Bitch had somehow gotten hold of a megaphone and as we rolled along, she kept encouraging the crowd to cheer and scream as we danced and waved. The atmosphere was electric, pulsing through my veins and making me feel like I was floating on air.

I still hadn't seen my family, but as we rounded onto the bottom of the High Street, I could see a little crowd by the side of the parade route.

And as we got closer, I realised they were all clustered around my parents. And I could see my dad giving out giant hug after giant hug to everyone around him.

"Your dad really is amazing," Bitch said to me quietly, lowering her megaphone for a second.

"Yeah, he's pretty cool."

"Way to undersell it, Sparkles." She grinned and handed me the megaphone. "Give him a shout out."

I took it, lifting it to my mouth and pressing the button, unable to stop smiling as I did. "Free dad hugs!" I pointed at him. "Get free dad hugs from my dad!" Everyone around me on the float cheered and a few of them even blew him kisses. "We love you, Alan! I love you!"

Dad was laughing and Christopher was obviously filming all of it.

It really was amazing to see and my heart swelled.

I was the luckiest drag queen in the world.

When they found me afterwards, Dad was missing half

his glitter and looked more emotional than I'd seen him in ages.

"You okay?" I asked as he gave me and West our own enormous hugs. He was a head shorter than both of us today, especially since I was wearing giant heels.

"Yeah," he said. "Didn't think a hug would make so much of a difference. I didn't mean to make people cry."

"It's not you," West said. He stood beside me with his hand tightly grasped in mine. "Not really… It's having a supportive parent here. A lot of us don't have that."

Dad hugged him again tightly and then shook his head. He reached up and gently patted West's cheek. "Well you should, and if I have to keep coming here every year to hand out hugs then I will."

"You know," Mum said and I could see her thinking. "I saw something on Facebook about groups who organise people to act as parents for LGBTQ+ people at weddings and other life events. Maybe we should look into that. I like weddings."

Dad hummed and leant over to kiss her softly, "And that, Lou, is why you're the brains of this marriage. We'll have a look at it later. I'll need a new suit though. Don't think I'll fit in the one I got for Ian's wedding."

"Oh lord, Alan, that was fifteen years ago. It's made of polyester," Mum said. "You're not wearing that."

"You always liked that suit. You said I looked very handsome."

"You did, but that doesn't mean I'd let you out of the house in it now."

I giggled and glanced up at West, who was looking at them fondly. "You realise you're stuck with us all now? We're your family."

"Good," West said, pressing a kiss to the top of my head. "I couldn't ask for better people to be stuck with."

ACKNOWLEDGMENTS

I've been wanting to write a series about The Court and the drag queens, and kings, who perform there since the bar first appeared in *Always Eli* two years ago, and I'm so excited the series is finally here.

Drag is an incredible, diverse art form and I'm delighted to be able to celebrate it here, and I can't wait to share the rest of these stories with you. Buckle up, because I think this series is going to be a long one!

I owe a lot to many people for this book, but I do want to start by saying an enormous thank you to Noah Steele for all his help and for making me howl with laughter. I'll never look at peanut butter the same way.

Another massive thank you to Charity, who is not only my PA but my person. The journey wouldn't be nearly as fun without you.

To Carly, Lily, Con, Toby, and Jodi, my awesome writing friends who remind me not to take myself too seriously and get things done. You're all amazing.

To Rosie, Beth, Blair, James, and Stuart, for offering your fabulous opinions. I love being able to share my author life with you.

To Meagan Thompson, for naming Peachy Keen and

gifting me Peaches, whose story I already know and can't wait to tell.

To Jennifer, for helping my to polish, shine and perfect my words, and reminding me time is a thing. And to Lori, for finding all the errant commas and typos that are determined to get through.

To Wander and Andrey for finding me the most perfect model, and to Natasha for creating the most gorgeous cover I've ever seen.

To Linda, and her incredible team, who is very good about me randomly sliding into her messages and asking random questions. Thank you for helping me share Rory and West with the world.

To Dan, who I know will breath the most incredible life into these characters.

To my husband, for always listening, for loving me, and for bringing me peanut butter pumpkins when I'm sad or so deep in edits I don't know which way is up!

And last, but never least, to you, my fabulous readers. Whether I'm new to you or you've been here since the start, I am grateful for you love and support.

If you enjoyed *Drama Queen*, please consider leaving a review. Reviews are invaluable for indie authors, and may help other readers find this book.

Until next time.

Love,
Charlie x

ALSO BY CHARLIE NOVAK

The Court
Drama Queen

Scene Queen *(February 2024)*

Heather Bay
Like I Pictured

Like I Promised

Like I Wished

Like I Needed

Like I Pretended

Like I Wanted

Roll for Love
Natural Twenty

Charisma Check

Proficiency Bonus

Bonus Action: The Roll for Love Short Story Collection

Roll for Love: The Complete Collection (Boxset)

Forever Love
Always Eli

Finding Finn

Oh So Oscar

KISS ME

Strawberry Kisses

Summer Kisses

Spiced Kisses

OFF THE PITCH

Breakaway

Extra Time

Final Score

The Off the Pitch Short Collection

Off the Pitch: The Complete Collection (Boxset)

STANDALONES

Screens Apart

Couture Crush

Up To Snow Good

Pole Position

SHORT STORIES

One More Night

Twenty-Two Years (Newsletter Exclusive)

Snow Way In Hell

Audiobooks

Like I Promised

Like I Wished

Like I Needed

Like I Pretended

Like I Wanted

Natural Twenty

Charisma Check

Proficiency Bonus

Always Eli

Finding Finn

Oh So Oscar

Strawberry Kisses

Summer Kisses

Spiced Kisses

Up To Snow Good

Translations

ITALIAN

Qui Neve Ci Cova

For a regularly updated list, please visit:

charlienovak.com/books

charlienovak.com/audiobooks

CHARLIE NOVAK

Charlie lives in England with her husband and two cheeky dogs. She spends most of her days wrangling other people's words in her day job and then trying to force her own onto the page in the evening.

She loves cute stories with a healthy dollop of fluff, plenty of delicious sex, and happily ever afters — because the world needs more of them.

Charlie has very little spare time, but what she does have she fills with baking, Dungeons and Dragons, reading and many other nerdy pursuits. She also thinks that everyone should have at least one favourite dinosaur…

Website charlienovak.com
Facebook Group Charlie's Angels
Sign up for her newsletter for bonus scenes, new releases and extras.
Or Patreon for early access chapters, flash fiction, first looks, and serial stories.

- facebook.com/charlienovakauthor
- instagram.com/charlienwrites
- bookbub.com/profile/charlie-novak
- amazon.com/author/charlienovak
- patreon.com/charlienovak

Printed in Great Britain
by Amazon